Wow! Fiction ought to be just... well... fiction. However, Jed Wright has done what most people can't do, to wit, he has written an intriguing and exciting fictional novel and, at the same time, has taught some important truths about culture, love, commitment and the Christian faith. This is a great read! It's fun and good for you at the same time. You'll rise up and call me blessed for recommending it to you.

—Dr. Steve Brown,
President, Key Life Network, Orlando, FL

Wake Up, O Sleeper is a contagious and inspiring read. Jed does a great job in telling a good story containing treasures of Godly truth. This book will hold your attention and heart at the same time. Its themes of love, truth, and honor carry the reader like riding on a breath of fresh air. A great book that will encourage people of faith and be inviting to the searcher.

—Dr. Jerry Russell,
Senior Pastor, Fairview UMC, Maryville, TN

Wake Up, O Sleeper takes you on an exciting adventure like no other with many twists and turns. It encourages and gives hope to the reader.

—Aaron Small,
former pitcher, New York Yankees, 10–0 as a starter in 2005

WAKE UP, SLEEPER

JED WRIGHT

WAKE UP, SLEEPER

Published in the United States of America

ISBN: 978-1-98350-193-7
1. Fiction / Men's Adventure   2. Fiction / Thriller / Suspense
09.12.15

SPECIAL THANKS:

To Mark (my fellow sword-waver), my sisters, and my parents for proofreading, suggesting, and encouraging me throughout the process.

For the heart-rattling poetry of the guys at Switchfoot. All of the cool chapter lead-ins are taken from *Oh! Gravity.*, with lyrics copyrighted 2006 by Publishing Schmublishing. *Oh! Gravity.* is available from Sparrow Records.

To my smart, beautiful, and inspirational wife, Debbie, who championed this story long after I had given up on it ever being published. This never would have happened without you.

To my writing-partner and King, this is for you. If this makes you smile, then it is a success.

"All of my world hanging on,
all of my world resting on, your love."
—Switchfoot

Wake up, O sleeper,
rise from the dead,
and Christ will shine on you.

Ephesians 5:14, NIV

CHAPTER 1

"Let the wars begin, let my strength wear thin.
Let my fingers crack, let my world fall apart."

Every boy must someday become a man, but most men cling far too long to their boyhood. The relentless pulling of a greater and more powerful force will always find a day when the grip is broken and the boy is lost forever. That someday came on a dark and rainy night when I buried my murdered father in a shallow grave next to a man who had just met the same fate. Murder is a strange word, separated in degrees by the intent of the heart. At that moment and on that day, the intents of my own heart were anything but clear.

For the past month, my father and I had been walking to the city to find Lori Applegate. She was the love of my life, or so I thought. I didn't know at the time how little I knew about love. My father and I had covered hundreds of miles together both during our journey and in our relationship. It seemed as if he was trying to cram all the fathering that he had missed over the last twenty-one years into that one month. He talked about life and love and all the important things about becoming a man, but all I could think about was reaching the city and looking for Lori. Looking back, I would give anything to relive just one of those days. His words were like gold, and I let them slip away. When we finally came to the little house at the perimeter of the city, he handed me a large package of papers and said, "You'll need to read this when you get inside." On that day, I still had a boy's heart and didn't take that package very seriously. I didn't realize that my father's papers and the events of the next four days would change my life completely.

When you are a boy that wants to be a man, you are bound by chains from all directions. The rules of life and society and the boundaries enforced by your parents seem to strangle and choke. Your natural impulse is to struggle to break free. When you become a man, you long for the comfort of those boundaries, seeking a rock to attach your anchor to in the midst of personal storms. A boy is always unpleasantly surprised to discover what it means to be a man and at that moment, I didn't want it. I just wanted my father back. I needed him to tell me what to do, to plan the next move, to make my next decision for me. We had finished our journey, and I was just miles away from finding Lori, but at that moment all I wanted to do was turn around and go back home to my mother.

The early morning darkness of my first day as a man found me in front of a bathroom mirror, looking at a strange reflection that bore little resemblance to my own. Two years of living without electricity weren't enough to break the habit of flipping up the switch. It was a dark world, but the darkness never seemed natural. The first rays of the sunrise filtering through the window were just enough to make out the features of a man's face, dark and serious, looking back at me in the glass. His forehead was drawn up with worries and his eyes were widened in fear. Even in the dim light, streaks of mud could be seen on the cheeks and chin where sweat had been wiped with the back of a dirty hand or forearm.

Things had not gone well the day before. The plan was to borrow an abandoned home and ambush the demolition inspector. We would tie him up, and I would take his place. My father was an engineer to the core. He had spent months working out every detail of what we had thought was a foolproof plan. Now I was the only fool left alive, and the plan was in shambles. To press on or to retreat? It wasn't the toughest decision of my life, but it was certainly the loneliest. It would be wonderful to say that all the amazing things that happened over the next few days came about because I stuck out my chin and steeled my resolve at that moment, but that really wasn't it at all. My father had given up his life to help me find Lori somewhere in this horrible place. He couldn't have died for nothing. Quitting was not an option. There was no other choice but to march on alone. I had an hour at best to assume the identity of the inspector buried in the backyard.

The only water for washing that was left in the house was in the storage tank on the back of the toilet. I scooped out a few cups, stopping to sniff the water before pouring it into the basin. To have been waiting in that tank for twelve years, it didn't even smell bad. Digging through the cabinets produced a wash cloth and some soap. My clothes were completely trashed and had to go. The shirt came off first. It was soaked in blood that had dried and then mixed with sweat. The pants and socks were completely caked in mud and quickly joined the shirt in the corner. The boxer shorts were my only option, so they would have to stay. After the scrubbing was over, muddy footprints and handprints marked the floors and walls around the bathroom. It was a good thing no one would ever see the room again.

I looked again at the mirror. Staying out of the sun and nearly starving for the entire journey had not worked. My face was too tan, too healthy for the charade that lay before me. Every detail of our plan had been worked and reworked, and now, at the cusp of its inception, the whole thing just seemed stupid. My hand was shaking uncontrollably as I bent to clean off the last streak of mud from my ankle. The shaking was worse on the inside. The next few hours lay in the hands of either providence or luck. My dad would have said, "Luck is for suckers." The events of the past day had led me to realize that much of what I believed and took for the truth was founded on what he said. But now, with him gone, nothing made sense anymore. There wasn't enough time for wavering. I needed to keep moving.

Dad had told me to look for an undershirt that was some shade of gray. I reached for the dresser drawer in the bedroom but stopped when a picture frame covered in a thick coat of dust caught my eye. They were an older couple, probably in their sixties—certainly the former owners of this house. Staring into their unfamiliar faces, the question rose in my mind, *Where were these two now?* "Likely dead," I concluded, just like most who had been there on that horrible day. The echo of my father's voice in my head jolted me back to the present. "Stay on task!" he would have said. I dug through the drawers and found a dingy old undershirt, far from white, but not as gray as my father would have liked. The shirt was neatly folded just as it had been since that day twelve years ago when everything changed for me and for everyone else. Slowly sliding the drawer back in, I scanned the room—the bed was made, the pictures were neatly hung, and there were a couple of unopened bills on the nightstand. Everything was left just as if the old couple would soon be returning.

It was a scene I had walked through a hundred times without stopping to notice.

My thoughts were jerked back to my own nightmare twelve years ago. I wondered what our house looked like. "Not so neat," I guessed, "unless someone came back and cleaned up the mess." Blurred images of the dark and painful day flashed through my mind. I remembered so little. My dad had ordered my brother and me to clean up our room that morning before everything happened, but we had never gotten around to it. The thought of a faceless uniform picking through our things sent chills up my spine. I struggled to stay focused and pulled the old man's undershirt over my head.

The shirt was at least two sizes too big. Tucking it tightly into my boxers, I paused for another look in the mirror. The shirt and shorts were definitely the wrong color and didn't look anything like the underwear on the inspector in the backyard. The suspicious eyes in the locker room where I would have to change would not be fooled so easily. There was no time to go back and unearth the only pair available, so this would have to do.

The light blue jumpsuit of the inspector was hanging from a hook on the wall. I had stripped his uniform from the body before burying him, trying my best to keep it clean. It was plain that the jumpsuit was too loose around my waist and a couple of inches too long, but when I stuffed the legs into the boots and wrapped the seal around, you couldn't tell it at all. The boots were size ten and needed to be eleven and my toes howled with pain. I zipped up the front of the jumpsuit and took another look in the mirror. Like father, like son, right? He had worn a uniform just like this for ten years, but I had never seen him in it. I sure hoped that everybody looked the same in these things. The gloves came next, and they fit tightly. I could easily move my fingers and proceeded to seal off all the seams in the uniform, following the airtight protocol my father had drilled into my head over the last four months. The hood was last. I slipped it over my head and tried to look out of the tinted face panel. My breath filled the hood and the cloud of stale, damp air brought on feelings of claustrophobia. That would take some getting used to. I took it back off for the time being.

The hour was up. I looked around one last time. The bathroom was a mess, but Dad had assured me that there was no need to worry about it. Within a few hours the house would be demolished, and nobody would set foot in this room again. It seemed strange to leave it in this state, piled with dirty clothes, blood and mud everywhere, the shovel propped up in the corner. The handle of the shovel was smeared with mud from my night's work. It was a gruesome scene, a murder scene even. Now I was to step outside and take on the life of my victim, literally walking in his boots.

What had I forgotten? I slipped the inspector's ID badge into its pouch on the front of the uniform and walked toward the front door. For the next three days, I would stop being Jack Wilson and would have to become M. Davis. I couldn't resist one last peek at the mirror in the hall. I was a total wreck on the inside. My face looked more like a madman than an overworked inspector. There was maybe ten minutes, I needed to hurry. That last something I was forgetting was picking at the back of my brain. There it was, on the kitchen counter, the package my dad had given me yesterday morning. How could I have forgotten that after the way he went on and on about it? I unzipped my uniform and slid it into the neck of my shirt under my armpit. Surely no one would see it in the baggy uniform. Resealing my seams, I stepped out the front door into the morning light.

It was a bright, chilly morning. The rain of the night before was gone. A light fog partially obscured the risen sun, cutting through and revealing a bluing sky above. It was sure to be a beautiful sunny day. The only sound during the long and dreary night of digging had been a light wind pushing between the leaves on the trees. This morning a mockingbird was singing loudly from the useless power line leading to the side of the house. His songs were mixed with the sounds of demolition crews working up the road. I looked all around the house, trying to come up with an excuse for the inspector to have spent the night away from the city. His light blue truck sat at the top of the long driveway. There was a fairly steep slope near the top that was concreted before turning into gravel as the drive flattened out. It was a long driveway, bordered on both sides by pine trees and a thick scruffy overgrowth. He had backed the truck up next to the house to avoid having to go backward down the hill. His keys were in the ignition, just like Dad said they would be. I slid behind the wheel and let off the parking brake. With one foot back out on the driveway, I turned the wheel slightly to the right and let my foot off the brake, jumping clear as the truck began to roll. The truck picked up speed on the short slope, veered off the drive and took a good-sized tree right in the center of the grill. *Perfect,* I thought, *it looks just like an accident.* Dad would have been proud.

My pride was scratched when I realized the hood of the uniform was still in the front of the truck. Hurrying down the driveway, I grabbed it out of the seat and took one last breath of natural air before pulling it on. I wouldn't last for five minutes if I kept this up. I grabbed a small duffle bag from the front seat of the truck—Davis wouldn't have left that. There was another bag in the bed that rattled when I picked it up. *Probably tools,* I thought and dropped it back down. The truck was halfway down the driveway, so I started walking toward the road with the bag over my shoulder, trying to look casual. Dad had said that the demo crews would have one house up the street to do before this one. I checked the clock in my head—they would be here any minute. The uniform was made from a vinyl-type material that was close to airtight. When the truck of the demo crew turned into the driveway at the bottom of the hill, I was already soaked in sweat, and the hood was so stuffy I could barely breathe.

Their orange truck was full-size, but with a standard cab, much larger than the compact truck of the inspector. Three guys were crammed on the bench. Each of them had jump-suits, like mine, but orange to match their truck. They had their hoods pulled back on their heads so their faces were showing. The hoods were hardened on top and made their heads look unnaturally long. The driver would be the lead of the crew, and his eyes caught mine as they neared. I had rehearsed this type of exchange time and again with my dad, but my throat was lumped over when the truck stopped beside me. There was a pop in my ear and the voice of the driver came in. I knew the hoods were wired, but wasn't ready for how much static and how loud it would be. "You must be Davis," he said. "What are you doing out here overnight?"

Short and simple, I thought to myself, barely remembering to push the button on my hip before talking. "Truck wrecked," I said, pointing up the driveway. "Parking brake went out on me."

He looked up at the truck and smiled. "Smashed her up pretty good, huh? I'll bet you had a good night's rest sleeping in your truck. Hop in the back. Yours is our last house out this way, and then we are back across to the west side of the city for the afternoon. We'll drop you off back at the bubble on the way through."

I climbed in the back of the truck, and he turned it up the driveway. I was shaking all over and was glad to be out from in front of them. There was a spot in the bed between their piles of equipment, and I stretched out my legs with my back to the cab, trying to look casual. The voice of the driver came back into my ears. "Hope you got enough room back there. You did mark for the charges, right?"

A second of panic rushed through me. "Yep," I lied, but it was just a little lie. My dad had marked everything the day before we met the inspector, taking the time to explain everything to me as he went. Three of the basement poles and four spots on the block walls, all marked with the light blue paint he had taken with him on the day we all left the city over two years ago. Dad's attention to detail was saving me. I held my breath, hoping the driver wouldn't ask any more questions. Holding my breath was a bad idea. I tried to force myself to relax and to take shallow smooth breaths.

As we passed the smashed truck, I cringed. The driver side door was left open. That was not smart; no one would have done that. If it seemed out of the ordinary to them, they didn't say so to me. As we came to the top of the drive, I could see in the daylight what wasn't visible from the rear bathroom window. Out the back door of the basement was a path of broken branches and trampled weeds. My only hope was that the monotony of the task would blind them to the obvious mess that was left. I thought of the basement floor. I had tried to mop up the blood, but it was very dark then and who knew what would be seen now? Things were not going well.

They parked their truck a good distance from the house, shut off the engine, and pulled down their hoods. I heard the whoosh of air as they decompressed the cab and climbed out. The driver leaned against the front of the truck, took out a pad of paper, and began to take notes. The other two smiled at me, grabbed their bags from the truck bed, and headed around back and into the basement. For a second, I thought about jumping out and running. I could hit the trees and be gone before they would think to chase me. Of course that wasn't an option anymore. The curtain was raised, the play had begun, and I was locked into my role. There was nothing to do but sit still and just let things happen. It was out of my hands now.

Providence, I thought, and said something like a prayer. The mumbled words were something my dad might have said and not my own. They didn't even make any sense. I didn't have a clue who God was and wondered if I ever had. The prayers had only ever been said to please my father. My head was swimming, and it was getting hard to breathe. My face panel was fogging enough that they would surely notice when they came back. I remembered the ventilator and pushed the button on the side of my hood. The little fan came on and almost immediately the fog was gone. I laughed grimly at my own stupidity and a tiny part of the tension inside me released. Maybe even bad prayers get answered.

The voices of the two men inside the house came into my ear. "All clear. We're coming out." They emerged jogging from the basement as the fifteen seconds counted down from the loudspeakers on top of the truck. The time ticked off, the small explosives fired in sync, and the house fell on top of itself. The setting for my previous day's nightmare was a level pile of rubble that would soon surely be grown over and absorbed by the jungle of green around it. As we pulled away from what was the house, I could see through the settling dust what they hadn't noticed: the uncovered soil of a freshly dug grave in between the green of the bushes and trees.

We were picking down the side roads between clusters of demolished houses. "You good back there?" came the voice in my ear.

No, I am not, I thought, but answered, "Fine, thanks." They must have switched frequencies, because their hoods were removed, and they were talking to each other, but I couldn't hear them. If my dad was right, I had about an hour of riding before we would even be close to the city. I shifted the bags of tools in the truck bed and tried to find a semi-comfortable position. My mind was reeling. I took in deep breaths of the stale, filtered air and tried to slow things down. Some semblance of reason replaced the frantic arm waving that had overtaken my brain for the last twenty-one hours, and I began to place together the pieces of what had just happened.

We had come to the house two days ago and slowly began to enact the plan that my father and I had been working on for months. Every detail was scripted, every contingency foreseen, or so we had thought. When I had come to Dad with my idea to go on this trip, I had expected him to try to talk me out of it. Instead, he had just looked at me, staring into my eyes, before beginning with the questions. "What were my plans once I got in?" "Why did I really want to do this?" "Did I understand the risks?" Like any twenty-one year old, I fired back what I thought were all the right answers. After an hour of interrogation, he stopped in midsentence and stared at me again, wrinkling up his forehead. "I'll go with you," he said, "and we'll do it right. But first we have to convince your mom." Of course, we never convinced Mom of anything. She cried and shook her head at "her crazy John Wilsons." In the end we went anyway. As we left, she said she would never see us again in this world. So far, she was half right.

I wondered what my father had seen in my eyes that would have led him to partner with me on this fool's quest. Part of me wanted him to say no to my request to leave. I certainly didn't expect or even ask him to come along. Ever since we left the city and came to the cabin, he and Mom had been happier than I had ever seen them. They plunged into our new life, learning quickly how to do the things that had to be done to live on your own in the relative wilderness. The community around us quickly became their best friends, and rightly so, for they were fine people, every one of them. The pallid somberness of the city had melted away from them in the vigorous work and sunshine of their new lives and within a few months each one of them looked ten years younger. But most striking to me was the shared joy and peace that I saw in the looks between them. I longed to have that for myself and thought every day of Lori.

The truck turned onto a main road, and we picked up speed as we rolled toward the city. I closed my eyes and tried again to see Lori's face. She had brown hair, cut too short like every one else's, but with just enough curl to be different. It would have lightened to a sandy blonde in the summer if she had ever gotten a chance to get in the sun. Her nose was small and turned up a bit between high cheekbones. Her face was natural and clean. Her eyes were blue and alive and seemed to see into my soul. I had all the pieces but I couldn't put them together. I couldn't see her face but could remember things she said and how she said them. I could hear the tone of her voice and see the cut of her eyes as she spoke. When we spoke together, it was like she and I were alive and everyone one else around us was dead.

But we had never kissed. I never even held her hand. From the words that were spoken, we had never been anything but good friends. I never told her how much I loved her. Had I loved her? Did she ever begin to love me? It seemed like forever ago now. She had left without a good-bye. And then we were gone too. I tried to forget her and start my new life with Mom and Dad, but thoughts of her consumed me. I couldn't bear the thought of my dear Lori chained to the dungeon wall in a room full of corpses. I had to go back to the city and rescue her and determined to approach my father with my plans.

So now at my hand, my father was dead, and my mother was a widow. Poor Mr. Davis, who had wished to have no part in my life, was just more collateral damage. It seemed so crazy now. I wondered why my dad had gone along with this. He was a serious and cautious man, and did nothing without carefully considering all the consequences. What had he foreseen that would have led him to volunteer for such a dangerous mission that seemed now to have only a selfish and foolish goal? My mind began to swim again, and I forced myself to come back to the recounting of the events of the previous day.

The evening before the ambush, we had walked for a mile in either direction up and down the road, stopping and going up each driveway, before settling on this house. It was an old split foyer from the eighties. Dad noticed the paint marks on the driveway entrance and counted back from the demolished houses up the road. He knew that an inspector would be coming to this house in the next few days to mark the blast spots for the demo team. The house was over a hundred yards from the road with no neighbors in sight through the thick brush and trees.

It had the unfinished basement we wanted. Dad was excited as we camped in the living room that night. We ate borrowed food from our long-departed hosts as he drilled me on the details of the next day's work one more time. In his mind, and mine convinced, it was the perfect house for the plan.

Dad had been through the routine himself hundreds of times and trusted that the inspector would follow the same steps he would have taken. We saw Davis work a house the day before up the street. He was working without a partner and was close to the right size—the perfect target. We would be his second house that day. He would hit us about noon. We got things set up and waited in the dim light at the base of the steps. Dad knew the inspector would crowbar the front door and turn down the steps for the basement without ever going upstairs. We had broken into a side door the night before for that very reason. Recon and inspectors used the front door; demo crews used the back door. We would hide in the shadows of the basement and ambush him as he came down the steps. The plan was for Dad to yank off the inspector's hood and pin him to the floor. He would be so shocked at the exposure to the toxic air and by the sight of an unsuited human that we would catch him off guard. I would jump in and help tie him up. I would borrow his uniform and truck and take his place in the city that same day. Dad would keep him company while he waited for our return. "It was a good plan," I said to myself, looking at the road pass beneath the truck's wheels. But good plans never seem to come to pass as we hope.

It was a bit past noon by my guess when we heard Davis working at the door. I was stiff from waiting but stood to my post. There was a hard rain streaking down the short and high windows of the basement. The inspector stomped his boots before he turned the knob and stepped inside. I stole a glance across the base of the steps. Dad's face was steeled with the anticipation of what was about to happen. The inspector paused for a moment before starting down the steps. Dad jumped out from the shadows and ripped off his hood, throwing it aside. The shock of the expected suffocation didn't freeze him like we expected. Instead he jolted backward, raised his pistol, and shot it directly into Dad's chest. Dad twisted backward down the steps and fell at my feet, cracking his head on the concrete floor. There was a shovel at the front of a stack of tools leaning against the wall to my side. Without really thinking, I grabbed the shovel and met Davis coming down frantically to grab his hood. I took a clumsy half-swing but got my shoulder behind it and planted the flat side of it into his forehead—crushing his face and pinning him against the wall. I took another full swing for good measure, and he was dead. Dad looked up at me, his eyes glassy and distant, and told me to turn the inspector downward on the stairs so he wouldn't bleed on the uniform. With that, he coughed up some blood, his body shivered once like he was cold, and my father was gone from my life forever.

The whole thing must have lasted ten seconds. I picked up the inspector and turned him around dutifully. No sound or movement came from him. His blood pooled with my father's at the base of the steps. I sat in the puddle on the floor and pulled my dad over so his head lay in my lap. My mind raced with a thousand thoughts. Nobody was supposed to have gotten hurt. We knew he would be carrying a gun in case of animals, but he should have left it in the truck. Something must have spooked him. What had we done wrong? The loud buzzing inside my head drowned out my thoughts, and my reason left me to grieve alone for a while. I cried and hugged my father's lifeless body as I rocked back and forth. The house darkened as the shadows overtook the patches of daylight and the rain slowly stopped.

I came to myself sometime in the middle of the night and wandered up the stairs. We had found an old oil lamp the night before along with some matches. Fumbling around in the dark, I found the matches and lit the lamp. I turned the wick up high, went back to the basement, and looked over the inspector. There was no sign of a pulse along his neck and wrists. His skin was already growing cold, and touching him made my head swim and I nearly fainted. I had killed an innocent man. Intentional or not, I was a murderer. Why had I hit him twice? Was the second swing out of anger or revenge? Shame flushed through me and my immediate instinct was to bury him and hide what I had done. I set the lamp near the back door of the basement, wrestled his body through the door, and began to pull him in the direction of the woods behind the house. As I went back in for the shovel, I found myself standing again over my father. Rage and fear and shame and anguish came together. Lights flashed on the back of my eyelids, and I reeled against the wall to catch myself.

Shifting in the back of the truck, I felt the soreness in my back, both from my uncomfortable riding position and from the work of the previous evening. It had been a long and terribly difficult night. The lamp was placed to the side of my digging and cast a dim light to my grim work. I knew in my head that no other human soul was within miles, but every rustle of a leaf stopped my heart. The impending sunrise had chased away my plans for a funeral and sent me back to the house with not enough time to clean myself. I thought I was strong, but the tangled mess of roots and rocks were too much for me. Two graves had been compromised into one. Six feet under was shallowed up to four. My father, Mr. John L. Wilson, the greatest man I had ever known, was laid side by side in the same hole with the unfortunate unknown of M. Davis. Their bodies were destined to rot together. I covered them with a half sheet of plywood and some spare cinder blocks I found pack-ratted in a corner of the basement. It was a poor attempt to try and keep out who or what might want to dig up the top two feet of dirt.

My thoughts were broken as we crested a small rise and I saw the city ahead. The early morning fog was long gone. The clusters of short buildings in front of me were wrapped in plastic like forgotten leftovers in the rear of the refrigerator. I had never seen any of the cities of refuge from the outside, and it looked ridiculous to me. The checkpoint booth was just ahead, as the road crossed a gap in a long chain link fence. I could see a small entry door carved in the wall of the plastic-wrapped city. Trucks and construction equipment were parked outside but still within the fencing. As the truck came to a stop at the checkpoint, I tried to collect myself. The lady in the booth was moving her mouth, and I looked to the driver to see him talking also. *She might know Davis,* I thought and tried to turn my face panel so it would pick up the glare of the sun and block my face. Her voice came into my ear, "Pass me your badge." I slipped it out and laid it into the transfer bin. She picked it up inside the booth with a pair of tweezers. Five seconds that seemed like forever ticked away, and she passed the ID back out to me. The driver and the booth lady waved to each other, and we rolled leisurely into the gated gravel yard.

The truck turned around slowly in a short arc and came to a stop near the door. I grabbed Davis's bag and jumped from the back. I hadn't taken the time to notice the driver's name and couldn't see his badge now. The lack of observation of him and his comrades had either saved my life or hastened its ending. His voice came into my ear, "Good luck, Davis. Enjoy your own bed tonight, huh?"

"Thanks for the ride," I replied. The orange truck bit its wheels and showered me lightly with gravels as it headed back out the road to those houses waiting their destruction on the west side. *I need a lot more than luck,* I thought. I heard my father's voice repeating a parade of a thousand details as I stepped to the entry door. The next ten minutes would have to be perfect. I leaned my badge toward the scanner at the door and shifted it from side to side so it could be read. All at once, the door opened with a beep and a rush of air. With that, I stepped inside the city.

CHAPTER 2

"What direction? What direction ... Life begins at the intersection."

The door closed behind me so quickly I almost jumped. Jets of air blew around me as they sucked out the contaminated outside air and pumped in the clean inside air. *Just the opposite of the truth,* I thought. The room I was standing in was only about three or four feet wide with the same length. A second door opened, and I stepped forward into another room that was the same width but a few feet longer and lit in a fuzzy light with a purple hue. The doors closed quickly again behind me, but this time I was ready for it. The drilling and repetition of the last months kicked in, and I went through the practiced routine without thinking about each step or even second-guessing myself. I set the bag on the ground at my feet and held my arms out in front of me. A hard blast of steam, lasting only a few seconds, came at me from three different directions at once. I felt the pressure and heat over every part of my body. It was uncomfortable but not painful. I counted to three slowly and then loosened the seal around my hood and boots. I pulled open a short door to my left and set the boots and hood in a bin inside the door. Remembering the ID badge, I switched it from the pouch on the uniform front to one on the side of the bag. I quickly unzipped the blue jumpsuit and stepped out onto the concrete floor. When I reached to put the jumpsuit into the bin, the package from my father nearly slipped out from under my armpit but stayed hidden beneath my undershirt. Why hadn't I put that into the bag? I quickly shifted the package back under my left arm, only holding that arm out halfway and extending the right out full in front of me as the second blast of steam came over me. This one wasn't as hard but seemed to be hotter without the jumpsuit on. I was neither wet nor dry but kind of sticky. The doors opened in front of me, and I picked up the bag with my left arm, digging my elbow into my side to hold on to the package of papers. Clean and safe by the standards of the gatekeepers, I stepped into a dimly lit locker room.

After two years, I was back inside the city. It felt like something between an escaped convict breaking back into the penitentiary and a resurrected corpse digging its way back into its coffin. The first impression of the room, before I saw anything, was the smell. It wasn't musty, and it didn't really stink; it was just stale. The filtered air in the hood of the uniform was hard to breathe, but at least it had recently been fresh. This air was dead and lifeless. My lungs rejected the first breath I inhaled, and I coughed involuntarily. I tried to cover it up and make it seem natural but it echoed in the open room. I surely did not want to draw attention to myself right as I walked in the room. I looked around and relaxed; the room was empty.

The locker room looked like it had been walled off from an old parking garage. The floors were painted concrete, and the ceiling was of waffled concrete squares with the lighting tucked up into the gaps between the vertical ridges. Just as my father had told me, there were clusters of lockers arranged in groups by color around the room. There were clumps of orange, yellow, green, and the same light blue of the uniform I had just left behind. It was midmorning, probably between nine and ten, too early for the crowds coming back in from a shift and too late for those going out. We hadn't planned it this way, but it was perfect timing for me not to be noticed. As I walked across the room, I saw the only other person there, a lady at the green lockers, out of sight from the door at the cleaning station I just left. She was hurrying quickly to cover up her standard-issue gray underwear with her standard-issue gray jumpsuit. She only glanced my way and turned away quickly. By the time I got to the light blue lockers of the inspectors, she had turned for the door without even looking my way. That was a good thing, because even in the dim light it was quite obvious that my borrowed undershirt and shorts were not standard issue.

I found the locker with Davis on the nameplate, slipped his badge in and out of the slot, and opened the door. The locker was surprisingly empty. We had kept our school lockers full of all sorts of junk, and I somehow expected this one to be the same. There were no personal items inside except for one faded picture taped to the side wall of the locker, probably years ago. At some time or another it had slipped sideways, now held on by only one piece of tape with its edges curled on one side. Davis and a woman stood smiling next to each other at what looked like a scenic overlook at a state park. "His wife," I supposed. The twelve-digit code on the badge listed him as single and living alone with no children. I wondered if she had been killed or if they had divorced in the stress everyone suffered through in the early days. The image of his dead face looking up at me from the grave rose into my mind. I pushed it away and grabbed the gray jumpsuit from the locker.

I left the city just weeks before officially becoming an adult and had never worn the gray before. The jumpsuits for everyone eighteen and younger were of the same material and style, but were navy blue for boys and maroon for girls. There was something very different about putting this jumpsuit on. I could only muster vague images of Mom and Dad ever wearing anything other than the same clothes I was stepping into. Every boy in school looked forward to changing from blue to gray. We had no freedom over anything in our lives, and the uniform switch had become a rite of passage for a boy turning nineteen. If I had put on the gray jumpsuit then, it would have been a very big deal to me. With the contrasted reality of living outside of the city for the past two years and the morbid realization that I was wearing the clothes of a man I had just killed, it really meant very little. As I zipped up the front, I was just happy to cover up my underwear and not be noticed.

I reached into the locker and pulled out the thin, leather shoes that everyone wore within the city. As I bent over to slip the shoe over my heel, I saw a man in gray walk through the room toward the orange lockers. I shut the door of Davis's locker, stepped away so as not to be married to a particular spot, and sat down on the long bench in front of the lockers to slip on the other shoe. The shoes were too small, just like his boots, and I curled my toes just a little as I crammed them on my feet. When I stood up, the gray man turning to orange caught my eye and smiled. I tried to act casual and smiled back. *He is demolition,* I thought. *He might have known Davis and probably certainly knew the fellows in the truck I had hitched on.* I looked away before he would have time to start up a conversation. Demolition guys always talked more than any other type.

I stood up, grabbed the bag, and headed toward the same door the man had come into. A small office, surrounded by glass windows, was cut into the corner of the locker room nearest the door out to the city. A woman in a green uniform was pecking furiously at her keyboard. I tried to walk normally in the poorly fitted shoes but was sure that the busy green woman and the friendly orange man could see that something was wrong with me. I turned my face away from the office and leaned over the computer at the small desk near the door. I had forgotten my dad's instructions and put the badge back into the pocket on the bag. I dug the badge out of the pocket and rubbed it over the scanner before putting it in my jumpsuit pouch where it belonged, hoping the green lady didn't notice my mistake. My new identity, M. Davis, came up on the screen, his face staring at me once again, not accusingly, just blankly looking over my shoulder. I needed to request two days of leave and prepared to type in the request form, trying to recall each step my dad and I had practiced. If the lady thought I was having troubles, she would come out and recognize that I didn't match the picture on the screen. My hands rested on the keyboard, waiting. Davis's time card came up in front of me with seventeen hours of "unauthorized overtime." I almost skipped ahead to the leave request before catching myself. The text across the bottom of the screen ordered Davis to take off the rest of the day and the following two days. *There's a stroke of luck,* I thought. If things had gone according to the plan, I would have been there the day before, and the overtime would never have happened. I quickly clicked "Accept" and logged out, scuttling out the door before the green lady even looked up from her desk.

The door from the locker room opened to a short hallway with a few steps up to another door that would end my journey back inside the city. I steadied myself and stepped through the heavy metal door onto the street. The sun was near to its peak by now, and the light from it trickled between buildings and down through the canopy above. The plastic canopy was draped loosely over support beams and columns above and sealed off to the edges of buildings to create a circus tent effect several stories high above the street. It was much brighter here on the street than the locker room, but several notches dimmer than the true outside I had just left, even without looking through my tinted face panel. The canopy was made of a clear plastic, but it was so thick that you could only see a milky white shade of the blue sky above. I could tell the position of the sun above by the brightness that spread in its spot on the canopy but could not distinguish its round outline through the plastic. Everything in the sky above was there to be seen, but only in a murky, filtered sort of way. I had lived in a city just like this for most of my life, but the past few years at our cabin in the mountains had changed my per-spective so much. Back inside the plastic dome, I felt smothered and oppressed by its weight above me.

I tried to walk as if I knew where I was going but had to stop in the middle of the street to gain my bearings. A large concrete building was in front of me, and a few people in green uniforms passed each other on the long stairs that led up to its double doors. *This would be their main city building,* I thought. I looked for the small plaque that I knew would be to the right of the doors. I stopped and squinted to see the writing on the plaque and read it to myself, "CR18." I had made it to the right place. This was where Lori had been sent.

I thought back to the day I had last seen her, at the steps of a building that looked very much like the one that stood before me. She had gotten her appointment card to be deployed a few days before and showed it to me at school. None of us knew what day we would turn nineteen or if the city officials just picked a day at random for each of us. Everyone in our class had spent the last year on edge, waiting for their appointment cards to arrive. Lori's card said she was scheduled to appear at the city building two days later at 10:00. When the morning came, she showed up at the door of the apartment I shared with my parents. It was my day off from school, and my parents had already left for work. She hadn't told me she was coming, but I was dressed and ready to go just in case she stopped by. When I came to the door, she just said, "Jack, would you walk with me?" and turned from the door, only glancing for a moment to see if I would follow her before turning down the hall. Of course I quickly locked the door behind me, jogging a few steps to catch her as she went down the steps.

We walked along quietly for most of the way, talking in short sentences about things that had happened in school the last few weeks or about something else that neither one of us really cared about and then dropping back into silence. As we neared the city building, she stopped and looked at me. "Should I be scared?" she asked as she pushed a piece of hair behind her ear. She was becoming a beautiful young woman but looked for that moment to be a little girl. Her eyes waited for my answer as if I would tell her how to feel and that would be that.

Scared? Of course I was and knew she should be too, but I shrugged my shoulders and said, "You'll be fine. You did every-thing you should've done, your grades were great, and you have never had a single demerit. They will just give you a clerical job here in the city. Nothing will change except you won't have any more homework to worry about." That was what I wanted to believe. She smiled and turned from me to resume her walking. Her question was out of character and caught me off guard. Normally she was confident, too sure of herself to need someone else's opinion. On that day, she seemed a bit shaken. I followed a step behind, just off her shoulder, letting her lead. She walked quickly and gracefully, as always, but with a heaviness that was not normal.

She stepped up on the first step of the city building and turned quickly around to me. She was walking at such a smart pace that I was stretching to keep up with her. When she turned, I nearly bumped into her and ended up closer than I meant to be. She was about six inches shorter than me, and with the help of the step, her eyes were just above mine. She didn't back away from me, so I stayed where I was. "You can't come with me, you know," she said. She looked directly into my eyes for just a second and then looked away, past me over my shoulder and then to the ground. She chose her words carefully and spoke deliberately. I often wondered if she knew what was about to happen to her. Her eyes caught mine again. "Please wait here for me, and hopefully I will be back out in a few minutes."

She put her arms around me and leaned against me, pressing her face on my shoulder. I was surprised but reached out and pulled her to me. I had never held her against me like that. My arms wrapped all the way around her, reaching almost under her arms on the opposite side. I felt her body pressed full against mine from her knees to her chest to her shoulders. Feelings of sympathy and worry wrestled with the pleasure of feeling her body pressed against me. She held me for longer than I would have felt right about holding on to her, but I waited for her arms to finally relax before letting her go. She smiled at me through clenched lips, and I saw the tears in the corners of her eyes just before she turned. She bounced up the short, flat steps two at a time and disappeared through the heavy double doors without looking back.

I stared at the doors closing behind her and sat slowly on the steps to wait. I had loved her for years but had never thought she felt anything toward me. I wondered what I would say to her when she came out. I practiced lines to myself, sometimes thinking that we were deeply in love and would surely be married and then convincing myself that the hug meant nothing and she was just emotional and worried. I had a few other friends but none as close as her. *If I come on too strong*, I thought, *she will be hurt and it might ruin our friendship.* I batted thoughts back and forth in my mind, not noticing the time slipping away. She didn't come out by noon, and I began to get worried. The sunlight began to fade and a stream of green uniforms filed past me down and up the steps as they changed shifts. I stood up, stiff from sitting for so long, and pressed back against the wall of the steps. I searched the faces that passed in front of me. She wasn't there. My stomach tightened. I was embarrassed at the foolish thoughts I had been entertaining. I tried to convince myself that she had gone out another door and I had missed her somehow, but in my heart I knew that Lori was gone. And I was right. I searched the city for a week in every spare moment I had, but never saw her again.

As I stood staring at the plaque on the building in front of me, I could almost see her thin frame in the faded maroon jumpsuit slipping between the doors in front of me. I could see the back of her head and her hair swaying from side to side as she jogged up the stairs, but I couldn't remember her face. How was I supposed to pick her out from thousands of people when I couldn't remember her face? I felt lost and foolish. What was I even doing here? I shook myself free from my thoughts. I needed to keep moving.

I scanned the buildings around me and tried to figure out where I was. To my right, an old hotel was backed against the outer wall of the city's plastic skin. A line of neon letters, unlit in the daytime, spoke a single word: "Entertainment." I was obviously at one end of the city. I turned to my left, walking up the street at a slight incline. Dad had assumed that CR18 would be laid out like the CR12 we had left. The entertainment building would be on one end of the city and the school and the apartments would be on the other end. If he was right, I had a long walk before me.

As I crested the small hill, I could see that my dad was right again. The city was really only one long street flanked on either side by buildings draped in plastic. The corridor only widened when a larger building required more of the canopy to cover its backside. I left the few government offices and passed between rows of nondescript buildings with few or no windows and with no signs or markings, just a number on the wall to the right of the door. These would surely be some sort of manufacturing or packing facilities. A building like one of these would certainly have been my destiny at CR12 if we hadn't left when we did.

Dad and Mom had been pleading with me for months to go with them when they left the city, but I refused. After Lori was gone, I had no reason to stay. As we prepared to leave, I asked Mom to track down Lori. She worked at the main city building of CR12 in personnel records. We both knew it was risky and jeopardized our escape, but I had to know where she was and Mom gave in to me. Mom found Lori's deployment to CR18, but no apartment number or job assignment. She did find a record with some old shipping directions for a uniform transfer between the two cities. When Dad and I decided to return to find Lori, we used the shipping directions and old road maps to figure out which city was which. Dad was good with the maps, but I just went along with him, not paying much attention to where we were. I began to wonder if I would even be able to find the way back home without him. First I would have to find her and try to figure out how to get back out without getting caught. At least I was in the right city.

So here I am, I thought, *but where is she?* The street was mostly empty, but there were a few men and women walking silently along the street. I walked in a funny stride in the tight-fitting shoes. I was sure everyone was looking at me and I was doing something wrong that someone would notice. But no one even lifted their head to look at me, no one spoke to anyone walking beside them, no one nodded a greeting to an acquaintance across the way. Instead they trudged along like lemmings, watching where their feet would next step. They marched not to a sudden death over a cliff, but to a silent and gradual dying within. From the looks of the faces I passed, most were already dead or nearly there. Lori was so alive when I had known her before. *Surely,* I thought, *she will stand out, and I will find her quickly.* It was the first shred of optimism I had dared in the last two days.

As I came to the cluster of apartment buildings, I pulled up the duffle bag and pretended to flick off a piece of dirt, looking one more time at the number on Davis's badge. Right in the middle of the long number there was 05–03–18. He was in the fifth building, third floor, room eighteen. I walked into the front door of the building marked number five and up the dimly lit stairwell to the third floor. I came to apartment number eighteen and stopped. His badge also said 100 for the three digits following the room number. That should have meant that he was living alone, but you never knew for sure. I didn't need any more surprises today. I listened at the door, not wanting to wait too long in case someone else came down the hall. If Davis wasn't living alone, I could always abandon his apartment and try to find an empty one to break into. *I've got to keep going,* I thought. I slid the badge through the lock and quietly opened the door.

I shut the door behind me, stepped out of the shoes, gently set the bag on the couch and quickly scoped out each room in case I needed to bail. There was no one there, which was a relief. I found only one toothbrush, looked for hairdryers, and poked through the small dresser and the closet. Davis was obviously living alone and didn't have much to show for that. His apartment looked more like a motel room he was staying in for the weekend than a place he had called home for the last twelve years. He was an odd man to be sure. *And dead at my hand,* I reminded myself.

The apartment was tiny, much smaller than the three-bedroom unit that I lived in with my parents for so long. The houses my dad and I borrowed for the night over the last few weeks of traveling had single rooms that were much larger than this entire apartment. I hadn't realized I had it so good. The living room was just wide enough for the couch and an end table. There was a narrow path for walking between the couch and the half kitchen. The bedroom adjoined the living room. Davis had taken down its door from the hinges and put it in the bedroom closet to make more room. The bedroom was just large enough for a person to walk on only one side of the double bed that filled the room. The only window in the apartment was on the wall of the bedroom opposite the door. I looked out the window through the thick plastic that wrapped tightly over the building to the ground below. It was tempting to lift the window, slit the plastic and try for a breath of fresh air. *Some sort of alarm would probably go off,* I thought and turned away.

A utilitarian bathroom was next to the bedroom. The sink, tub, and toilet were crammed together efficiently with just enough room to open and close the door. The only things in the bathroom that would let you know that someone was living there were Davis's toothbrush, a comb, his razor, and a bar of soap. The thought of a shower was too tempting to resist. I took the four steps back to lock the apartment door, pulling off the jumpsuit and borrowed underwear as I walked. The package of papers from my dad fell onto the floor. I pitched it onto the couch next to the bag and got into the shower. I had forgotten how weak the water stream would be but remembered that I had to hurry. I scrubbed up the parts that needed it most and just got rinsed off before the water trickled dry. *The creek back home was way better than this,* I thought as I toweled myself off.

The thought of the word *home* made me stop. Where was home? I had been the child of three different worlds: the primitive cabin of the past two years, the cramped apartment of CR12, and the almost mystical place of my early childhood that I could barely even remember. That earliest world was the one that I wanted the most. Part of me was still eight years old, waiting for this nightmare to just go away and for the peaceful happiness of our life to return. That life was fading away to a mist of memories. A chill came over me. I needed to get some clothes on.

I wadded up the borrowed underwear that had caused me so much grief and stuffed them under Davis's bed. He only had two sets of underwear in his drawer. "The other set is buried," I thought. I pulled on the undershirt and shorts and got back into the jumpsuit. I needed something to eat. His refrigerator was as empty as his drawers and closets. I found something already cooked and half eaten in a sealed container and stuffed it down. I didn't like the taste it left in my mouth, but I was too hungry to care. There was something that tasted like ginger ale in a plastic bottle and I washed it down, drinking straight from the bottle. My mom wouldn't have liked that.

I looked at the clock on the wall in the kitchen. It read 11:42. I had about four hours before anyone would be changing shifts. I sat down on the couch and picked up the package of papers from my dad. He had stuffed the papers into a large plastic freezer bag, probably a gallon size, and pressed out the air before sealing the zipper at the top. He had written front and back on pages from an old yellow legal pad, and from the thickness of the folded-over pack of papers, it looked like he used the whole thing. There was a single page of paper, folded and wrapped the opposite way around the rest. His words were written in all caps and tightly packed together in the generic style that we were all taught to use. In spite of the forced uniformity of style, I could see in the letters the little nuances of my father's hand that had showed up in the notes left around the cabin in the last two years and in the sketches and lists that we had used in the planning of our trip. Seeing his personality glowing up off the papers uncovered the fresh scabs of the painful experiences of the night before. I fought away the tears and pulled out the single paper, setting the others on the floor in front of me.

The other papers were all written in black ink; this one was written in blue. On the paper was the imprint of something that he had used to write on, maybe the wrinkles in a book cover. Scribbled across the top of the page in large letters were the words, "Read this before you meet her!" I looked to the first line of writing and began to read:

Dearest Jack,

I am glad you are reading this because it means you made it safely inside. I am watching you sleeping beside me as I write this in the light of the lamp we found. I have enjoyed this trip with you so much, more than you will ever know. Tomorrow we will "meet" the inspector and your real adventure will begin. In just a few days we will be back together again, and you and I can take Lori back to meet your mother. I too am anxious to meet someone who you care so deeply for. You may be wondering why I agreed to go with you on this trip. I wondered the same thing myself, especially as these past few days approached. This trip is riskier than you realize, and there is so much for us to lose.

So often I have wondered if we made the right decision to come. But then I remembered the look in your eyes when you came to me to ask for my permission to go. It was the first time I had seen you stand up like a man. I realized then that you had a right to chase your own dreams and make your own future. The life we have at the cabin is good, and I hope you can make something like that for you and for Lori when we get back, but it needs to be you making your own life for your own family. God's plan for you is not the same plan He has for me and you have to follow His way for you or you are just wasting your time. I hope you can see that. Even if I somehow lose you in all this, it is worth it just to try. It is part of you becoming a man and part of my job as your father. I don't think your mother understood that when we left or ever completely will.

I have been such a poor father to you. You grew up under my nose from just a boy to a man, and I missed it all. I wasn't there for you. With all that we went through in the beginning at the city, you never got a hug or a word of encouragement from me. I was torn apart inside and never even thought that you might be struggling too. I never helped you with your school work. I didn't know the names of any of your friends. I can remember hearing you cry out in your dreams at night and standing outside your door, wanting to go in but not knowing what to say, and just walking away, letting you cry. Please forgive me for all these failures.

For the last two years, there has been so much to do just to survive. You have been such a help at the cabin to your mother and me. I have tried to be a better father these past years, but how can I give you advice or steer you along when I barely know how to be a man myself? So here you are about to make the biggest decision of your life so far. Do you really know her and do you really love her and does she love you? I am guessing you are asking yourself the same questions. I wish I had some good answers or could tell you something profound that would help you to understand, but I don't know much myself. All I know to tell you is what love has been in my own life. So please read this before you meet her. You owe it to her to know in your own mind what you are doing before you try to talk her into risking her life and leaving for another world.

So here you are. This is a rambling mess, I know, and my handwriting is tough to read. My hope is that you can see that what you are reading is from my heart. Please know that I love you, my son. I would give all that I am for you. I am so proud of the man you are becoming.

Love, Dad

I dropped the page to the floor and rolled back onto the couch, pulling my knees against me. It was too hard to read, too much to take in. I couldn't stand the thought of him being gone. I felt so alone. The tears I had held back all day finally broke loose. I sobbed uncontrollably, shaking all over. Exhaustion finally overtook me and I fell into a deep, dreamless sleep.

CHAPTER 3

"I want to wake up kicking and screaming.
I want a heart that I know is beating.
It's beating, I'm bleeding."

I woke with a jerk and looked over at the clock in the kitchen. It read 16:03. I was late. I jumped from the couch and grabbed for the shoes. My left arm was half asleep and wouldn't respond when I asked it to the first time. I crammed in my feet and slapped myself in the face, bumping into the wall as I reached for the door. I remembered to check for my badge in its pocket and tried to steady myself as I stepped into the hall. There were a half dozen people walking toward the stairs, and I fell into the line, trying to look casual. This was not what I had planned.

The small line of commuters on the stairs merged into a larger line as we came from the front doors of the building, and I found myself in heavy traffic on the main road. I remembered what I was doing and began to look around at the faces of those walking beside me. I was the only one without something in my hand and the only one with my head raised. I tried to look down and glance up at the same time and the effect kind of made me dizzy. I was pressing along quickly in a sea of gray jumpsuits. We were all heading back toward the other end of the city that I had just left that morning.

Although I couldn't create an image of Lori's face in my mind, I knew without a doubt that she was not among the faces that surrounded me. As the mass of people moved along, I realized my mistake. I was only getting a small picture of all the people here. Those in front of me and behind me were escaping my scrutiny. It was too late to change directions, and I trudged along in my little pocket of traffic, disgusted with myself for this wasted opportunity.

Men and women slipped from the line of walkers and turned into buildings to the left and right. As we neared the end of the road, our group had dwindled to a few stragglers. I found myself standing at the entrance to my new place of employment back in front of the city building and entertainment building. Startled at my own stupidity, I walked away quickly before Davis's nametag might be noticed by a co-worker. I found a spot to the side of the entrance to the entertainment building where the current of people would not sweep me along and tried to observe.

It was now surely already past 16:30 and the workers leaving their shifts were pouring out of the buildings around me faster and heavier than the throng I had walked in the other way. I had been in the mass of night shifters going to fill the slots of the day shifters. At this end of the city, the day shifters were certainly the larger group. I stood completely still, unnoticed in the corner, and attempted to study each face that passed in front of me, searching for a face that I would remember to be Lori's.

Most of those coming from the buildings trudged up the hill toward the apartments, but more than a few turned toward the entertainment building, passing by me through the double glass doors. *Where were they going?* I wondered. I could never have gone into the entertainment building at CR12, no one underage was allowed in, but here, in my new identity, I was old enough to enter. A mix of curiosity and guilty desire pulled me toward the doors. I stepped away from the building and stared through the glass, trying to catch a glimpse of what might be inside. A man jostled against me as I wandered into his path and looked at me with annoyance. I turned back toward the street leading the opposite direction and realized that I had missed a few hundred people by looking away for just that moment. The mass of people coming from the buildings was slowing to a trickle, and I quickly stepped into the rear of the line and headed up the hill again. I was really disgusted with myself now. I couldn't have handled the last hour any worse than I did.

The group ending their workday walked more slowly than those getting started. I stared at the back of people's heads in front of me, looking for something familiar. I tried to pick upward in the line without being pushy. I needed to see more people if I was going to find her in this mob. As we passed between noisy manufacturing buildings, I noticed that no one was leaving or joining our group. I was at the end of the line and all the workers from these buildings had gone on ahead. I kicked myself inside as I realized just how stupid I had been. Ten to twenty thousand people, pretty much the whole population of the city, had just passed up and down this street, and I had seen only a few hundred. I was never going to find her this way.

My feet were screaming at me as the apartment buildings came back into sight. Where the work buildings ended and the apartment buildings began, a small patch of grass and a few short trees formed what they called a park on either side of the street. Exiting from the line of traffic, I plopped down onto the grass, leaned forward against my knees, and slipped my heels out of the shoes. I searched the last few faces that passed in front of me as the sunlight through the canopy above began to fade and the orange streetlights came on.

The street widened and curved to the right toward the schools as it passed by the apartments. A young lady walked back down from the direction of the schools, holding the hand of a girl that must have been her daughter and looked to be six or seven years old. It was odd to see young children in the city, and I couldn't help myself from staring. I studied the face of the young mother in the habit of the last hour, and her eyes caught mine. She was definitely not Lori but was still quite pretty. Like most everyone I had seen that day, she looked tired and sad. When she saw me looking at her, she steered the little girl to the other side of the street and headed down to the other end of the park. They slipped off their shoes and walked in the grass. The young girl grinned and giggled softly. The look on her face reminded me how I had felt at the same age walking barefoot with my own mom in our backyard. It was oddly encouraging to watch this young lady trying to find just a moment's worth of happiness for her daughter in this cold and lifeless box of existence. I wondered if Lori might have a family of her own. Maybe she too had found a way to steal happiness from this world. Maybe she wouldn't want to see me, and this crazy charade was for nothing. The two girls slipped back into their shoes and walked, almost skipping, back toward the apartments. They were alive in a dead world and the contrast was striking.

The street was empty, and the daylight was completely gone. I stood and stretched, looking instinctively up to the sky. In the past two years at the cabin, I had fallen in love with the stars, digging through old books, memorizing constellations. I spent hours outside at night, lying on my back, just staring up at the sky. When I looked at the stars, everything my dad had tried to tell me about God and life and meaning seemed to make a lot more sense. Something about all those points of light being so far away made me feel really small and insignificant, but it put me in my right place in the universe. Someone else was directing the movement of those stars, so maybe they were directing the chaos around me, too. As I looked up, trying to catch a glimpse of the sky, the orange glow of the streetlights reflected off the canopy, and it seemed lower and more suffocating than ever. *No way of seeing anything through that thing,* I thought to myself.

CR18 was laid out a lot like CR12 and had a market at the corner of the park. Back in school, we had traded off IDs dozens of times without ever being caught. The guys working the checkout never even looked at our badges. I thought about the lack of food back in Davis's apartment and considered getting something better to eat, but I didn't even know if Davis had any money left in his account. *Better to not risk a scene,* I thought and turned away from the market for the apartments. I had totally wasted this day of searching and needed to see more faces in the morning if I was going to find Lori. I also had some reading to do and desperately needed a good night's sleep.

I climbed the stairs, found the door to Davis's apartment, and locked it behind me. I looked around again at the apartment of the man I had murdered the day before. This day seemed to be a lifetime in itself. The whole universe seemed tightly compressed into this little bubble while everything outside it seemed murky and distant. I felt lonely and cold and intentionally brought an image of my mom and dad to my mind to try and comfort myself. Their faces I could see easily. I closed my eyes, remembering movements, glances, tones of voice, smells. "That is what is real," I said out loud to no one.

I should have been starving, but I wasn't. The clock in the kitchen read 19:22. I needed to read some more of what Dad had written. I picked up the papers and sat down on the couch, pulling off the shoes and socks I had borrowed. My feet were red, my toes were numb, and the heel of the shoe was beginning to dig a trough into my skin. I rubbed my feet a few times and laid back on the couch with my head propped up under the lamp on the end table. I had suffered through blisters worse than these on my hands the first few weeks at the cabin. Swinging that ax had grown thick calluses in the line across the top of my palm at the base of my fingers and in the crease where my thumb joined the rest of my hand. I pulled a little tab of skin from one of the calluses and smiled. *Bad shoes I can handle,* I thought. Turning on my side, I laid my dad's stack of yellow papers on the little pocket of the couch cushion in front of me and began to read.

My story begins with my awakening. I could say that I had been asleep for many years, but that would not be completely true. It wasn't sleep, like we sleep each day. Nor was it like a coma, a trance, daydreaming, or even normal dreaming at night. It is only fair to say that now I am most definitely awake and to say also that before I woke up I was not awake. That statement is very true, but certainly hard to get a grip on. The description that works best for me is to remember years ago when I had a 45-minute drive from work to home. On many afternoons, I could remember starting the car and pulling from the parking lot and the next thing I knew I was in the garage at home, shutting off the engine. In between, I had navigated several stop lights, turning both left and right, had stopped and started in heavy traffic, had merged onto and off of the interstate, and had probably even stopped for a dog to cross the road but could recall nothing of the entire trip. My mind had been totally focused on a project or issue at work or some argument I had with someone and the details of driving had been left to my subconscious, which obviously did just fine without the help of my thinking brain. That description works great for me, but not so well for you, I suspect, considering that you have never driven before or perhaps have only driven the inspector's truck yet today. Let me just reconcile myself to saying that I was asleep and then I awoke, and I will let you adjust the meaning of the word sleep or any other unworthy phrase in your own understanding as you read.

It would be an easy excuse to say that the sudden trauma of losing part of my family and the collapse of my world around me had driven me to this state, but that would be a lie. I had begun to fall asleep years before that day, nodding and drifting away from reality and from all relationships, creating a wall around myself to shield out sound and light for my slumber. The events of that day only pushed me off a ledge that I had been standing on the edge of for some time. I had already begun to separate myself from anything and everything in my world that was real. I have heard people say that they were cheating on their wives, having an affair with their jobs, but for me it was something different. I never loved my work, but I knew I was good at it. Work was black and white, and I knew if I did things a certain way, I could have a measure of success. Real life and relationships were tougher. I knew that no matter how hard I tried, I was going to fail a good part of the time, and I couldn't stand to fail. So instead of escaping to an affair or to drugs, liquor, or pornography, I just began to work more and more. To me, it seemed so much easier, less destructive, and less harmful to Abbie and you and to everyone else that I really did love and care for. Or at least that was the line of reasoning that my subconsciousness used to slowly and incrementally lull me into my state of drowsy disconnect. I was under the hand of the hypnotist, or a gentle and subtle anesthesiologist, or more accurately, I became the proverbial frog in the pot, just sleeping to death instead of boiling.

And so, crossing from one world to another, I was not aware of anything other than one day at a time. One job, one family, one marriage morphed into another with some of the same characters, but so different in every other way. Life unfolded and unraveled around me and I made no attempt to determine its beginning or end, allowing it to pile about me like a jumbled mess of unmanaged hoses. All of a sudden, I awoke and found myself choking in this pit of snakes with everything remaining in my life that I truly cared about but had ignored for so long dying slowly on all sides of me.

I had been asleep then for most of my life and to have awoken in a space of a few hours was quite a shock. Two events woke me up completely and suddenly. One was the worst moral failure of my life and one was a chance meeting with the most extraordinary man I have ever met. One event led to the other, but I cannot be sure that one without the other would have done anything more than make me roll over and fall back asleep. Looking back on that day, I often wonder if I came to on my own or if God himself shook me awake. At the time, I would have written it all off to chance, but with each passing day, I realize more and more that nothing is left to chance. The hand of the Shepherd is always around us, shaping and guiding. I just wonder why he let me sleep for so long and why so many others fill these cities, sleeping soundly as their lives slip away. I also wonder why and how something so wicked would have been the beginning of so many good things. But such is life, and it has always been so, and the arms of my mind are much too small to reach around these things and grasp them.

Without a doubt, what first woke me up was the sudden realization that I was in the act of committing a murder. I know, in fact, that it was on the count of seven. It was a beautiful sunny day, cold and crisp. I can remember now that the sky was clear and beautiful, but I surely didn't notice at the time. I do remember that it was cold. Our jumpsuits and long underwear were too hot in the summer, but not thick enough to cut the draft and cold out in the winter. I have often wondered if they have better gear in the CRs up north. At the insistence of Jackson, my inspection partner, we had just done a final check of our charges as they readied for the countdown. This was a building that actually needed to be destroyed. It was an older retail building in a downtown section of a little town about an hour's drive out of the city. The building was two stories tall with self-supporting two-brick thick walls that were bulging outward on all four sides and especially so along one wall. The place probably should have been condemned even before it was abandoned on the day. Nine years of no upkeep only made it worse. It was a tricky job for us and for the demolition crew. We worked together to try and make sure no one got hurt. It was noteworthy enough of a demolition job that our supervisor had come to see the place fall in. That was what had led Jackson to go back into the building one more time.

Jackson was young, no more than two years out school. I had been doing the inspector job before he hit his teen years and had been a licensed structural engineer for years before that, but on our two-man crew, he was my superior. He was a riser, and I was a flatliner—he knew it, and I knew it. I learned the hard way that I was not going to get anywhere in this game. I put in the extra hours, filed the perfect reports, blew the top off every quota put in front of me, and kissed all the right butts, but got nowhere. He was a prototype riser, just the guy that they wanted at the top. He was out of their schools, was completely self-centered, and had never known the rules to any other game but the one they wanted him to play. I was the backup quarterback that was smarter, stronger, and more experienced, but was watching from the sideline as the kid got all the snaps. It wasn't that I hated him, because I didn't. He was stupid, arrogant, and annoying, but not deceitful enough to be worthy of hate. It was just that he saw me as another head to step on as he climbed to the top. There was something about his attitude that represented perfectly a system that inspired me and everyone else around me to just shut it down and quit caring. It was guys like Jackson that made getting up in the morning and going to work feel so meaningless.

Jackson and I had already done a "final" walk-through with the head of the demolition crew, but that was before our supervisor showed up. I knew it was all for show, but I went along anyway, walking behind as we passed from charge to charge in the bottom floor, neither of us commenting in our radios, neither of us even looking again at our marks or at the work of the charge setters. I was annoyed with him, not because he was showing out to the supervisor (I was used to that), but because it was cold in that building and I was anxious to get back in the cab of our truck and warm back up. We had set up a series of anchors and cables along the bulging wall to cause it to implode instead of blowing out bricks all over the place. It was really a nice piece of work, my work along with the demo supervisor. Jackson had done little or nothing on this project except try to look important. He and I ducked and weaved between the cables and headed for the back door.

We were the last out and were only a few steps away from the building when they gave the "all-clear" and started the countdown from fifteen over the loud-speakers of the truck. The exit door was in the rear of the building, and everyone else was gathered around the front, a safe distance away to observe the building's collapse. Our truck was parked to the side, and I jogged to it and turned around, leaning back against the grill to watch and ready to get inside the cab and warm up. I knew that Jackson would be finding his way to our supervisor, to be sure they were standing together to watch it fall. When I turned around, the count had hit eleven, and I saw Jackson, lying at the threshold of the door, a look of desperation on his face. He had apparently jammed his boot between two boards near the door and tripped, falling forward. I never could figure why he went back to the door, maybe he had left something inside and gone back for it, I don't know. But there he was, twisted in a heap, stuck, and in trouble. He must have fallen hard, because his hood had pulled loose and was lying a few feet from his head. His immediate struggle was as much to put his hood in its proper place as it was to try and pull his foot loose.

It is amazing how much information can flow through our brains in a very short period of time. I processed the situation before me and considered the implications through twice or more in the space of a second. You don't realize that you think that way until you are on the timer and the seconds are recorded. By the time the count of ten came through the loudspeakers, I had determined that no one but me could see him, that no one would know that I could see him, that he was not going to get his foot loose in time, and that he was not going to get his radio re-attached in time. My first thought was that I could likely get back to him in time to give him a good yank and pull him loose before the building collapsed on top of him. My second thought was that I could easily switch my radio frequency to call the demo supervisor or even just run around to the front and wave my arms and have him call off the detonation before the building collapsed on top of Jackson. My third thought was that I didn't really care if the building collapsed on top of him. My fourth thought was that it was strict policy not to go back toward a building in the midst of a countdown. And so then, I ran back through all those thoughts again and decided that I would stand there, lean back against my truck, and do nothing. The count of nine came, and then eight, and he looked up at me, his unhooded face sucking in breaths of what he thought was poisonous air, staring death in the face and screaming at me to help him. Between eight and seven, I wondered to myself if anyone else could hear him screaming over the countdown, and then I realized that I couldn't hear him screaming and that I only knew he was screaming because I could see his mouth open and see the veins straining in his neck and that I was somehow relieved at that thought that no one could hear him. As the count of seven came over the speakers a new thought came into my head, "This is a murder. I am killing this man." I reached for my radio and then let my hand fall to my side and looked away, listening to the seconds count down to zero. I looked back in time to see the building collapse on top of him, crushing him completely and instantly.

The sight of him actually dying was something different than the thoughts of indifference and subtle hatred that I had nursed in my mind as the final six seconds ticked away. A burst of guilt shot through me and mixed with fear as I realized what I had done. I quickly looked to the group at my right to see if anyone else could have possibly seen him there or if they would really have known whether I could see him. I looked again back toward Jackson, straining through the dust to see the spot where he had been. If he was not really dead, he would take me before the review board and cut me down for sure. Instinctively, I rushed toward the building to see if I could get to him first. I had no thought of finishing him off; I just needed to know if he was alive or dead. A massive mound of bricks covered him and only his arm was left poking out from the bottom of the pile. I ripped off his glove and tried to feel for a pulse through the fingers my own gloves. Of course I could feel nothing and probably wouldn't have felt anything if he had been alive. The demolition crew saw me run toward the building and followed me in. They reached him within a few seconds and shoved me aside. Following their man-down protocol, they pulled bricks off by hand and then quickly brought in equipment that uncovered his crushed and lifeless body within a few minutes.

Except for Jackson's untimely death, the demolition had been a great success. The building had folded in upon itself neatly without a single brick falling more than twenty feet from the building's perimeter. I stood quietly to the side, watching them pull his body from the pile of bricks. I was shocked at how cold-hearted of a man I had become. Two men in orange suits loaded up his flattened light blue body into a dark brown bag and gently laid him in the back of my truck. I waited for the rubble to be marked as a crime scene, but no tape or paint came out. Our supervisor walked over to me and laid his gloved hand on my shoulder. He was about my age, but had started his ascent early on. I suppose he had the remnants from our previous life of the habitual phrases and facial expressions that are exchanged when someone dies that we know. He at least intended to show some disturbed sadness, but it was obviously not genuine. Like me, but for different reasons, he didn't care whether Jackson lived or died, and his poor attempt to act as if he did just showed him to be all the more oblivious to the value of Jackson's life. After passing off a few phrases like, "what a horrible thing to have happened" and "such a loss to the department" or "he was great fellow," he calmly reminded me that since Jackson was my partner and according to regulations I was to be off for the next two days and that I would need to report to the City Building that afternoon to answer questions and file a report on the incident. I nodded silently and passed off a few sad and mournful facial expressions that were just as phony as his words.

It was a strange and somber drive back to the city. My senses had been jostled into awareness by the realization of the murder I had just committed. The shame and fear of my current situation was mixed with the adrenaline rush of suddenly being awake. A parade of thoughts rushed through my mind at a pace too fierce to comprehend. It was as if I was Rip Van Winkle, awaking from a deep sleep into a world I did not know, but into a brew of dangerous and fearful circumstances that old Rip didn't have to contend with. I didn't know where to begin to focus my mind and instead let present remembrances bounce against those from the near and distant past, not bothering to process or organize the information into meaningful patterns of thought.

When I arrived at the checkpoint in front of the yard, two men were waiting to collect Jackson's body from the back of the truck and waved me over to their end of the building. After carrying the body bag inside the building, one of the men reappeared. He waited silently as I segregated Jackson's tools and personals from mine in the cab of the truck, stuffing each into our respective duffle bags. I grabbed my bag, leaving his in the cab, and picked up my tool bag from the back of the truck, tossing it over my shoulder. The whole process of handling his body seemed to me to be too familiar for these guys, even in a world full of death. They picked up the bag of his body the way I picked up the bag of tools. From the little we had spoken of personal matters, I knew that Jackson had no family in CR12, no wife, and no children. There would be no autopsy, no investigation, no funeral, and no memorial. Who even wanted to know how they would be disposing of the body? These thoughts I considered, but I only nodded to the fellows as I walked the long walk back to the entry door and washdown at our locker room.

I had the locker room to myself and changed quickly, as always. At the check-in computer station, my work schedule had already been adjusted, and I could see that I had an appointment with the review board in room 212 at the City Building that afternoon at 1:30. I had two hours before the meeting, but I didn't even consider doing anything other than just walking over and waiting out the time. The streets were empty as I stepped past the door and into the large City Building.

I had been in the building many times in the last nine years, but had never until that day noticed the high ceilings and marble floors. This had been a courthouse before the collection of everyone to the city, and it continued to serve a similar function. The details and architecture were expensive and stunning, especially in comparison to the drab utilitarian buildings that were normal to the rest of the city. I caught myself gaping up at the ceiling and twitched my neck to one side, correcting the angle of my head to the more typical and expected in case anyone was watching. This building was where Abbie worked, up in the records department on the third floor. I went to see her office a few times, but years had passed by since I had been there last. She would be on lunch break and would have the time to talk. I was surprised at how much I wanted to tell her how I felt inside, but as I prepared opening sentences to the conversation, they were all odd and uncomfortable. What would I say to her? Maybe something like, "Abbie dear, I just watched a man die because I wouldn't hit the button on my radio and seeing his body crushed in front of me has made me realize that I have been missing so much all these years." She was only one floor above me, but I could feel the force of the divide between us. I stopped on the stairs at the second floor, found room 212, and sat down on the polished wooden bench that faced the door.

I stared at the numbers of the heavy-looking double doors and thought about the interrogation that awaited me. I had been questioned by a review board one time before, when a defective charge I had set had blown up prematurely, nearly killing a man who was working nearby. The questions then had been tough, but I knew I had done nothing wrong. In the end, the board agreed with me, and I was not disciplined or reprimanded. This was obviously a different situation. They would be considering me as only a bystander to the incident and would be asking a few basic questions to go into the accidental death report.

I closed my eyes and leaned my head back against the wall behind the bench. An image of Jackson's crushed and lifeless body, but with his head still alive and his face straining in a silent scream came into my head. I shuddered and opened my eyes, staring again at the numbers on the door, just to see something else. That same image still comes into my dreams from time to time. Son, I hope that you never have to deal with a secret sin like I have. You will drag the guilt around with you like a sack of bricks for the rest of your life. It has helped to confess everything to Abbie. It has helped to pray to heaven for forgiveness. But even after all these years the guilt has never left me completely. I suppose something like a murder can't just go away. My only hope is that I will meet Jackson in heaven to apologize, but I don't suspect that day will come. It doesn't seem fair that the killer would be redeemed and that his victim would be condemned, but what I know of his heart would lead me to no other conclusion.

I sat staring passively at the door, alternately considering guilty recollections of the day's events and practicing answers to supposed questions of the board when the offices around me opened for lunch. A stream of people, mostly women in clerical positions, filed past me. They were used to seeing people sitting on that bench, and I knew that no one would look my way, but I looked down and stared at the floor to avoid making eye contact with anyone. I supposed that some would see me sitting there and wonder what small or large crime I had committed. Knowing in my heart that my crime was heinous and wicked, I hung my head and waited for them to pass.

As the crowd around me thinned, a tall, slender black man quietly sat down on the end of the bench opposite me. He was the sort of man it was hard to pin an age to; somewhere between forty-five and sixty was my guess. His hair was cut short, but still all there and there was more than a little gray around the sides. He was smiling and the lines around his eyes cut deep furrows in the sides of his face. I watched him as he sat down, but looked away before our eyes met. I sure didn't want to talk to anyone. The bench was big enough for three and he had left the space between us, but there was also another empty bench a few feet down the hall. I was annoyed that he would sit so close. I leaned forward and looked down at the floor, trying to make it plain that I wanted to be left alone. When he cleared his throat to talk, I groaned inside. What I didn't know was that the conversation would change my life.

"Name's Wiley Fisher," he said, sticking his hand out for a shake, but down near the floor so I would have to see it even with my head lowered. I couldn't refuse such a deliberate greeting, so I sat up and took his hand. It was rough and calloused, he was a man that had worked, and he gripped it firm and solid. It was a handshake my grandfather would have given me as a boy, followed, of course, by an admonishment to shake his hand like a man. I was half-expecting him to say the same, but as I looked into his eyes, it was as if he was laughing at me. I was almost annoyed again, when I realized that he had said his name and was expecting me to say mine back.

"Wilson," I said, and then added after a pause, "John Wilson." It felt odd to say it. I hadn't been called by anything other than Wilson since that day nine years previous.

"Pleased to meet you, John," he replied and grinned from ear to ear. "I was afraid for a minute there that you had forgotten your name." It was as strange to see someone smile as it was to use first names. Needless to say, his odd behavior had caught my attention. He chuckled softly and went on. "You look like you woke up on the wrong side of the bed. But at least we're awake, right?" I didn't really know what he meant by awake and I wasn't sure when he and I had become a "we." I almost answered but then thought I shouldn't and instead tried a smile, not sure where the conversation was going.

"What time is your appointment?" I offered, trying to be nice.

"One forty-five," he said.

"Mine's one thirty," I said. "You in two twelve like me?"

"Yep," he replied. "You must be getting off easy, only being in there for fifteen minutes. Not like you got a murder to explain, huh?" His question stung, and I cringed involuntarily. I saw him notice, but he didn't comment. "I'm the last one on the docket," he went on. "I guess they have more than a few questions for me."

"What are you up for?" I asked. The question seemed rude once I said it, but I just wanted to get the conversation away from myself. It was good to actually talk with someone and Wiley was definitely an interesting person.

"Unlawful assembly," he answered. "All of the awake people in the city like to get together every so often. Kind of like an old-time church meeting, you might say. I guess they didn't like us having so many people in our apartment."

His use of the word "church" was odd. Church was something that had just gone away with everything else from the old world on that day. I thought of a bunch of people jammed into an apartment. "It isn't safe to have that many people in there," I said without thinking. "What if there was a fire?"

Wiley laughed at me when I said that, but when he laughed it wasn't like he was laughing at me, more like he was laughing over my head at something bigger. I wasn't offended in the least bit. "Fire?" he said. "Fire? John, what do you do for a living?"

"Inspector," I replied.

"Oh, inspector, smart man, I see," he said. "And how many fires have you seen in this city in the last nine years?" The answer was none; he and I both knew it. I had worked with the design team in the beginning to insure it. A fire in this place would be catastrophic, and we had done everything possible to try and make sure it would never happen. Before I could answer the obvious, he came back with another question. "And where, do you think, would be a good place to be in this little Ziploc bag if anything in here was ever to catch on fire?" I looked up and smiled at him, he had me for sure. I hadn't thought of Ziploc bags for years, and I imagined in my mind a big "yellow-and-blue-makes-green" seal across the middle of the canopy. In the midst of that thought, he came back with another question. "So why do you think they don't want us awake people to be meeting together?"

It was a question without an easy answer, and I dropped my smile and turned to stare at the door in front of me. For all these years I had never really thought of the people running this city as a "they" and had never considered the motives behind the thousands of rules and regulations that molded and shaped every moment of every day. He had used that word "awake" again, and it was getting to me. The thought in my mind came out of my mouth. "Wiley, what do you mean by 'awake people,' and why do you keep using the phrase 'us' and 'we'?" He might not have been including me in his us and we, but I thought he was and I really needed to know why. I would never have normally asked such a question, but this was not a normal conversation.

His face softened, and he looked at me with a look that I can't remember from anyone other than my father. Jack, your granddad had looked at me just the same way at the hospital on the day you were born. It was a look that can't be described in any other way, and I hope that you will see me giving you that same look someday about something. It is the look of a heart knowing a heart. When Wiley looked at me that way he had me hooked. I was firmly awake, and he didn't have to say another word—I wanted to have in my heart what he had in his. But he did say another word or two, and those words I will never forget either.

"John," he said, "all the people but just a few in this city are sound asleep. They pass from day to day without a clue of anything that is going on around them. I woke up six and a half years ago, and it has changed my whole life. Somehow, I have been given the job to round up all the awake people I see and have been given the gift along with that job to see who is awake and who isn't. Now it really isn't all that hard to tell who is awake and who isn't. I can tell, for instance, that someone woke you up pretty roughly, and from the look on your face, it happened pretty recently. Now in the next little bit," he went on, "you need to figure out why that someone woke you up and what job that someone has for you to do. You didn't get woke up for no reason, that's for sure. If we both make it out of that little room alive this afternoon, come find me and my group, and we will see if we can help you figure out what it is you are supposed to be doing."

He smiled again, and we both turned forward, leaning with our elbows on our knees, alternately looking at the ground and the door in front of us. I was lost in my thoughts and didn't reply. What he said made a lot of sense about being awake and asleep. It was a lot to process all at once, and I did my best to get my rusty brain back in order and try to run through and think about where to go from here. I don't know how long we sat there without talking when I realized he was humming softly to himself. I hadn't heard anyone hum, whistle, or sing in the nine years since that day. It was a beautiful sound to thirsty ears. I can still hear the tune in my head, but I have never been able to place it to a song with a name. Maybe I will meet Wiley again someday, and he will tell me what song he was humming.

I was just about to ask him when they opened the door and called my name, "Wilson." No John from them. I turned to Wiley and smiled, stopping to shake his hand again.

"Good luck," I said.

He smiled back at me, squeezed my hand firmly, and held onto it for a second. "Luck," he replied, "is for suckers."

I was in and out of the review board in ten minutes. I can't even remember any of the questions except that I remember that I didn't have to lie with my answers, which I surely would have done if it had come to it. The whole matter of Jackson was written up in a report and filed somewhere in a cabinet, probably along with his body. After the questions were done, they sent me out by another door into the back hall. I circled around as quickly as I could but when I got back to the bench, Wiley was gone. I waited outside the City Building until quitting time that day and looked for him off and on for the next year, but never saw him again. I never had a clue of where or when the "awake group" might be meeting, or if they even still existed. But I was a member of the group for sure. I had been recruited and initiated by Mr. Wiley Fisher.

When I got back to our apartment that night, I was on fire inside. I was just ripping at the seams to sit down and tell you and your mom everything that had happened that day. But when I got in and looked at Abbie, I opened my mouth and just closed it back again. She wouldn't understand a single word I was saying. Abbie was sound asleep and had been for years, and it was completely my fault. I had broken her heart, crushed her spirit, and put her into this coma. It was at that moment, Jack, that I first realized that being awake was not so much fun, especially if everyone around you was asleep. In the months ahead, I would also realize that waking someone else up is no easy task.

I put down Dad's papers and rose to the surface for a breath of air. I looked around the tiny room in front of me. The clock read 20:44. I was hungry and needed to process some of what I had been reading. I remembered well the night he had come home "awake." I knew he had changed but didn't know why. Until now, he had never told me the details. I remembered too well when Mom had fallen asleep. He was right in saying it was a lot of his fault. Everything he said rang with truth, but dragging out boxes of past hurts just made them hurt again. It was a good thing to read what he was writing. It was almost like hearing his voice. *It would be better to have him here with me,* I thought. For just a second, it seemed as if the apartment was all that was left of the universe and the door to my right opened to nothingness. I stood from the couch and reached for the door, just to make sure the hall was still there. Instead of opening the door, I turned around and went into the bedroom. The room was dark. I went to the window and peered through the glass and the thick plastic behind. There were no lights on the outside of the building. The sun had already set, but what was left of its light trailed around the curve of the earth, leaving a bright corner in the western sky. I couldn't see the color of the sky through the plastic, but I could see the shadowed silhouette of the trees and growth against the dimly lit sky behind it. I needed that moment but I also needed to eat, so I turned around and went back to the kitchen.

CHAPTER 4

"So you walk outside and everything's new.
You're looking at the world with new eyes.
As if you'd never seen a sky before that's blue.
As if you've never seen the sky in your whole life."

I rummaged through Davis's cabinets and fridge, looking for something that might have some taste to it. I found a large box of something that was between toast and a cracker, choked down a few slices and washed it down with what was left of the ginger ale stuff. It had only been two days since Dad and I had shared a good meal together. As we traveled, we shared a steady diet of corn, beans, tuna, saltines, peanut butter, soda, and juice. Every house we came to was like a convenience store full of leftover food. We always made a point of reading the expiration dates and laughing before opening up the cans or boxes. Warm or cold, it still filled the belly. Even back at the cabin, the garden-grown vegetables, cornbread, and an occasional squirrel or rabbit had plenty of taste and always filled you up. Every house and store within reasonable walking distance of our group of families near the cabin had been cleaned out of canned, boxed, or bagged food. In the same way, there was a circle of cleaned-out houses around each CR with a radius equal to the driving range of the trucks. In between, the homes and stores were full of food. At the cabin, we had learned to live off the land again. Here in the city, people were living on the stale cardboard food that they made in the hydroponic farms in the basements of the factories. It looked like food, but was a plastic substitute. If I was going to be in this apartment for the next two days, I would need to do some shopping tomorrow and see if I could find something with some taste to it.

I took Davis's badge and went to the small computer mounted to the wall. He had left it on, and I touched a key to wake it up out of sleep mode. A pop-up box came up immediately. It was an invitation to a meeting at the end of the work day on my first day back. *Probably to explain the wrecked truck,* I thought. I certainly wasn't planning on going to that meeting. I hit the "accept" button for the meeting, and the pop-up box disappeared. Davis had left his account manager program open from two days ago. I scrolled down the ledger to the bottom of the screen. His balance was big, he had been saving for something, or nothing maybe. I scanned back up the list of expenses for the last month, reading backward in time from the day before I killed him to about thirty days before. He hadn't bought much; it was mostly food. "Crappy food," I said out loud. Mixed in between the food orders and a few odds and ends were some entertainment orders. Those would come every fifth day—on his day off I would guess. There was plenty of money in the balance for me to buy whatever food they had at the store and to get a new pair of shoes. I only had the risk of not looking much at all like the picture on the badge.

I pulled out two more pieces of the bad toast and munched on them, pacing back and forth between the two rooms, leaving a trail of crumbs behind me. The ginger ale had gotten my saliva going again, and the toast didn't seem so dry anymore. I walked back into the bedroom, hoping for another glimpse of the outside world, but it was too dark out now and my own reflection stared back at me from the bedroom window. I tried to sort out my thoughts. I kept having the strange sense that Lori could be next door to me that very moment. What a silly thought—and useless too. I sure wasn't going to go knocking on doors. I paced from room to room, looking at the blank walls of Davis's sad and empty life. I stopped pacing and leaned against the wall, closing my eyes. *What should I be doing right now?* I wondered to myself. I knew the plan for the morning; that had been worked through thoroughly in the few minutes on the grass after today's failure. A good night's sleep would do me some good for sure, but it wasn't late enough to give up on my assigned reading. *First things first,* I thought. *Dad has more to say.* I reached over and set the alarm clock for an early morning. It wouldn't do to make the same mistake twice. I ate the last bit of toast, took a glass and filled it with some of the water from the jug marked "for drinking," took a swig, and sat back down to continue my reading.

There were a lot of pages left in the stack; it was plain that I was just getting started. It was strange that Dad had begun his story with murder, and here I sat reading about it wearing the clothes and eating the food of a man that I had murdered myself. I think I might have judged him harshly for what he had done if I hadn't just become a member in the same sad brotherhood. *Which of us was worse?* I wondered. He hadn't premeditated his killing, hadn't touched Jackson, but had acted in cold blood. I had brutally beaten Davis to death with a shovel, but I was acting in the heat of the moment, in something like self-defense. To me, both murders seemed the same. The bodies of Davis and Jackson were piled along with my father's and countless others into the corner of a dark and dusty courtroom waiting for justice that would never come. Maybe my father's death was the price paid for the death of Jackson. Perhaps my payback would be coming shortly. At that moment, I saw no meaning or value, no justice or balance to the lives lost. Each of them was a casualty of a cold and heartless system that ate men's souls and infected us all with an indifference to the value of life. At the same time the day before, I was starting to dig a grave. Tonight, I was reading a story. I found where I had left off, set my glass on the end table, settled into a comfortable spot, and sank back beneath the waters of my father's tale.

My first fourteen days being awake were odd to be sure. For starters, since I had no partner, I was working alone. Every bird, every green leaf, every cloud in the sky sang to me as if I had never seen it before. The whole world around me awakened to my awareness, and I felt as if I was a child again. I found that I could do my job in half the time. I spent so much time checking and rechecking everything I did for no good reason. I knew how to do my job, did it carefully and correctly the first time, looked it over once to be sure it was right, and was done. I only had a few houses to do each day, so I spent the rest of the time wondering and wandering around outside, soaking in everything that I had been missing for the last nine years. Driving out of the city each day, I felt like a kid on his first day of summer vacation. I was free inside, and it was invigorating.

My days outside at work were contrasted with a deep guilt back inside the city. I walked in a cloud of paranoia, always wondering if anyone knew my secret. I had the strange sensation that every young woman I passed was Jackson's secret lover and that I had crushed and ruined her life. I peered into every face I saw, looking for Wiley or for any other someone that might be awake. I felt like an alien in every crowd and knew that my strange actions would eventually betray me to some spy of the city fathers.

Along with the joy and guilt was a very new emotion that I wasn't expecting. I was lonely. For all these years, I really had nothing to say and nothing to share with Abbie. Now, when I came home from work I had a million things I wanted to talk about with her and no way to start up the conversation. It was like we didn't speak the same language. I tried several times to tell her what I had seen and how I was feeling, but she simply couldn't process what I was saying.

The time at home was also full of a different type of guilt. Every time I saw Abbie, every time I saw you, all of my failures as a husband and father slapped me in the face. Just as much as I dreaded walking the streets, I began to dread being at home. I wanted nothing but to be in my truck, be outside the baggie of the city, and be away from everything that was wrong and complicated and hard to deal with. My job had been an escape from home before and for those few days I let it become that again, but for different reasons.

But by this time, my life was not my own—I had been taken over by a force external to myself that could see beyond the day-to-day existence that still drove my thinking. Just as Wiley had been placed in my path, I met another soul that would draw me deeper into my new life and further away from the old. It had been only fourteen days since the murder, the meeting with Wiley and the rebirth of my life. Those days had been so full of experiences that they seemed longer than the past nine years combined.

The joy of being awake was tempered by the image of Jackson's silent scream. Try as I might, I just couldn't shake the picture from my mind. Each second of his death was played over and over again with the countdown echoing in the background. Those were the images playing through my mind when I pulled up to the last house I was assigned on that fourteenth day. As I finished marking the house for destruction and went back outside to look around, a strange new question came to my mind as the familiar image rose up into my thinking—*Why was he not having any problems breathing?*

At first I reasoned that the toxic air hadn't had enough time to kill him, but that didn't fit at all with what we had been told. The handbooks and safety videos all stated firmly that we would be dead in a matter of seconds if we took even one breath. That was plainly not true for Jackson. He had taken several good, strong breaths and had screamed them back out. He was still screaming and looked pretty healthy right up to the moment he died. He didn't even turn a shade of blue or cough or anything. So, as Wiley might have said, "Why would they tell us a lie about the air?"

I stepped out the back of the house onto a little concrete patio they had built, still pondering that question. I had a couple of hours before I would need to head back to the city. It was a beautiful blue sky day, one of those warm winter days in the south that tricks you into thinking that spring will be there sooner than it will. The concrete patio created a little pocket between the house and the familiar clumps of briars, bushes and trees that had overgrown what once had been their backyard. I was admiring the beautiful day and was pondering the quality of the air on the out-side of my hood and just decided to take it off. I don't really know why I did such a thing. I don't even think I stopped to think about it; I just did it. I pulled off the hood and took in several deep breaths of the toxic air, waiting to die. After about ten seconds and a few more inhales, I began to laugh. I don't know why that was my reaction, but it was. I lay down on the ground and laughed and laughed and stood back up and let out a big whoop. I didn't even stop to think if another work crew might be in the area, and for that moment, I don't think I cared. Those first breaths of real air were a freedom that I hadn't known in years, maybe ever. I had been afraid of so many different things for so long. Taking off that hood was like being set loose from a prison.

I set my hood against the wall, took off my uni-form and boots, and lay back down on the concrete, staring at the sky and taking deep breaths. The air felt so fresh and clean it almost burned my lungs. There was a light breeze and the air felt cool as it passed over my sweat-soaked long gray underwear.

I must have lain there for at least fifteen minutes, just watching the clouds drift by before even thinking about moving. It was great to have been aware of things, but to see them with my own eyes, not through a dirty visor, was so much more. When I finally stood back up, I noticed a little patch of grass that had escaped the growth of the bushes. I pulled off my socks, flipped them toward the uniform pile and stood in the grass. I was facing back toward the house, wiggling my toes and bare feet, when I noticed a back door to the garage.

I had marked all the charges in the crawl space under the house and hadn't had a reason to go in the garage. I opened the back door and stepped inside to look around. Like every other house, it looked like a scene frozen in time from nine years ago. It was a two-car garage. There was one car parked in its spot and a large pile of junk occupying the other stall. A tall red tool box with the slide-out drawers was to one side. It looked just like one my dad had given my uncle for Christmas the year before he died. A bicycle hung from hooks on the ceiling. I wondered if I could still ride. The tires were probably flat. Lawn chairs and camping gear were piled together in a corner. There was a half-sized freezer against the wall, plugged into a lifeless socket. I knew better than to open that for a look. No telling what smells might be trapped in there. There was a fifty-pound bag of generic dog food stacked up on a shelf next to some old paint cans. A baseball bat had been left against the wall with a couple of gloves underneath it. In the pocket of one of the gloves, the faded yellow of an old tennis ball caught my eye.

I grabbed up the ball and glove and headed back outside. The concrete patio was long and skinny, and there was a brick wall at one end. I backed up to get the full length of the patio and began to throw the ball against the wall, scooping it up with the glove as it bounced back. The first few throws were just sad and went nowhere near the target I had chosen on the wall. My shoulder felt as rusty as would be expected for not having thrown a ball for so long. It was a lot more than nine years, to be sure. After a couple more throws, I began to loosen up and throw a bit harder. The ball came back in only one bounce now. I got into a rhythm, hitting the wall in the right spot so that it would bounce once and come back on my glove hand side. After each catch I would flip it out of the glove to my bare hand and throw it again to the same spot. Every once in a while, I would hit a mortar joint in the brick or just have bad aim and I would have to stretch my glove to one side or the other to scoop it up. The flow and rhythm of the throwing was cathartic, loosening both body and soul, and I lost myself in the moment, thinking of absolutely nothing but the next throw and catch.

I don't know how long I had been throwing when one got away from me. It bounced over low and hard and I reached across to backhand it too late, letting it slip under my glove. "That's a two-base error on the third baseman." I laughed out loud and turned around.

Standing on the edge of the bushes was a very skinny and ragged dog with the tennis ball in its mouth. Who knew how long he had been standing there, watching me, waiting for a miss. The remnants of a collar were on his neck. This was probably his fetch ball, probably his house. I walked carefully toward him, squatting lower as I came near. He took one step toward me, dropped the ball at my feet and stepped back into the bushes so that I could only see his nose.

I picked up the ball and backed up, looking at him the whole time. I waved the ball a little, and he stepped back out of the bushes. I stepped toward the side wall to give him a free path to run and bounced the ball softly against the wall. His eyes lit up, and he leapt after the ball, catching it on a bounce in the air. I think it was a reflex for him, because he dropped the ball at my feet and retreated again to the bushes. We repeated that for about five throws, and then I squatted back down low when he brought the ball back to me. I reached out slowly and patted the side of his face, saying "good dog" softly over and over. He pulled back a little but let me pet him for a few seconds. We had made friends with each other.

I pulled his collar around and noticed there was no tag as I scratched him behind the ears. I thought about giving him a name, just for the afternoon, but then thought better of it. "You've got a name," I said to him, "I just don't know what it is." He liked me talking to him and looked back up at me, almost barking, choking off the sound as it came from his mouth in the sort of sound a smaller dog would have made. He picked up the ball in his mouth and dropped it again at my feet. He wanted more fetch.

The fetch game continued on for a good while, more vigorously now, and both of us were panting and needed a break. The dog looked mostly like a golden retriever, but its long nose had a collie look to it. Its fur was matted with cockleburs, and he let me pull a few out while I petted him. I thought of the big bag of dog food in the garage. How sad that he would nearly starve all these years with that full bag of food in the garage! He had probably been scratching by on whatever rabbits or possums he could catch. From the looks of him, he hadn't caught much. Surely there was some stream or spring nearby for water. Most dogs would have left their home and caught on with a pack of dogs for survival, becoming wild and wolf-like again, but not this one. I imagined him watching my truck pull up the driveway, hoping his family had finally come home.

I stepped back into the garage and wrestled the food bag down from the top shelf. I opened the bag and took out a handful of food, setting it on the concrete at his feet. He just whimpered and looked at me, not eating. *Only out of his bowl,* I thought. *What a good dog.* There was a stainless steel feeder next to the garage door with two bowls side by side, one for food, one for water. I scooped the handful of food back up off the ground and put it into one of the bowls. He ate it up in two bites. I filled the bowl to the top and stepped around to my truck. There was a whoosh of compressed air released as I opened the door, and it startled me. It had only taken a few hours of breathing real air for me to forget that the truck would do that. The air smelled bad to me now. I looked down at myself standing there in my underwear and laughed. I found the two bottles of water I was looking for, grabbed them up, and left the door open for spite. I took a couple of swallows from one of the bottles and poured the rest into the other bowl. The dog took a breather from eating and lapped up the water. "Probably not as good as what you are used to drinking," I said to him. He cleaned out the bowl of food, and I filled it up again.

I was standing there, watching him eat when I heard the radio beeping in my truck. We didn't even have radio contact out this far until about two years ago, when they upgraded the tower. I jogged around to the truck and picked up the receiver. I answered with a simple hello, trying to collect my thoughts and not say something stupid that would betray what was going on. It was the dispatcher doing a late check. I should have been back already.

Her voice came through with some static, "Everything all right out there, Wilson?" I considered a few excuses but just said I had finished up my last house and was about to head back. I didn't tell her that I was breathing real air, playing fetch with a dog, and standing there in my underwear. But then again, she didn't ask.

It was time to leave; they knew how long it took to drive back to the city. I ran back around the house and grabbed up the various pieces of my uniform, not paying as much attention to the seals as usual. The glove was returned to its spot in the garage. I topped off the food bowl one more time and left the open bag up in the bushes. *Surely his hunger would eventually overcome his manners,* I thought.

He stood there with the ball in his mouth watching me put on the uniform with a puzzled look, as curious with my suddenly hurried disposition as with my changed appearance. I patted him on the head one last time and jogged toward the truck. He followed me as I went and stood in front of the bumper as I got in and started it up. I couldn't risk him chasing me, so I got back out, took the ball from his mouth and threw it as hard as I could into the bushes. The dog dove through the thick briars in a line for the ball. As soon as he was clear, I jumped back into the truck, slammed the door shut, and sped off down the driveway and out onto the road.

The cab was hissing as it filtered out the dirty air I had just been enjoying, replacing it with the good clean air that met city standards. I instinctively waited for the yellow light to come on before I removed the hood and laughed at myself. What a day it had been. The truck had a speed limiter to conserve gas, so I had no way to make up time. I looked at the clock and saw that I was going to be good and late. I was sure to get bad marks for it, but I didn't care. It was worth it to have tasted real air again. It was worth it to have spent the few hours with another living and breathing being, even if it was a dog. It went further back than before the day that we were taken to the city. It went back to before I was working, before college, before high school, back to when being a kid was more important than what everyone else thought about you. It went back to when throwing a ball against a wall was time well spent and not time escaping from whatever assignment or project you really should be working on. It went back to a freedom of the soul and to a corner of myself that I had forgotten even existed. Just taking off that hood was only the half of it. It was a good day.

I finally got back to the city, nearly an hour later than I should have, and hurried through the steam spray and into the locker room, knowing that the sooner I logged out on the computer, the less trouble I would be in. As I changed from light blue to gray, I noticed my underwear was completely soaked in sweat. Hopefully it wouldn't show through the gray bad enough that anyone would notice. Part of me didn't care, and part was terrified of my afternoon being found out. I changed and checked out without being questioned and hurried up the emptying street to our apartment.

I burst into the apartment, determined to tell you or your mother all about the day, all about the air, all about the dog. I peeked in at you in your bedroom. You looked to be in deep thought, working on homework, and didn't notice me. Your mom was in her bedroom, leaning back on propped up pillows, sifting through papers from work. It was the normal post-supper routine. Abbie looked up at me with a thin smile, or more nearly looked over my shoulder at nothing, and said, "Your supper is in the fridge."

I remembered all the times in our former life that I had come home late from work, sometimes hours late, and had gotten the same look, the same reply. Back then she cared and was actually upset at me. Now, I don't even think she noticed I was gone. I lost my nerve to talk and just replied, "Thanks, I think I'll get a shower first."

I stepped into the small bathroom and closed the door. Pulling off the jumpsuit and my suit of under-wear, I looked at myself. My socks were clean on the outside and dirty on the inside. My feet were covered with dirt and had stained the socks. I noticed my hands were dirty and looked like they had a little sunburn. I looked quickly up at my face in the mirror. My fore-head and nose were red. I hadn't even thought of that as a possibility. We were all so pale from living in the city. Those of us that went outside were always cov-ered from head to toe. This would be hard to explain. A little bit of fear came across me, and I thought that maybe I had been a bit foolish to do what I had done.

I hurried in the shower, of course, and it was tough to get the sweat and dirt off of me. I thought to push in the plug before I started. The water that pooled in the bottom of the shower helped to wash off most of the dirt from my feet. As I toweled off, I looked at the dirty socks in the corner. The sweaty underwear I could explain, but the socks would be tough. We took our dirty laundry to work and just picked up clean clothes there. I didn't have a clue how to clean the socks. If the laundry lady snitched on me, I was in trouble.

I went to the kitchen and heated up my plate in the microwave. Abbie always made us dinner every night when she got home from work. She didn't have much to work with but always did a good job. When we got to the cabin, I asked her if she had cooked all those meals out of love, but she said at that time she had no love for either of us and just did it out of habit. I don't know if I believe that or not. I took the plate of food and a fork, picked up my socks from the bathroom, and went to the bedroom where she was working.

I sat at the foot of the bed, laid the socks out in front of me, and ate my dinner, waiting for her to notice me. I don't really know why I did that, I just wanted to see if it would have any affect on her. She looked up from her work, saw the socks, and asked, "How did you do that?" It was the opening I had been hoping for, and I started to talk, telling her everything. I told her about Jackson, about meeting Wiley, about waking up, about breathing the air, about taking off the uniform, about playing fetch with the dog. I reeled it all off without stopping, completely excited as I spoke. I don't think I had talked to her like that ever, even before we were married.

She sat there through the whole thing and didn't say a word. I stared at her face, looking for something, anything, to connect with. Her face changed for a minute, maybe just a bit of softness. She opened her mouth and then closed it again. Her eyes left mine and drifted to the wall over my head and then back to the socks. "We will need to get those socks clean," she said. "The laundry people will wonder where the dirt came from."

She got up from the bed, slipped her papers into a file, stacked everything into a pile, and set it in the floor in the short hallway outside the bedroom. She picked up the socks and went into the kitchen, leaving me to pick up my plate and follow behind her. Taking a bowl out the cabinet, she filled it with water and put the socks in. She rubbed them together a few times, squirted in a little dish detergent, and rubbed them some more, making a few suds before rinsing off her hands and drying them on the towel lying there. When she turned back around, her eyes caught mine for a second. I looked hard for some sort of spark. "You better finish your dinner in here," she said. "I need to get on to sleep."

I followed her suggestion, rinsed off my dish, brushed my teeth, and flipped off the lights, double-checking the lock on the door, following the same routine as every other night. Your light was still on in your room. I thought hard about going in and telling you the same story but thought I would probably get the same response. I turned instead to our bedroom and climbed into bed, trying not to wake her up. As I lay there, I could hear her slow and steady breathing as she slept. I could hear you turning pages in your books in your room. Abbie's lack of response had taken some of the wind out of my sails but not all of it. I felt the stiffness in my shoulder and the slight burn on my nose and knew that the events of the day were real.

I woke up early the next morning and dressed quietly in the living room. This was Abbie's fifth day, and she was off from work so I didn't want to wake her. The socks in the kitchen looked to be much less dirty than the day before, but I left them there, letting

Abbie decide when they should come out of their bath. I had to be at work before you had to be at school, so I grabbed a breakfast bar and slipped out of the door.

The best time in the city was the early morning, especially if I was out before everyone else. The thin gray light filtering through the plastic seemed more natural in the morning. It was almost like a normal morning before we were taken to the city, especially if I imagined that the canopy was only a light fog. The closer I got to the locker room, the more excited I grew. I couldn't wait to get out and breathe again. When I got into the truck, I wanted to put the windows down but they had taken the handles off. I was so entranced with thoughts of the day ahead of me that I almost missed my turn. Halfway to my first house assigned for the day, I got a call from the dispatcher telling me to go back to the last house I had marked from the day before. I doubled back most of the way to the city and headed out toward the house. Fearful thoughts ran through my mind. Had I forgotten to mark for the blasts? Had I not put something away from the romp with the dog?

When I pulled up the driveway, my fears were realized. Parked next to the house was the smaller orange truck of the demo supervisor. The larger crew truck was parked next to his. I knew it was trouble. He wouldn't have been out there if he hadn't been called in from the crew. This particular supervisor was a hard guy to work with. He stood at the end of the driveway, waiting for me to drive in. I couldn't see through the hood and visor, but I could see his attitude in how he was standing. An inspector was up in rank over a normal construction guy, but a supervisor always had authority over a normal, no matter what color uniform he was wearing. He had the dog bowl in one hand and the empty bag of dog food in the other. He was waiting to chew me out.

I pulled to a park several yards away from his truck and took my time sealing off my uniform and hood before getting out of the truck. I looked down and tried to collect my thoughts and think of reasonable excuses that wouldn't sound like lies. I flipped the door handle and stepped out. When I turned around to face the inspector, I saw the dog from the day before running toward me. It had the tennis ball in its mouth and appeared to be grinning around the ball in a way only a dog can. He must have heard my truck, grabbed the ball, and come running back to resume our game of fetch where we had left it off. The supervisor was walking toward my truck and was geared up to tear into me. He never saw the dog running behind him but must have heard his feet on the concrete patio because he turned halfway just before the dog shot past him, bumping into his leg. The impact knocked him to one side, and he nearly fell over, catching himself with his gloved hand against his truck.

The dog came straight to me, dropping the ball at my feet, and I reached down and petted his head, almost as a reflex. He was being a good dog, just doing what he should. As I looked up, the supervisor had pulled his pistol and was moving toward the dog, motioning me to step aside. I didn't have time to move or yell or even think before he had put a bullet through the dog's skull and into the sheet metal of the bed of my truck just in front of the bumper. The dog hit the ground immediately, and the supervisor put one more into him for good measure and then turned toward me, glaring through his visor close enough that it was almost touching mine.

The shots had happened so fast that I froze. He had shot the dog from less than ten feet away and my hand was inches from his head when the first shot went in. I was startled as much as anything, but then rage rose up into me and I erupted. I lunged toward him, shoving him backward and knocking the gun from his hand. He was a bigger man than me, but I had caught him off guard. Stepping as quickly as I could in the bulky uniform, I followed him as he stumbled and pushed one more time, knocking him to the ground. I jumped on top of him, driving my knee into his chest. For some reason, I had one thought: to take off his hood and force him to breathe the air he thought would be poison. If I had succeeded at that, I would surely have been charged with attempted murder. All the events that were yet to follow never would have happened. You would not be sitting where you are, reading this, close to finding your Lori. For all I know, your mother may have never been awakened. As you know now, that was not part of the plan for our lives.

Before I even got my hands to his hood, two workers standing nearby grabbed me by my shoulders and threw me to one side. Another following close behind grabbed the supervisor's gun from the ground and pointed it at me. The supervisor stood up and dusted off his uniform. He had collected himself and was talking through clenched teeth in something close to a civil voice. He knew that he didn't have to dress me down now, I had done myself in. "Get yourself together, Wilson," he said. "It was just a dog. You're acting like it was the family pet or something." I could see his slimy smile through the visor. "I guess you can go on now," he said. I could hear him chuckling softly to himself as he turned around and walked away. The other men followed his cue, put away their guns, and walked away also. My rage was gone, replaced with dread. I knew I was in deep trouble.

I stepped around the dead body of my friend from the day before and got back into my truck. The supervisor had gotten what he wanted and more. I had fallen right into his hands. I watched in the rearview mirror as one of the men picked up the dog by two legs and swung in a half circle, pitching him into the bushes on the side of the driveway. My heart sank, and I fought off tears. I had killed the dog as surely as if I had pulled the trigger myself.

A dozen rules had been broken with this episode. It was proper procedure to kill a dog on sight. The dog could be aggressive, could be carrying diseases or contamination, or could easily puncture or tear a uniform with its claws if it jumped up on someone. These were the reasons drilled into us in training. I never should have coaxed the dog from the bushes. I was sure to be called down for not killing the dog the day before. One question would surely lead to another. How many lies would I have to tell to get out of this? What about my sunburn? What if I was transferred away from my family? I was busy chewing on these questions when I got the second call of the day from the dispatcher telling me to bring it in and report to a meeting. That jerk had barely let me get out of sight before he called me in.

Less than an hour later, I found myself sitting on the same bench in the city building, staring at the same door to the same room where I had been questioned just fourteen days prior. This time, I knew I was in for a grilling. The reviewers hated the same person coming back so soon, no matter the reason. They didn't like disregard for well-known rules. They especially didn't like insubordination. I thought of Wiley. He was smiling before he went in for his review. He was in as much or more trouble than I was. Why had he been able to be so completely at ease when I was sitting here with my insides tied up in knots?

I thought about the guys I had known over the years that had really blown it like this. Some had been severely demoted. Most were just gone. They didn't come back and we never saw them again. I couldn't help but think about you and Abbie while I waited. If I was sent away or killed, I would never see either one of you again. My heart ached for Abbie. I had told her everything the night before, and she had sat there, looking at me without expression. I had hurt her so much already. Then I thought something worse, *Maybe she won't even care if I am gone.* The thought was too close to the truth. We had no relationship, not even a friendship. For all intents and purposes, our marriage was dead. She was nearly dead herself on the inside. I felt the weight of my mistakes. My actions had killed my co-worker, had killed a very nice dog, and had put my wife into a deep sleep. I whispered to myself, "If I was gone, would she ever be able to wake up again?"

In the midst of that thought, the door opened in front of me, and they called me in. The room was dimly lit and my sunburned face wasn't noticed. The same collection of men lined one side of the table. I moved to the other side and sat in the same seat I had taken before. They started with a few basic questions about the events of that morning. I tried to dodge some of the questions and ended up going with a sort of lie. I said that I went after the supervisor in a fit of rage because he shot so close to me and very nearly hit me. That seemed to stick with a couple of the reviewers, and they shifted their questions to the dog. That one I couldn't cover much for. I had clearly spent time with the dog the day before. I tried to make up something believable, but I couldn't. I just owned up to petting the dog and took my lumps. I never volunteered the fact that I had taken off my hood and uniform, and they, of course, never asked. I left out the hour-long game of fetch, but they were mad enough that I hadn't shot the dog. After about a half hour of being told how reckless and stupid I was, they sent me away with a reprimand and a demotion to assistant inspector with the matching cut in pay. I was also scheduled for rage management training for my next day off.

I was sent back out to the field and marked two more houses that day before heading back in a few minutes early. I didn't even take off my hood for a quick breath of real air. I was kind of numb from the whole day. I realized that I was more upset over the dog than I was over letting Jackson die, and that brought in more guilt to add to the rest. Mostly, I felt overwhelmed about everything.

Back in the apartment after work, I just let things be the sad normal they were before I awoke. None of the events of the day were brought up. Nothing from the day before was rehashed. The conversations were short and meaningless. The evening passed quickly, we all went off to bed, and I found myself staring up at the ceiling in the dark. In the quiet of the night, my mind settled down and began to see things clearly.

Once you have seen the truth, you can't unsee it. Once you know you have been lied to, you keep looking to see what else the liar has been lying about. My whole structure of right and wrong, my whole purpose of living was being turned upside down. More properly, I was turned right-side up. Something like a kayak rider that had flipped his boat in the river and then, after much struggling, had flipped it back around to the breathing side of the water. It had become clear on that day that the city was my enemy. I needed to get myself and my family out of it.

Up to that point, Jack, my days awake had been enjoyable, but meaningless. The death of the dog, the reprimand, and the demotion set my life into motion and gave me a purpose. For more years than I even knew, from long before we were taken to the city, all of my drive and energies had been focused toward my work. My marriage and all other parts of my life were secondary sidelines. On that day, my focus shifted to waking up my wife and saving her life. I knew that our time of safety was slipping away. If I messed up again, my chances of saving my family would be gone.

It was hard to sleep that night. I was exhilarated with the task before me even if it seemed impossible. Most men spend all their lives on worthless and meaningless tasks. We turn a screw or push a piece of paper over and over again. We empty a trashcan that will just fill up again. We spend a lifetime building something that will only be torn down, replaced, or pushed aside. The task before me from that point on was different. It was personal, it was permanent, it was a matter of the soul. I don't know why, but in that moment, I fully grasped that I was finally working on a project that meant something.

I listened to Abbie breathing quietly beside me. I loved her and wanted with all that I was to wake her up. I had wooed her before, but back then it was different. My efforts at romance were mostly just to try and get her in bed. I wanted her love, her admiration, but it was all about what she could give to me. Certainly I still wanted those things, but this was more the way a husband really ought to love his wife. I think it was the first time I wanted what was best for her instead of just wanting to feed myself.

Even with all the guilt and worry of the day, I felt more peace on that night than I had in years. I was sure at that moment that my love for Abbie was perfect and pure, but I know now that it wasn't. I thought I had arrived at the pinnacle, but I was just getting started on my climb. Even after all the years we had been married, I barely knew her, much less loved her in any real way. Jack, I am a little worried for you for the same reason. You are sure you love Lori, but you barely know her. You think what you feel for her is noble and pure, but it isn't. Real love isn't about fairy tales and princesses and happily ever after. It is messy and complicated with mixed-up emotions and hurt feelings. But the fairy tale stuff is plastic and fake, and once you get a taste of the real stuff, the other just won't do anymore. If you really want to love Lori, then roll up your sleeves and get ready to work and fight and be hurt. If you are willing to do all that, you might just have something worth all that you are going through.

I leaned back on the couch and closed my eyes, drifting. Dad didn't know that I had listened to every word that he told Mom on that night he came home with dirty socks and a sunburn. I had lain awake just as he had the next night, but with much less peace, wondering what the future would hold. I felt a similar uneasiness at that moment on Davis's couch, but I drew some peace from my purpose. I had a clear, well-defined plan for the next day. I ran through the steps I would follow in the morning, counting backward as I fell asleep.

CHAPTER 5

"These dreams started singing to me out of nowhere"

I was startled from my sleep by a light pecking on the apartment door. Something in my head told me it was Lori before I even opened my eyes. The room was dark, and I stumbled toward the door, trying to remember where I was. I was about to ask "Who is it?" when I heard a whisper through the door, "Follow me." It was a female voice, but I couldn't be sure who it was because it was a whisper and not her normal voice. I had enough sense to quickly grope the top of the kitchen counter and pick up my badge, locking the door behind me and shutting it as quietly as I could.

The hallway was lit only by a security light on one end. I could just make out the outline of a person near the stairs. The figure was definitely female, but I didn't see the face. She turned back toward me and whispered again, "Follow me," as she went down the stairs. What else was I to do but follow? I took the stairs two at a time, trying to catch up and be quiet at the same time. She swung the exit door open widely, and I caught it just in time to keep it from slamming shut. I wanted so much to catch her, but I sure didn't want to wake anyone up. It was forbidden for anyone to be on the street at night. If they caught me out, it was all over.

By the time I had let the door close quietly behind me, she was twenty yards in front of me, in a light jog. I ran to catch up to her, but I wasn't gaining at all. In fact, she was getting farther away. She looked back over her shoulder just as she came under a streetlight, and I could see her face.

It was Lori; I could see her clearly. She was smiling at me, almost laughing, and I knew it was her without a doubt. "Follow me," she said in a normal voice this time and turned around, going faster, running instead of jogging.

I struggled to keep up. We were past the park area and between the factory buildings. I was in a dead sprint now, laboring to breathe in this noxious air and still a bit dazed from just waking up. She was running in front of me, gliding effortlessly, gracefully. She was a beautiful woman. Her hair was longer than I had ever seen it before. She had always kept her hair short; it was required. I was confused as to what she was doing and what I was doing, but just trying to catch her was consuming my thoughts. I focused on keeping my feet moving and taking deep breaths.

I was running out of gas and out of wind. My legs burned, my lungs ached, I was beginning to lose stride and stagger to one side, and she was pulling farther away from me. We came to the end of the street, and I lost her. She was too far away, and she just faded into the darkness between streetlights.

I came to the end of the road, wheezing loudly, and bent over with my head between my knees, searching first for some air, hoping I wouldn't pass out. I raised up again and looked around, walking from building to building in the dark, looking for any sign of her and seeing none. The city building was dark and lifeless, and I climbed the stairs and peeked through a glass door. There was a night watchman inside, but I stepped quickly away before he noticed me. The locker room I had first entered the city from was even more lifeless. Its doors were locked, and it was completely dark inside.

I turned to the entertainment building. Its lights were on, but it looked quiet and empty. No one came or went from its front doors. I could hear soft remnants of insipid techno music coming from inside. It was crazy to go in. I was setting myself up to be caught. But she was so close, and this was the only building that showed any signs of life. It was the only building on the end of the street that didn't have its doors locked. I had to try.

I stepped through the front doors. I had never been inside the entertainment building back in CR12; no one under age was allowed to go in. I looked around quickly, trying to gain my bearings. Lori was nowhere to be seen. The building had been a nice downtown hotel in its former life, and it still looked like what I remembered vaguely from the two or three visits I had made to hotels as a child before we were taken to the city. The front desk was unattended and the lobby was empty. An elevator was to the right with a hallway beyond it around a corner. There was a small sitting area straight ahead, also empty. I could hear the music coming from beyond the sitting area, so I followed its sound through the room, to the left through a short hall, and into a larger room that I guessed was the bar, though I had never seen one or even had one described to me.

The room was dimly lit and full of round tables with four chairs at each table. There was a large, chubby, older fellow keeping the bar, polishing glasses with a white towel. He looked up with no expression when I walked in and turned back down to his task. The room was completely empty except for a threesome near the back wall. A voice hailed me from the table, "Jack, it's you! Come on in." Confused, I walked toward the table, straining to see who it was. I stopped behind a chair when I was yet two tables away, speechless at what I saw.

The voice that had beckoned me was my father's. He sat between two men, playing cards. From the pile of chips between them, they must have been playing poker. One man I knew, the other I didn't. My father was wearing the clothes he had on when I buried him, and there was a fist-sized hole in his chest with a ring of dried blood around it. There was dirt around the edges of his face and hair. It looked as though he had splashed a bit of water on his face to clean off and hadn't done such a good job of it. He was grinning in kind of a goofy way like he did when he was happy. He waved to me and said, "C'mon, son, pull up a chair, we need a fourth." A dog was sitting next to him, and he was patting its head as he spoke. A good part of the dog's head was missing, but Dad rubbed behind the ear that was still there. My dad continued, nodding toward the dog, "This is my friend I was telling you about. Before we get back to our cards, son, I got to tell you, your mom needs you back home at the cabin. You had better go on and leave and get back to her while you still can." He looked back at his cards, laid two down on the table, and held up two fingers to the man on his right.

The dealer to the right I recognized as Davis. He handed my dad two cards from the deck lying on the table in front of him. His head was partly mashed in, but the first thing I noticed about him was that he was wearing only his underwear. His back and shoulders were smeared over with mud. He looked up at me coldly. "How about giving me back my jumpsuit, pal." He took a drink and went on, "What are you doing here anyway?"

Without thinking, I answered back, "I'm looking for Lori; I just saw her. Did she come in here?"

Davis answered back with a wicked grin. "I was with her just a few days ago. Haven't seen her tonight, but I hope to later." He laughed and sneered at me and turned back to his cards. Half of me wanted to pound him in the nose for what he had said, the other half of me felt guilty for having killed him two nights previous. As it was, my feet were frozen to the floor, and my mouth was glued shut. I couldn't have spoken or moved if I wanted to.

The third man was sitting to Dad's left, wearing a standard-issue light blue jumpsuit. I could see his nametag, but I knew who he was without reading it. His body was thin and flat like it had been crushed. His face was twisted with his mouth wide open as if he was in terrific pain and screaming, but no sound came out. He turned and spoke to me in a normal voice that I heard in my head, but his mouth wasn't moving. "She isn't here. You are wasting your time. Just leave! Haven't you done enough here already! Just look at what you've done!" His voice escalated with each sentence, and he finished with a scream that matched his face. My feet unfroze from the floor, and I turned and ran out of the room and through the lobby. Something in my mind knew that I was being followed, but I didn't look back. I burst through the front door and back out onto the street, breaking into a sprint as I hit the pavement.

I looked down and noticed for the first time that I was barefoot. I heard men yelling at me from behind to stop, and I tried to run faster. I pumped my legs faster and faster, but I was running in place, getting nowhere, my feet burning and bleeding on the road below me. I realized I was dreaming and began to scream—softly at first and then louder to wake myself up. I sat up straight from the couch in the dark room of the apartment in a cold sweat, breathing hard, in a state of complete panic, not sure if the screams were audible, not sure where I was.

I knew it was a dream, but it seemed so real that I checked the bottom of my feet for cuts and blood, rubbing them for a moment to see if I had indeed just been running barefoot on asphalt. They were clean and cold, but the false sensations of pain and heat from the dream were struggling with reality. I stood up and wiggled my toes to try and get a normal feeling back. The clock across from me read 05:29. The alarm was set to go off a minute after that, so I quickly stepped across the room and flipped it off before it would sound. I turned on all the lights in the apartment, trying to wake myself up. I hadn't planned to take a shower, but I wanted to clear my head, so I washed off quickly, turning the water to as cold as it would let me to try to shock my senses out of their stupor.

When we were on the road, just Dad and me, I had struggled with a recurring dream of Mom calling out from the darkness, warning us to turn around and come home. I didn't tell Dad about it for the first several nights, but when the dream kept coming back, I was worried it might be a sign of something. In his typical analytical way, Dad explained that dreams didn't really mean anything and were just a manifestation of our hopes and fears mixed with what we had eaten for dinner the night before. In fairness to him, I never had the dream again, but it still bothered me. Now my dad was part of the dreams instead of being here to reassure me.

I chewed on what each of the three ghosts had told me. They couldn't all be true. Each ghost was merely spelling out a different fear that I was carrying. But the dream was about Lori, what did they have to do with her? I decided to go with my dad's advice while he was still living and try to put it out of my mind.

One huge positive, considering the task before me that morning, was remembering Lori's face. I had searched my mind so hard for months to bring it into focus, and to have it come back to me in this way was both exciting and disturbing. The brief glimpse in the streetlight was enough to open the file folder it had been tucked away in and to replace the white blur in the visions of my memories with the proper picture of her face. "It was in your mind all along," I said to myself, "you just needed to dig it out."

The water ran out while I was thinking, and I stepped out of the shower without even getting to the soap. I stood dripping on the mat in front of the mirror, staring at my own face. It had been quite a ride the last few days. The face looking back at me didn't look the same as it had in the house the morning before. There was a desperate look that better matched the appearance of others in the city. "A little stress and some bad air was all I needed," I said out loud. I needed a shave, so I picked up Davis's razor, rinsed it off in the sink, and looked around for some shaving cream. There was none to be found, so I grabbed the bar of soap from the shower and tried to lather up my face. I took a swipe with the razor upward along the right side of my neck, and it sliced me good, bringing up blood immediately. I looked carefully at the end of the razor and saw the warped edges and little barbs in the well-used blade. *The tightwad won't even spring to have his razor sharpened,* I thought to myself. I tried another swipe, this time barely touching the skin, and I cut myself again. I put the razor down and rinsed the soap from my face, plugging up the cuts with a little pressure through the towel to stop the bleeding. The shave would have to wait.

I covered the cuts with scraps of toilet paper and dried and dressed, finding a single change of clothes in the dresser. I was a good half hour ahead of schedule but decided to go ahead anyway. This was what I was doing today, so I might as well get started. I grabbed up Davis's badge and stuffed Dad's papers back under my armpit again, zipping up the front of the jumpsuit. I brushed my teeth with my finger and headed out, adding toothbrush to shoes to razor to shaving cream to palatable food in my mental list of items to buy as I locked the apartment door behind me.

I hadn't planned on stopping at the market until after the morning rush, but I was ahead of schedule and hungry, so I stepped inside. The store was empty and apparently had just opened up. I walked up and down the aisles slowly, looking to see what the choices were. I had been in the store back in CR12 many times, but had only popped in to buy something quick, never shopping for anything. I found the razor and shaving cream and a toothbrush that looked a little used near the back of the store. Each item was an obvious leftover from before the day, probably scavenged by a supply crew from another store or demolished house that was within the circle around the city. The things could have come from someone that had died within the city. Not a pleasant thought.

I looked around for some shoes, but the only clothes of any kind for sale were socks. I picked out a pair, also used, of course, just to have an item of clothing on that didn't belong to Davis. Too bad they didn't have underwear. I had never bought clothes before and really hadn't even thought of where my clothes had come from. Mom had always taken care of it. I guess there was some sort of clothes distribution office somewhere in the city. I had no idea where to find that office and suspected that they would check my badge closer than they would at the convenience store. I resigned myself to the fact that I had no chance of getting any new shoes.

At the checkout counter, I picked up something warm that looked like a biscuit. There was a squeeze tube of hydroponic jelly that I remembered from CR12. It was actually pretty good and had some taste to it. I grabbed two tubes and got myself a cup of coffee. I never drank coffee, but bought it to look the part, figuring that someone who was up this early would probably want something to help them get going.

I laid the biscuit and the other items on the counter and waited for the clerk to ring me up, more than a little nervous, anxious all of a sudden that I would be recognized. She swiped the badge and handed me a receipt back with it, never looking at my face or the picture on the badge. I took my bag and my cup of coffee, paid for with Davis's paycheck, and stepped triumphantly out onto the street, excited to have beaten the system. The rush of fear, the anticipation of the day's events, and a few sips of the hot coffee pushed the odd images from the night's dream to the rear of my mind.

It was still early and mostly dark, and I was alone on the street. I went on to the little park from the night before and found a spot on the grass to eat my biscuit. "The most peaceful time of the day," my granddad would have said, "and the best time to fish." The morning in front of me was more about hunting than fishing. I drank about half the cup of coffee and dumped what was left with the biscuit wrapper into a trash can near the road and headed for my station.

I had picked out a spot in the park after the failure of the previous afternoon. There weren't really trees in the park, more like overgrown bushes. I wanted to be off the street and up, but I needed a line of sight to see the entire street in both directions. The park was just a wide spot they had chosen where the fronts of the buildings were off the street more than normal. The building on the left had concrete stairs on one end leading up to a door that had no markings. On one side of the stairs, there was a brick wall with a concrete cap that stepped up until it was higher than the top of the door by a few feet. I climbed up the steps and scrambled up on top of the wall to take a look back toward the road. The canopy above was lightening a bit, and it looked so close. I couldn't resist the temptation and stretched to try and reach the sagging plastic just above me, but I was still a few feet short, even on tiptoes. So I sat down and surveyed the scene from my catbird's perch.

It was as I had hoped. Even sitting, I was at least twelve feet up off the level ground of the park. I could see the street in either direction with a clear sightline beneath the canopy and between any large bushes. From here I would be able to see every person that passed by on the street that morning. I settled into what I hoped would be a comfortable position, letting my legs rest on the top of the wall out in front of me and leaning on the brick wall behind me. I was excited, but it was early. I looked down at my watch. I had just over a half hour before the morning's massive pilgrimage would begin.

I decided to read what I could with the time that I had. I unzipped my jumpsuit a bit and pulled out the folded wad of papers, finding the corner of the page I had turned over the night before. I flipped the unread pages with my thumb—there was still a lot to go. *What if I find her today?* I wondered. *How did he expect me to read all this and still have enough time to find Lori?* I didn't even know where he was going with all this, but reading was better than sitting there and doing nothing, so I turned to the marked page and picked up where I had left off.

The time following those first few days passed quickly and without event. My efforts to wake up Abbie were not working well. I spent every day trying to talk with her. I went on incessantly about what I had done at work that day, what I had seen, and where I had gone. I talked about the politics of the office and replayed the story of my meeting with Wiley and with the dog. Mostly she just sat there and listened, replying only in short sounds, being polite, but clearly disinterested. She never stopped to ask me a question or to make a comment. Whenever I started asking her questions about her day or trying to bring her into the conversation, she would just get up and walk away. *At least I am annoying her,* I thought. *That is a something like an emotion.*

The cool day of my awakening and the warm day that I had taken off my hood had given way to the mostly cold days of late fall. I had been assigned a new partner, a young boy named McAllister, not much older than you. He had grown up in the city and was another riser, so he thought. With my demotion, he was my superior, even though he knew nothing about engineering or about demolishing buildings. At first he went along and watched, occasionally asking questions about where to put charges and how things worked. As cold weather came on, he stayed more and more often in the truck, to catch up on paperwork, so he said, though I usually found him sleeping when I came back.

That was fine with me. I appreciated the time alone. I could mark for the charges in the crawl space or basement quickly and spend the rest of the time looking around the house. Only once did he come in on me and find me upstairs. I just told him I was up there looking for load-bearing walls. He didn't know the difference and went back out to the truck. On other days I had taken off my hood to get a real breath, but by God's grace I had left it on that day. It was enough to discourage me from trying again. I wanted so badly to breathe real air again, but it was just too risky. This wasn't about me anymore.

I started to look for things to bring home that Abbie might find interesting. I could get small things and slip them into my uniform. I found little paperbacks she had read before, little pieces of jewelry, bottles of perfume, interesting pictures, and even a hat just like one her mom had worn, but nothing seemed to interest her. When I brought them home, she would look at them briefly and then always say, "Why did you bring this home? What if someone finds it?" One day I found a high school yearbook. Not from the same school she graduated from, but from the same year. That was a trick to hide in my uniform. That evening I tried to read some of it to her, but she just walked away. Each night, I would just slip whatever I had brought home that day into my bag and then pitch it into a closet of another house the next day. The world was my trashcan.

I saw a glimpse of interest from her one day. I had brought home a Little Debbie Oatmeal Cookie that someone had stashed in a drawer in their nightstand. It was still squishy inside the package even after all those years. Her face lightened a little as she turned it over in her hands and said, "Jack used to love these things. He ate one every day with his lunch." You were in your room working on school work, and she turned that way. I thought for a minute she was going to call for you to come into the kitchen, but then her face darkened again. "It's too old, it would make him sick," she said as she pitched it into the trash can and walked away. I pulled it back out and thought about taking it to you anyway, but decided against it. I pulled back two books from the shelf, not read in years, and hid the cookie behind them. That was as close as I had gotten to a reaction from her.

As winter drew near, I had to make a conscious decision to not get discouraged. I was getting nowhere with her. I felt the pressure of time passing, wondering how much longer I had left, always in fear of messing up again and being reassigned away from Abbie without having succeeding in waking her up. That pressure of time led me to another mini-breakthrough and the first real glimmer of hope I had with Abbie.

As I was reading, I caught some motion in my peripheral vision, and I looked up at the street in front of me. There was a man walking alone. I looked back up toward the apartments and saw a wave of people forming. Not a good place to stop reading, but it was time to get going. I quickly folded over the papers and tucked them beneath my leg. As the sea of people approached, I forced myself to concentrate and focus on each face. The flow of people picked up quickly, and within only a few minutes, the street was filled. Though no car had driven the street since the day, the walkers instinctively stuck to the right of the yellow line, refusing to enjoy the luxury of the full width of the road. As expected, they were entirely flowing one way—from the apartment buildings to the factories and offices. Almost everyone who worked in that city would be walking past me that morning, and I was in the perfect position to see each one. I leaned forward and quickly sorted out rows of people, first picking out women from men, then eliminating each face as a "not Lori," taking advantage of the image I had regained from the previous night's dream.

I was looking down slightly into the mob and could see each face clearly. I worked quickly, scanning through about fifty people at a time and working slightly back up into the flow. From my elevated seat, I could see even more strikingly what I had seen the night before when I was trapped within the flood. Each person that walked past trudged silently with their eyes to the ground, not looking at each other, not talking to anyone. It looked like a procession of corpses. If the ground had opened up and each had fallen into their own casket, it wouldn't have been surprising. But no one looked like Lori.

I sat there for what felt like an hour, but it was only about fifteen minutes before the river of people began to thin. As the outgoing lanes died down, a few going against the flow began coming up from the other way. The ingoing and outgoing lines of traffic parted seamlessly without sign or direction. My back and butt were getting numb from sitting on the wall, and my neck was locked into a cramp from the concentration, but I forced myself to hang in there until I had eliminated every face going both ways.

In less than an hour, it was over. The entire city of CR18 had passed right in front of me, and I hadn't seen anyone who even vaguely resembled Lori. It was discouraging to be sure. *Is she even here?* I thought. Maybe they had sent her to another city. Who knew if she was even alive? I leaned back against the wall and lifted up with my shoulders to let in a little blood flow to my rear and thighs. Remembering Dad's papers, I slipped them back into my uniform, always keeping an eye out for any stragglers that might be trudging past.

I stayed in place until midmorning. No commuters walked by now, only a few policemen and some women in pink suits picking up trash. I studied each face just to be sure. If Lori was in this city, she could be doing anything.

I was just about to abandon my post when a golf cart pulled up in front of the park and turned to go down the sidewalk and directly toward me. A short, thin fellow with glasses in a nice suit jumped out quickly from the passenger seat just before it came to a stop. He was the first person I had ever seen in real clothes in the city. He caught sight of me as he strode up the steps two at a time and glared oppressively my way before opening the door and putting on a fake smile. "Mr. Mayor, good morning," he said cheerily to a man in a much nicer suit stepping out from the door. The mayor was reading something and drinking a cup of coffee as he walked. He took the thin man's seat in the cart, and they talked for a minute.

I tried to blend into the wall and disappear, but the mayor saw me sitting there. He nodded his head in my direction, saying something to the thin man that I couldn't hear. The thin man turned toward me and said, loud enough for me to hear, "I'll take care of this one." As the golf cart pulled away, he stepped my way and looked up at me. He had a look on his face that reminded me of my first grade teacher when she caught me playing in the sink in the bathroom.

"Why isn't your badge on your uniform?" he asked as he stepped quickly to the top of the stairs.

"It's my day off," I offered as I dug out Davis's badge from my pocket and handed it to him. I tried to turn my face away from him so he couldn't get the same frontal view that was on the badge. It had the effect of making me look like I was ignoring him. He scowled menacingly at me and pulled a small computer pad, long but narrow, from a pouch on the side of his leg. He scanned the badge through a slot on the machine and read Davis's file.

Without looking at me, he said, "You shouldn't be sitting here, you haven't shaved, and if you don't have any paperwork to do on your day off, you probably aren't working hard enough." He grinned as he looked down on the screen of his little computer. "Looks like you are going to have a review down at the city building day after tomorrow, Davis, for destroying the city's truck." He continued, "Maybe I should show up for that review and bring this little incident onto the table." He smirked triumphantly as he handed me back Davis's badge. With that, he spun on his heel and marched off importantly.

Mostly I wanted to punch the little twit in the nose, or maybe hit him in the head with a shovel, but I knew that wouldn't get me anywhere. Instead, I tried to look remorseful and hung my head until he was gone. I slipped down from my perch and walked away from the park, wondering what my next move should be. I had lost my perfect spot for the afternoon commute and for tomorrow. At that moment, it didn't seem to matter. Dad and I had been planning this for months and the plan had worked beautifully. Just as we had laid it out, the whole of the city had walked right under my nose. I saw every face clearly. I had truly expected to be talking with Lori at this moment, or at least have a meeting time for when she got off of work. To say I was discouraged would be an understatement. As I passed the market, I started to turn back toward the apartment but thought better of it. Hiding in there all day wouldn't do me any good. The road continued to the right and I could see a brick building ahead. "Their school—of course," I said out loud. Plan B began to form in my mind.

CHAPTER 6

*"You watch the sun rise. You saw the darkness
had no choice before the dawn."*

The apartment complex was at the head of the city, or the foot, depending on your point of view. The road leading away from it led to all the factories and offices. Separate from the rest of the city, and forming an L-shape to one side of the apartment complex, was the school building. I walked toward the school, sizing it up as I ran through the plan in my mind. Back at CR12, our school had been a renovated group of offices, but here they had an actual school building. It looked like it had either been an old high school or maybe even a small college. Only one building was used for the school. If there were other buildings on the campus before, they were on the other side of the plastic now. But even with only one building, they had a much nicer setup here than I had at my school. I could see the gymnasium at one end of the building. The road leading to the school narrowed down to just a walkway, and there was grass on either side of it leading up to the door. It was a long brick building, with three stories and tall, paned windows. A single tree, full grown but short enough to fit under the plastic canopy, was to one side of the sidewalk. It was a nice scene, an island of serenity in the midst of the oppressive weight of the city. I really hoped that Lori would be inside the school in front of me.

As I grabbed the handle of the front door, I had my plan firmly set. If I had learned anything about the city, it was that you could go anywhere and do anything if you just acted like you knew what you were doing. So long as I didn't break from protocol, I could walk through any door. I knew the routines from when I was in school, I just had to play it smooth and act disinterested.

The main entrance was near the center of the building, and the front doors opened into a short hall that stubbed up to the primary hallway going left to right. The outside of the building was completely different than CR12, but the inside was nearly identical to the school that Lori and I had attended. The floors were polished white, the block walls were painted a cream color and the white ceiling tiles were dropped into a white tray. The bright fluorescent lights reflected off all the whiteness, giving the hall a serene, heavenly glow. It was brighter inside than it was outside under the canopy. Sounds of teachers talking in their classrooms mixed together into an incoherent, rhythmic melody. The familiar antiseptic smell filled my nose. It was the same generic cleaner from CR12, and they must have used on it every surface in the building.

The office was directly in front of the entrance and the secretary looked up and caught my eye when I walked in. I looked away and scanned the walls of the short hall, finding the panel with the teacher's names listed. There were about thirty teachers listed. I didn't see anyone named Lori Applegate, didn't see anyone with the first name Lori. Even if she had gotten married when she moved here (a thought I hadn't considered), she wouldn't have changed her last name. Very few people even bothered to get married anymore; they just floated from mate to mate, picking a temporary partner to sleepwalk with. I picked a name from the list and locked it in my mind as I walked toward the secretary.

"May I help you?" she asked. The secretary was young and pretty but dull and lifeless in her eyes.

"I have a meeting scheduled with a Ms. Taylor," I said.

She put on a plastic smile as she directed me to room 14 on the third floor. "She's still in class right now and will be unavailable for another twenty minutes," she offered.

"So I guess I am a bit early," I replied, looking around the office. There were three other rooms in the office, each with a name on the door. I scanned them quickly and none were named Lori. There were a lot of people working here besides teachers, and I needed to eliminate all of them if I could.

The third floor was perfect for what I needed to do. I started down one hall, knowing the stairs would be at the end. As I passed each classroom, the doors were open and I could see inside. The first few doors passed were younger grades, the rooms nearly empty of students, with less than ten children in each room. The four-year-old class only had three kids in it. The door of each classroom had the teacher's name engraved on a small plaque with the name of their aide just below. I scanned each one as I passed, hoping to see Lori's name. I peeked inside each room, looking for a glimpse of her face. Somehow I could sense that she wasn't in the building.

I worked my way to the end of the hall and then up the stairs, stopping to pass down the second floor hall in the same way, lingering near each door just long enough to look inside. I stepped into each boy's bathroom and walked slowly past each girl's bathroom, listening for the sounds of any adults that might be inside. I found the custodian, an older man, in the boy's bathroom on the second floor. I just went on in, did my business, which I needed to do anyway, and tried to act natural, not speaking to the man.

By the time I reached the third floor, I realized that the younger children were on the lower floors and the upper floors were for the older children. I had apparently chosen to meet with a high school teacher. I thought to myself that perhaps the secretary might figure out that I was much too young to have a child this age and didn't have an appointment with this teacher after all. I would do well to hurry and get back out on the street.

The classes for the upper grades had a lot more students in them than the younger grades. I could see the faces of the boys and girls as I passed, involuntarily searching the girls for Lori's face, even though I knew she couldn't be a student anymore. I heard the tones of the teachers' voices rising and lowering as they lectured, picking out phrases about factoring binomials and renal systems and objects of the preposition as I passed the rooms. Part of me felt like I could slip into the back of the classroom, right where a Wilson would be sitting, and pretend to take notes, just like always, and not miss a beat. But the other part of me felt more separated from these young men and women than ever, almost as if they were from another planet. I had changed so much since we left the city, and I was not the same person who had sat in classrooms like these just a few years ago.

Seeing the students, hearing the lectures, walking between the rows of lockers, brought back memories of Lori and how we first met. She and I were in the same grade and had been in classes together from the beginning. We had both come to CR12 on the same day, just like everyone else. It was the summer before our fourth grade in school. By late in the fall, things had stabilized enough in the city that all the kids were called in to go to school. We had three classes in our age group, and she and I had been in the same class for both the fourth and fifth grades and then in some individual classes when the classes were split in the sixth grade and on. I was shy and reserved, especially in the early years, and had never even spoken to her until near the end of the seventh grade year.

She was an Applegate and sat near the front of the class, and I was a Wilson and sat in the rear. All the kids were numb for the first year or so, and no one really even tried to make friends. There were a couple of kids who talked all the time, really to no one in particular, just because they didn't know what else to do. Other kids were violent and lashed out at the teachers and the other kids, but they were usually gone after a few episodes, sent away somewhere. Every one of us had to try to find our own way of dealing with the things we had gone through. After a few years, most of us had boxed away the pain, going on with the life that had been presented to us, trying to make the best of the situation with a sleepy numbness of denial and self-absorption. For whatever reason, I never made it to the fully numb state, and neither did Lori.

By the seventh grade, my hormones had overcome my grief, and I had certainly noticed Lori. She was a natural beauty, and she actually smiled on a regular basis. Most of the girls were either angry a lot of the time or were fiercely cliquish, but Lori had a quiet, easygoing way about her. The boys didn't pay her as much attention because she was quiet and hadn't filled out her figure as much as some of the other girls, but she had a peaceful way that was very attractive to me, beyond the physical attraction that was already there.

I was too shy to say anything more to her than "hi," but one day in the spring of our seventh grade year, I got my opportunity. Reed Preston was one of those kids who talked loud and picked fights, always one step away from serious trouble or expulsion. As he walked past Lori in the hall that day, he leaned in and clipped her with his shoulder, bumping her hard against the lockers. I was to the center of the hall and just behind Preston and saw the whole thing; he had bumped her intentionally. I didn't like him anyway and sure didn't like to see him going after my Lori and a flame of rage erupted. I was a bit shorter than him and lighter by at least twenty pounds, but I was so mad I didn't care. I reached out and grabbed him by the shoulder, spinning him around. "What are you doing running into a girl?" I said, poking my finger in his chest. "Tell her you're sorry."

He bent down slowly, looking me in the eye as he set his books in the floor. "I would like to see you make me do anything," he growled in my face, shoving me backward with two hands as he said the last word. I reeled backward about three steps but caught myself from falling before setting down my books and balling up my fists. The kids in the hall around us backed up traffic in each direction, forming a pocket around me, him, and Lori. She was standing to one side with her mouth open. I bull rushed him in five steps, building up speed and driving my shoulder under his ribs, picking him up off his heels as he struggled to stay on his feet. I drove him backward, and his head hit against a locker door that was partially open. It slammed shut like a gunshot ringing through the halls. He pushed me off and drew back his fist to take a swing, but Ms. Swisher grabbed his arm and pinned it behind his back before he could fire a shot. She was a large woman, heavier than either of us, and was the type that didn't take any business off anybody. She gripped down on Reed's arm and gave him a look that would have made any-one else melt as she shoved him down the hall toward the office. As she walked away, she gave the onlookers a similar look, and the crowd dispersed quickly, leaving only Lori and me standing in the hall.

I went to her to see if she was hurt but was surprised at the look on her face. She was obviously annoyed with me. "I wish you hadn't done that," she said. "You should have just left him alone." I couldn't believe what I was hearing. I had been her hero and defender, and this was the thanks I got? She turned away from me and bent to pick up Preston's books that he had left, wrapping one arm around his books and the other around her own. The stack of books looked bigger than her, but she carried them without wavering. I followed her down the hall, opening my mouth to offer to carry his books and then just clos-ing it back. She certainly didn't want my help. She quietly set his books down beside the office door and breezed past me without saying a word or even looking at me. She was walking quickly now, almost running, and slipped into our third period class-room ahead of me. The tardy bell rang as I walked in the door, and I slunk into my seat in the back of the class. The teacher gave me the eye, but didn't send me back to the office. I didn't hear a word that was taught that period; I was too dumbfounded by what had just happened.

I would like to say I had noticed the fact that Preston had the whole world crashing down on his head and I got noth-ing, but the thought never occurred to me until after he was gone. He had been in trouble again and again. If he and I hadn't scuffled that morning, he probably would've gotten something started farther down the hall. The way I saw it, he was trouble and deserved whatever he had coming. That's why Lori's answer surprised me so much when I tracked her down that afternoon.

She was leaving the school, walking alone ahead of me toward the apartments when I caught sight of her. I jogged around a couple of kids and came up by her side. "Hey," I said. "How're you doing?"

"Fine, I suppose," she replied. My first impulse was to leave it at that, but I had been thinking about her and what had happened all day and my curiosity overcame my shyness.

"Why did you carry Preston's books to the office?" I asked her. "He bumped you on purpose. You acted like you were more upset with me than you were with him."

She stopped walking and turned around. Her face was sad, but not angry. She looked back toward the apartments and asked, "Do you see the last building of apartments?"

"Sure," I replied.

"I live on the third floor," she continued. "I had a roommate until last fall, and they transferred her off somewhere. Her name was Melissa; you might remember her before she got sent off." I nodded my head, but I really didn't remember her much. She had been quiet and just stared at the wall most days. One day she had started crying in class and hadn't stopped. They took her out, and we hadn't seen her again. "All the girls without parents live on the third floor," she went on, "and all the boys live on the second floor. Reed Preston lives, or used to live, I guess, on the second floor. He watched his mom and dad die on the day. Sure, Reed is a pest sometimes, but he just doesn't know how to deal with all this. Maybe if you had to watch one of your parents die you would understand." She was firm in her tone, but not angry, and she continued with her walking as she finished the last sentence.

I should have shut up, but I didn't know any better, so I kept after her. "Hey," I said, "all of us have been through a lot. Why did he have to go and hit you like that?"

She smiled a little as she replied with a question. "Reed picks on people all the time. Why did you decide to fight with him when he picked on me?"

She had me with that, and I stopped in my tracks, watching her walk ahead of me and letting the flow of students file past on either side. As she slipped away, I thought to catch up with her and ask her why she had said that Preston used to live on the second floor, but I was embarrassed at her question, so I let her go. In the days ahead I found out that she was right. Our almost fight had been his last straw, and we never saw him again. I always hoped that he had been transferred to another CR, but who knew for sure what happened to people when they were sent away.

All these years later, I finally understood a bit of where a guy like Preston was coming from. Even though my parents barely spoke to me, it gave me comfort just to know that they were still there when the tough days of doubt and painful memories came. With all that had happened in the last few days, I sure missed my dad and wanted his advice and support with what I was going through. Reed had no one to turn to, and he caved in under the stress and pressure that plagued us all. The strange thought that Reed Preston might actually be somewhere in CR18 came over me. He might have walked in front of me on the street that morning. *If he did,* I thought, *I wouldn't have recognized him anyway.*

By this time, I was deeply distracted by my thoughts and had stopped walking down the hall. I came to myself suddenly and realized that I had been staring aimlessly into one of the third floor classrooms. A girl in the second row was looking back at me with a curious look. It was evident from her face that she was the only one that was awake, to use my father's term, in the entire classroom. Everyone else was gazing blankly at the teacher or taking notes mechanically and hadn't noticed me. She gave me one of those "What are you doing standing there staring into space?" looks. I smiled back and walked away down the hall. Seeing her sitting in that room full of zombies gave me a shiver. There were awake people scattered throughout the city, isolated and alone. I remembered feeling just how that girl felt when I was in school. Lori was probably in some office or factory right now, feeling the same way.

I walked the rest of the third floor, checking the nameplates and scanning over each room as I passed the door. I took the stairs at the end of the hall to the first floor and finished the other half of that hall before scooting out the front door without saying anything else to the secretary or even looking to see if she saw me leaving. *Just look like you know what you are doing,* I repeated to myself as I stepped back outside.

I had hoped to find Lori in the school. She was a perfect fit to be an aide and probably would have made a good teacher, but she wasn't there. The disappointment of another miss in my search was tempered by the excitement of the resurrected memories. It was good to see her face in my mind and remember her words again.

From that first real meeting, she had me hooked. I was madly in love with her with as much as I knew what love was. The fact that she knew it and never said anything about it was equally maddening and invigorating. Looking back on it, she and I were probably the only two in our class that were awake, though we didn't know what that meant at the time. We talked with each other a lot, mostly about nothing, but sometimes we had deep conversations. We talked about what the future might hold; we even shared with each other about our families from the normal days before the city. Though we spent time together most every day, she always kept a distance between us that allowed for the friendship to stay strong but never grow into anything more. It is hard to describe it, but she would only let her guard down and be vulnerable for just the right time to keep our relationship close without fanning the flame she knew I had within me. Looking back on it, I think she subconsciously wanted to preserve our friendship above all else, because in some ways it was all she had to hold on to. Whether it was intentional or not, her prudence in dealing with me built a friendship that escaped the normal jealousy and fiery ups and downs of a normal boy-girl teenage relationship. My desire for her physically burned hot, as it does for any teenage boy, but steady, and it was insulated on all sides by the respect and admiration I had for her character. Even as a girl, she was a lady, and I never thought but to treat her that way. The downside of it was that I never really knew exactly how she felt about me. I knew she cared for me, but I wouldn't let myself believe it would become more until we shared the hug on the steps of the city building the day she was taken from me.

I was thinking of all this as I walked, and I found myself back at the park, looking down the empty street in front of me. Filling my mind with the thoughts of Lori renewed my resolve to find her but salted the wound of disappointment in the search so far. I had been from one end of the city to the other and had seen every soul pass in front of me on the street that morning. I even saw the mayor. But I had no sign or hint of Lori. In all the months that Dad and I had prepared for this mission, it had never dawned on me that she might not be here. If she was in another CR, I would have no way to figure out which one or even how to get there. The only option I had was to keep looking here. I would take advantage of the extra day off I had been given and hope for the best. The thought of the days off reminded me that this might have been her day off. "So I stand watch on the street this afternoon and tomorrow morning and try my luck at that," I mumbled to myself, trying to generate some optimism.

Dad didn't believe in luck. I wondered what he would have thought of all this and realized that my last thoughts might have come from his mouth. It was so like Dad to just plow along and make the best of whatever he had in front of him. At least that was the Dad I knew after he woke up, especially after we got to the cabin. I found a place on the other side of the road, this time safely away from the mayor's house, and found a comfortable spot to sit in the grass. The ground was soft, much better than the concrete stoop from that morning. I looked both ways sitting and standing and found that I could see between the bushes enough to catch a wide window of any walkers coming from either direction. Right now it was mid-afternoon and there was no one on the road. I put my trust in my peripheral vision and pulled out the papers to do some more reading. I had left Dad in the midst of his thought when the mayor's effeminate thug had assaulted me that morning, so I went back and reread the last page before picking back up on his story:

I think my main mistake with your mother, Jack, up to this point was that I misunderstood the nature of waking up. Just like every person wakes from a sleep differently, so it was never the same for anyone who managed to wake from the something-like-sleep that we were all in. I had awakened quickly, with a hard jolt, and I just assumed it would be the same with Abbie. It was not. She came back to me in small steps.

I do remember the one day that I believe was the beginning of her returning to self-awareness. It began about a week prior to that with the news that my young partner, McAllister, was scheduled to go through four days of in-house training. He and I were both on our scheduled day off, and I got the memo by computer that afternoon about his training. The class he would be attending was one that I had rotated in to teach before my demotion. The fact that he was my supervisor ticked me off enough, but him attending that training and me not teaching it just made it worse. I don't think being demoted really bothered me much until that day.

On top of that, it seemed to me that I was getting nowhere with Abbie. I had tried for day after day to get some sort of response out of her. All the gifts and attempts at conversation weren't doing a thing. She barely even spoke to me. Even a smile or something like a conversation would have been nice. The constant rejection was really kind of depressing. The harder I tried, the lonelier it made me feel. The whole thing just got me down.

That night I didn't talk much with you or with Abbie. I didn't have the heart to try. I let the night be like it was before I woke up. We passed the evening away, not saying much of anything. I lay there next to her in bed, listening to her breathing, but couldn't sleep myself. Abbie was right next to me, but she might as well have been miles away. I tossed and turned and woke up about six or eight times that night, still angry and depressed. The last time I woke, it was close to the time when I would be getting up anyway, so I dressed quietly and snuck out while you two were still asleep.

It was a cold morning, and I remember that I beat everyone else out that morning and walked the streets alone. Even under the plastic, I could see my breath in the cold air. I had a long drive ahead of me that day and had four houses on the schedule, so I had a good excuse for starting early. I was the only one in the locker room and the first one to the trucks. The guard hadn't yet gotten to the checkpoint, so I got out of my truck and scanned my badge to open the gate. The truck was still cold, but I hurried back anyway, urging on the slow-starting heater as I started off down the road. I drove in silence, letting the solitude feed my simmering self-pity. The directions to the first house were difficult, and it was still pretty dark. I had to concentrate on each turn, getting out twice to hack at the growth around the road signs to make sure I was headed in the right direction.

I finally came to the entrance of what was once an upscale subdivision with tall, expensive-looking houses spaced tightly along the slope of a ridge. In typical fashion, we would start at the end of the road and demolish them backward. The road switched back a couple of times and rose sharply as I neared its end. As I came to the cul-de-sac at the top of the hill, the sight took away my breath. The last house at the end lot had not been completed and a panoramic view of the surrounding countryside spread out before me. The mist of the morning clung around the houses in the valley. They poked their heads from amongst the mist like prairie dogs in tall grass. In the distance, the mountains formed a shadowy silhouette behind the curtain of morning fog. The trees alternated from the wiry nakedness of the hardwoods to the sagging green branches of the pines and their cousins. High on the farthest peaks, the white tops showed evidence of snowfall in the previous few days.

I hadn't seen anything but a glimpse of those mountains since the day. The sight of them pulled me from the cab of my truck to stand on the road. I stood staring with the driver's door left open, the heater now trying to warm up the whole world. I glanced quickly around to make sure I wasn't in sight of anyone else and slipped off my hood. The real air was shockingly cold compared to the recycled air inside my uniform and the first breath burned the inside of my nose, melting off what was left of my morning sleepiness. The view unobstructed by the visor was even more enticing. The mountains had been an anchor of my world before the city. It was the mountains as much as Abbie that had pulled me away from the city. She had talked me into the move by choosing a home with a view when we moved back to Tennessee.

Abbie and I had met in college. She was smart and pretty, and I was going to set the world on fire and make a million dollars. I never really knew what she saw in me, but I wasn't arguing with her. I had married up in looks for sure, and that was most of what attracted me to her at the time. We got married a month before I graduated in December. I took a job as an engineer in Atlanta, and she enrolled to finish her last semester in accounting at Georgia State. It was a tough change and a poor fit for a small-town girl from Tennessee, but I convinced her that my job offer was too good to turn down, so she left her family and followed me to Atlanta.

The first month there, our second car broke down. It was an older car that she had borrowed from her parents, and I was too proud to let her call them and ask for help. We had already borrowed money from them to cover all of our deposits for moving and had taken an apartment in a nice neighborhood up around Alpharetta that we couldn't afford. By this time, I had only gotten one paycheck. I convinced her that she could ride the MARTA downtown to her classes for just a month until we could afford to pay the repair bill or trade for a newer model. One month turned into six, and we finally got another used car for her to drive. By then, she was done with her school and had taken an intern position with an accounting firm downtown. My job was closer to our apartment, but I was gone more than I was home. I signed up for every out-of-town assignment I could, traveling two weeks out of every three, looking for project bonuses and per diem overruns to try and catch us up with our bills.

Abbie hated the traffic and hated being alone in the apartment without me. On top of it all, it was the first time she had been apart from her family. We had no friends and never had time to join a church. The weekends I was gone, she would usually drive the three hours back home to her parents. Looking back on it, I know she had to have been depressed. I was so busy working and was gone so much; it is amazing that our marriage survived that first year. I steered every conversation we had to something about a project at work or how we were doing on our bills. I don't know why I neglected her so much. Maybe I thought that once we were married, I didn't have to work on our relationship anymore. Maybe I just figured that the Abbie project was done and I could go on and focus in on the next one.

She had only been at her job with the firm for a few months when I came home from another week-long trip to find her waiting for me at the door. She had a pensive look on her face, and for that one brief moment I was scared she was going to tell me she was leaving. When she told me she was pregnant, I was as much relieved as I was excited. I had been away a lot, but it never crossed my mind to wonder if she had been unfaithful to me. It just wasn't in her nature. Your mom is a wonderful lady, Jack, but it took me a long time to figure that out. When I got a look at your face and held you in my arms, I never would have doubted her faithfulness anyway. You were a chip off the old block and had my complete attention, at least for a while.

I think Abbie knew how smitten I was with you, and she took the opportunity to suggest that maybe we couldn't afford to live in Atlanta if she wasn't working. We hadn't had the conversation about her staying home, but she wisely slipped it past me as she went around it to the next point. Two weeks after you were born, she called and got me three job interviews nearer to home. The challenge of a new job and the flattering and wooing I received at the interviews played to my ego, and I went along with her plan. When she found our pretty little home with the view of the mountains, the deal was delivered. Faster than I could even think, we were moved out of Atlanta and back to East Tennessee. It was a few counties south of where I had grown up, but it was the same line of mountains—the same mountains I was looking at that morning.

Even on a cold day like that one, there is a warm aliveness about these mountains that is hard to describe. The valleys and hollows roll and breathe as they crawl along between the hills and ridges that gather at the foot of the mountains. Everywhere in sight were trees and creeks and rivers and ponds with homes scattered between. Nowhere could you see even an acre that was flat. There is a robust strength and vigor about that land that exudes a noble masculinity. Years after that day, when we came to our cabin in the midst of the mountains, I never felt more like a man, more like who I was created to be. Standing there that morning, looking out over the scene before me, it was as if the land was rolling beneath a blanket of mist, waking from the sleep of the previous night. The mountains were beckoning to me, inviting me to come to them. I realized at that moment that I could drive the truck until the gas ran out and just walk the rest of the way and no one would ever bother to come after me. My moment's temptation was broken by the tip of the dawning sun rising over the peak of the far off mountains.

It was a beautiful sight. I had of course seen many sunrises, but it had been so many years. Breathing in the cold air of the morning and drinking in the sight before me, my depression and self-absorption melted away. In that moment, I began to understand that I was nothing and that God was everything, but that was really an okay thing. If he could make all of this then he could take care of my little problems. I never prayed a prayer, never made any great confession or signed a letter of commitment, but at that moment I subconsciously shifted all my burdens and worries from my shoulders to his. When I saw how easily he carried them, I laughed and the depression was over. I would like to say it was an epiphany experience that cured me of my depression and started me on the pure and pristine path, but God doesn't work that way. It was just another little step that was leading me to become someone that I had never planned on becoming. At any rate, it was a moment of clear thinking, a temporary escape from self-absorption, and I often still will call up its memory when I am feeling down.

I happened to look down at my watch just as the sun first peeked over the hill. The time in the truck was synchronized with the main clock in the city, and I checked it against my watch to make sure it was right. My thought at that moment was just that it was 7:52, and I had been standing here gaping at the mountains for a long time and had better get my hood back on and get to work before anybody else came up this way. But that little glance at the watch was perhaps as important to Abbie and to our family as the clarity of the moment had been to me.

The rest of the day passed quickly. The houses were large and complicated and took a good bit of pondering to figure out and mark. It was good to work and move about to try and stave off the cold. I didn't think so much about the thoughts of the morning until I climbed into the truck that evening and headed back toward the city. I resumed my prodding and tugging at Abbie that night at the apartment, showing her an old photograph of a couple and a gardening magazine. She looked at the magazine for a few minutes but didn't say much to me before heading off to bed. It was more of the same, but I had a peace about things that had been missing for a while.

I woke early again the next morning and slipped out at about the same time, anxious to try and catch another sunrise. My jobs for the day were at the same subdivision, just further back up the road. I drove past my next house to the end of the road again for the view of the sunrise. The demo crews were following me in that day to knock down the houses I had marked up the day before, so I took off my hood with caution, watching the entrance road below me to catch their orange truck coming in. The sunrise was just as beautiful that day as it had been the day before, this time with a bit less fog. I looked again at the clock to see how much time I had left, and this time it read 7:53.

That got me thinking back to eighth grade science class, and I could barely sleep that night as I prepared for another early morning. It was awfully cold for the days to still be getting shorter. I only had two days left to try and test my theory, but it was worth a shot. When the sun came up the next morning at 7:53 again, I let out a whoop that echoed in the valley below. On my last day to myself, I hurried out again, knowing I had to get to the same exact spot to know for sure. The fog was thick that morning, and I was afraid I wouldn't be able to see the sunrise, but I drove up and out of the fog as I climbed up the switchbacks and topped out at the cul-de-sac. I glanced back and forth from the point of the rising sun to the clock and back again. This time it rose at 7:52. I had found the winter solstice, or at least something very close to it. The short day before was probably December 22nd. That day had to be the 23rd, so the next day would have to be Christmas Eve. It was also my fifth day, so I was at home. Instead of working on paperwork, I got busy getting things ready while you and your mother were gone to school and to work.

I got up early again on Christmas Day, but this time I woke up you and Abbie too. I taped together some papers I had found and colored in with some crayons a green Christmas tree with red lights and stuck it up to the wall. It was about four feet tall, and the size of it made up for my lack of artistic ability. I had tried to make a Santa's hat from red colored paper and some cotton balls, but it tore when I put it around my head, so I just laid it to the side, hoping to add to the holiday mood. I made for breakfast some of the hard biscuits we had, dyeing them with some green and red food coloring I had found. I had also found a little plastic container of honey, unopened. It didn't have an expiration date, so I figured it was safe.

Jack, I remember clearly your face when you walked into our little living room. For just a moment, you were the little kid from before the terrible day, innocent and excited. You looked at me with your eyes shining and asked, "How do you know it's Christmas?" Abbie's face was a bit more skeptical, but at least she was interested. I made the two of you sit on the couch. I had found your gifts weeks earlier and used the Christmas as an excuse to give them to you. If you remember, I got you two Hot Wheels cars that looked like something you would have played with back then. I also got you the letter *M* from a set of encyclopedias. I am not really sure why, but you seemed to like it. Lastly I pulled out the Little Debbie oatmeal cake I had saved from the trash can and stashed away several weeks before. Abbie frowned when I brought that out, but she didn't say a word and even almost smiled when you opened it up and ate it in two bites. You did not get sick, if you remember.

Abbie's gifts had been much harder. I had several small things I had already found for the warm up gifts: some magazines, pictures, and a pair of slippers that weren't very worn. I had been bringing her little gifts for weeks now, and I knew I needed something special for Christmas morning. I really only had the one day to find something so I said a quick prayer at each house I came to as I took a moment to rummage around after marking for the demo. At the last stop, I found the perfect gift.

From the pictures on the wall, the house appeared to have belonged to a wealthy, older couple, just what you would expect for such a ritzy neighborhood. Tucked away in a drawer by the nightstand on the woman's side of the bed, I found an oval pendant on a thin gold chain. The pendant was about half the size of a woman's thumb and had a green colored stone embedded on the front. It looked like something that Abbie would have worn, so I put it back in the box I found it in and took it back to the apartment for wrapping. I colored in decorations on the paper and even cut out a little paper bow to go on top.

She smiled at the package and carefully removed the paper from around the box so as not to tear it. As she opened it, I asked her if she remembered the last time she had opened up a Christmas present, but she didn't answer back. She didn't smile or frown when she pulled out the necklace, but immediately slipped it around her neck, fastening it behind. "It's long," she said as she looked down at the pendant hanging below the neckline of her nightgown.

"Yeah," I said, "that was on purpose so you can wear it under your uniform without it being seen." My reply sounded made up, and I don't think she believed it, but it was actually true. The pretty green stone was just a bonus—the long chain was what I had looked for.

She sat still for a moment, staring at the stone on the front of the pendant and then she flipped it over. I hadn't looked at the back, but engraved in cursive in the gold was the one word, "Dawn." "Your sister was named Dawn, wasn't she," I said absently. I hadn't bothered to get to know her family very well, but I had liked her sister and her husband.

"She was named after my Granny," Abbie said. "What would Granny have thought of all this? What would Mom have thought?" A tear rolled down each cheek, and she began to cry.

She rolled the locket in her hands and stared off at nothing, tears and sobs flowing freely now as she came to herself and pulled in all those years of repressed memories and emotions. I was crying too, not for the memory of her grandmother, who had died two years before the day, but because I knew that Abbie's tears were real and that she was finally awake.

She broke from her crying and looked at me pointedly. "Where did you find this?" she asked.

I stammered for a moment, realizing what she was really asking. "It was from north of the city," I replied. "It couldn't have been from your Granny or your sister. I didn't even know your Granny was named Dawn, she was always just Granny to me. I didn't even look at the name on the back when I picked it up." I stopped and looked into her eyes, reaching to wipe off a tear. "Abbie, honey, it was just a coincidence."

She smiled at me in a way I had waited months to see. "Well, it was very sweet anyway, and I like it a lot." She leaned over and gave me a kiss on the cheek and gave another to you. "Boys, this has been exciting, but we had better get going or we will all be late."

And with that, our Christmas morning was over. The red and green biscuits were too hard to eat, but Abbie strung them through with thread, and they hung over the kitchen sink until February 14th, when they were replaced by pink paper hearts. I would like to say we celebrated Valentine's Day like a married couple should, but things didn't work that way. I wanted her as my wife, but it was a wonderful start to just have her as a friend. I am sure you noticed that she still wears the necklace every day. As you are reading this and I am waiting for you outside the city, you should know that I am really looking forward to seeing it around her neck when we get back to the cabin. That Christmas was a new day for Abbie and me, a gift in itself. I know now that the "Dawn" scratched in the back of the pendant was no coincidence. In this life we live, there are no coincidences and no luck, just a God with a strange, but perfect sense of timing.

I folded up the papers and sat still for a moment, remembering well the Christmas Day that Dad had just described to me. It had been a good day, the first time we had felt anything like a family since the day. It hurt to hear Dad talking so much about how lonely he had been. I had been awake the whole time, but he was so focused on pulling out Mom that he never took the time to talk to me about things. I thought about the cars he had gotten me for presents. Up until we left the city, I don't think he ever saw me as anything other than the nine-year-old boy that had rode the bus into the city with him on the day.

I had been lonely too, and for a lot longer than Dad. I think in some ways, my relationship with Lori, or friendship, or whatever it was, was an attempt to fill in the gap that my father should have filled. It was a deep thought, and a disturbing one at that, considering all the pain and suffering it had taken for me to come here to find Lori. The thought was broken up by the first person walking along the road in over an hour. Behind him walked several others. The evening commute had begun. I tucked away the papers and stood to my feet to get the perfect view in each direction.

CHAPTER 7

"Does it have to start with a broken heart,
broken dreams, and bleeding parts?"

My vantage point wasn't nearly so good as my morning perch across the street, but it was good enough to see what I needed to see. I focused almost mechanically now on each person as they passed by, eliminating each face like a sharpshooter knocking down targets. I didn't miss a face and never looked down, but as I studied the crowd, my interest in the task began to fade. I realized, even as I was standing there, that I had no expectation of seeing Lori in the crowd that evening. And, as far as I could tell, my intuition was correct. It was necessary to be in this spot at this time just to make sure she didn't walk by, and this was part of the plan we had laid out months ago, but in my heart, I knew she wasn't there.

So my mind drifted, bouncing back and forth between wondering about where Lori might be and processing the thoughts my dad had just laid out before me. I remembered everything he was talking about, of course, and I wondered what he was up to with his story. He had started the whole thing with "read this before you find her." Here I was with only one day left, and that day a bonus at that, and I was only a little past halfway through what he had written. How had he expected me to finish reading all this and still find Lori? It wasn't like Dad to spend all this time writing down a story that he could have just told to my face as we were walking down the highway to CR18.

To think that he would be anything other than thoroughly practical and planned was impossible. He was a consummate engineer, no thought or action wasted, everything working toward a goal or plan of meaning or substance. He knew the ending of his story before he started it, that was for sure, and he was leading me somewhere, although it was anything but plain at that point.

Whenever my dad started talking about God, it made me uncomfortable. It was like he expected me to know an old friend from his childhood that I had never met. Part of me really wanted to see God in the same way Dad did, it just never clicked like that for me. Dad and I had numerous conversations, "arguments" my mom called them, but we never saw eye-to-eye on the subject. I think it hurt Dad that I didn't think like him, but believing in something is not a thing you can just make yourself do—it is either there, or it isn't.

It's not that I didn't believe in God. When I was walking alone at night, with all the stars above me, I always felt really small, but in a cozy sort of way. It was a relief to be reminded that there was something bigger than me, and that he would bother to put each star in its own place. The constellations painted on the evening canvas could only have been laid out by the hand of an artist. Dad would have pointed out that some of the things that had happened in the last few days were just too much to be a coincidence. It never entered my thinking that there might not be a God and that he might not be in control. I knew God was real; I just didn't see God in the same way my dad did.

If something good happened, Dad would say that God was blessing us. If something bad happened, he would say that it was part of a greater plan and everything would work out for good in the end. Looking at life that way just seemed silly to me. It was like God got a free pass and didn't have to answer to anybody. What about my dad getting killed? How was that part of the greater plan? How come Davis had to get killed? How was that good for anybody? Why was God letting all these people suffer in these horrible cities, with no hope of anything else? I had no problem believing that God was capable of fixing things; I just didn't understand why he wouldn't go ahead and do it.

I remembered the little prayer that Mom would say with us over lunch back in our house. "God is great; God is good. Let us thank him for our food." I could certainly identify with the God is great part; I just didn't buy into the part about him being good. It started, I guess, when we first were taken to the city. I ached over my friends from school, my grandparents, and especially my little brother, Jeremy. I was only a boy, but I was seriously angry with God. Mom and Dad were both asleep, and I felt so alone. I can remember curling into a ball in bed at night, crying myself to sleep and spitting out angry prayers at God, sure that he either didn't hear or didn't care. It was the only time I was able to let my anger out and as my prayers piled up, I slowly gave up on there being any goodness in God. When I lost Lori, all the old anger kindled again. I spent many a night at the cabin, tossing and turning in the bed, rising to wander through the woods, mentally shaking my fist at God. My only peace was a clear night when I could stare up at the stars, but it was a fleeting peace. My dad both loved and trusted God and I could do neither. I just never could believe that God was on my side or even that he cared about me. It was a disconnect between Dad and me, a broken bridge that would never be rebuilt now that I had lost him forever.

"Well, I guess Dad knows the truth about God now," I said out loud. "I hope he was right." The sound of my voice shook me from my thoughts. I had been eliminating faces throughout my musing, and by now the crowd had dwindled to a few scattered singles. It baffled me how I could be studying each face, even concentrating, and having a conversation of such deep magnitude with myself. Hopefully, finding Lori was part of "God's greater plan" as Dad would have said. Even if that plan had nothing to do with what was right or fair, maybe for once I would find myself on the good side of God's game of chess.

The flow of commuters had almost dried up when I saw the mayor's golf cart coming up over the hill. It wouldn't do for me to be across the street again when he and his lackey pulled up. As they came to a stop, I slipped along the rear of the grassy area and stepped back out onto the road with my back to them, walking along with the thinning flow of stragglers away from the apartments. I squeezed my elbow against my ribs, holding onto my dad's papers.

Walking this way wasn't such a bad thing. I was facing the few people making their way home and could see their faces clearly. Only a few of the second shifters were walking the same direction as me, each of them with their heads down, staring at the road in front of their feet. No one even raised an eyebrow when I stepped from the bushes into their group.

I had no hope of seeing Lori in the crowd of commuters, but I hadn't given up hope on her being in the city. There was enough of my father in me to see it as a challenge, not as a discouragement. I knew that she wasn't in the mainstream of people in the city, so I forcibly tried to think outside the box, trying to come up with another place she might be. As I walked along the street, I studied the buildings on either side. I was looking for any sign of another place that someone might be—a door, a side alley, an opening to a place away from everyone else— somewhere that Lori might be living or working. I didn't see anything that looked like anything other than what I expected. Building after building was marked with a string of numbers that signified what the space was used for or what they were making inside. Every so often a brick wall had been formed to close off the gaps between buildings or to bridge across streets and alleys, but all the walls were solid with no doors or windows. The city was a tunnel of long, straight buildings, lining up at attention on either side of the one main street and encased in a canopy of plastic.

I was studying everything around me so intently that I didn't notice that I had come to the end of the road. I also hadn't noticed that my feet were on fire. I could feel the blisters on my curled up toes rubbing against the inside of my shoes. There were still a few people walking around me, and I needed to act like I was going somewhere, so I walked as naturally as I could right into the entertainment building on the end of the street.

As I stepped inside the doors, my mind was flooded with images from the dream of the night before. The real rooms were inexplicably similar to my dream considering that I had never been in the building before. The lobby, desk, and hall were nearly identical, but when I stepped into the scene of the poker game—it was not the same at all. It was a large room, about three-fourths full with men and not a woman in sight. Each man was sitting at his own table, slowly sipping from a mug, no one looking up or talking to the person next to him. I sat down at a table against one wall where I could see most of the room without drawing attention to myself. I slipped my heels out of the tortuous shoes and looked around the room.

The waitress walking toward me was the only woman in the room and was not a friendly lady. She never spoke to me or even asked me what I wanted, reaching instead for my badge, swiping it quickly across a machine on her hip. She stood too close to me while she did it, and I cringed at the smell of what was probably already a long day for her. The machine beeped in approval, and she walked away without looking at me. Her next time my way, she left off a mug full of a thin, yellowish liquid and a bowl of big, doughy pretzels.

The pretzels were tough and hard to chew, but at least they had a salty taste. It was definitely better than anything I had found so far back in Davis's apartment. I tried a sip of what was in the mug, my second taste of anything with alcohol in it. I had never had a beer before, never even had the opportunity. I suppose that there is some beer that tastes good—this was not it. The lingering taste it left on my tongue was worse. I tried to wash it off with another sip and a bite of pretzel, but it didn't help.

My first taste of alcohol had been back at the cabin with Dad, about four months after we had gotten there. Harkey Simpson, an old man of about eighty, lived down the valley from us. Others lived nearby, but he was our only shouting distance neighbor. He and his now deceased wife had somehow escaped the roundup and cleanup that brought everyone else to the cities. Even with their old age, they had slipped away and hid out in a hunting cabin on the side of the mountain for about a month before coming back down. Mr. Harkey, as I called him, taught us how to live off the land that first year, and he probably had as much to do with saving our family as anyone else.

Dad and I had worked with him for several days, cleaning up and preparing his fields for the winter. When we were done, he handed my dad an old mason jar full of what looked to me like water. "Good cough medicine," he said with a laugh.

"Is this moonshine, Mr. Harkey?" my dad had asked.

"Call it what you want," he had replied, "but it makes for a real good cough medicine. Good for washing out cuts and sanitizing things too—your wife will like it."

"Well," my dad had said, twisting off the lid, "I guess we had better try a taste of your cough medicine. Would you like one too, Mr. Harkey?"

"Don't mind if do," he had replied, and he and Dad each took turns taking a tiny sip.

My dad coughed three or four times, his eyes watering. He looked at me for a minute, pondering the situation. "You have sure worked like a man for the last few days," he said. He handed me the jar and whispered quietly, "Only take a sip." And so I did. I coughed a few times more than Dad did. A sniff of that stuff had more kick than the whole mug sitting in front of me.

That was the only time I saw my dad drinking from that jar. He had his faults, but he was no drunk. The best use we got out of the moonshine was being able to get the old tractor running, even if it locked up the engine after about thirty seconds. That tractor was a project I hoped to take back up when I got home. A better trick I had learned from Mr. Harkey was how to eat cornbread sopped in a glass of milk. They tasted better together than they did apart. I looked at the mug in front of me, shoved the pretzel down into the beer and let it soak for about fifteen seconds. I pulled it back out before it got too soft to hold on to. The pretzel was much easier to chew and the salt drowned out the bad beer taste a little. It was about four pretzels down the hatch before I realized how strange I must seem to everyone else in the room.

I tried to chew casually and looked quickly around the room. No one seemed to have noticed me. I caught eyes with one man halfway across the room, and he looked away quickly. I kept an eye on him and noticed he started doing the same thing with his pretzel about a minute later. *He's awake,* I thought, *but doesn't have much to show for it.* I noticed he was the only man in the room trying to get drunk. There were at least nine or ten mugs lined up in a row on his table. What a tortured, hopeless life! How much of that nasty-tasting beer was he going to have to drink to try and fall back asleep like everyone else?

Lori was obviously not in this room, so I grabbed three or four pretzels from an abandoned table nearby, crammed my achy feet back into Davis's shoes, and headed out the door like I knew where I was going. The entertainment building had been as useless a trip as the school, but I was in a different mode now. I was searching my mind for options as much as I was searching the city for Lori's face. I patted my pocket as I walked along, feeling the pretzels in my pocket. "If nothing else, that was worth the walk down here," I said to myself. As I started up the hill, my feet disagreed with my conclusion, but of course they didn't know anything about pretzels.

I studied the buildings and walls again on my return trip, looking for any sign or clue of another option. I had lost a whole day with no sign of Lori and was putting off beginning the debate of whether I would leave the city if I couldn't find her the next day. In the months preparing for every possible scenario, Dad and I had considered the fact that I wouldn't be able to find her right away. We had thought about buying an extra day or two by me faking the inspector's job, but that had been a last resort. The review meeting scheduled by the mayor's leech for the first day back to work made it near to impossible to stay the extra day in the city. My cover would be blown for sure if I went to that meeting. The next day, my extra day of leave, was the last chance to find her. I was digging hard for options but was coming up with nothing.

I crested the hill at the top of the street and went back into the convenience store. I bought another cup of coffee, partly to wash out the taste in my mouth and partly for the caffeine. I determined myself to finish my dad's story that evening, if for nothing else than to accomplish something useful for the day. Maybe the reading would clear my mind and open up some kind of new thought on how to find Lori. There was just a bit of light left filtering through the canopy and I wandered back to the park again. It had become a comfortable place for me. I chose a seat in the grass where I could lean against a wall near a streetlight that would be coming on soon. It made just as much sense to read there; I certainly wasn't going to find Lori if I holed myself up in Davis's apartment.

I looked around as I pulled out the papers, checking to see if anyone was watching. The doors were closed at the mayor's house and the lights already on, seen dimly through the window drapes. Across the street from me, the same pretty lady and her daughter from the night before had slipped off their shoes to wiggle their toes in their grass. I realized that I had seen her face on the street both times that day and that I had seen the little girl at the school during my walk through that morning. I was so focused on looking for Lori that I didn't process who they were until I saw them again. They followed the same routine, playing and dancing the troubles of the day away in their sanctuary of grass. *Both of them are surely awake,* I thought to myself. I was tempted to go over and talk with them, but I let the moment go. They skipped away again to the apartments.

An older man came by pushing a load of supplies for the store, doing his share for the city, and then the streets were empty for the evening. The streetlight came on with a buzz, and orange light showered over my shoulder onto my lap. I had at least another hour I could sit out here before they would run me off to the apartments. My eyes had adjusted to the funny light so I pulled out Dad's papers to pick up where I left off, just after our Christmas morning surprise:

The next few months were wonderful and tortuous at the same time. Abbie and I would talk for hours, remembering the time before the day, trying to piece together the years we had lost. She was vibrant and alive, funny and smart, and I saw in her face the same pretty girl I had met in college. Sometimes I would just lose myself looking at her and forget what she was saying. She would smile and look at me in an annoyed but resigned sort of way and just repeat the parts I had missed. I was struck at how immediately her focus was on the future, on reconnecting with you, Jack, and how little time she spent hashing over painful parts of our past. I saw a beauty of her soul and a sharpness of character that I had missed in our previous life. I was in love with her in a way I could never have imagined before, but it was a one-way street. Your mother was awake for sure, but I was convinced that she did not love me in return.

We were cordial, friendly even, but it stopped there. We shared our meals, shared our future, and even shared our bed (for sleeping only, of course), but whatever love she had once had for me was gone, crushed and killed completely either by some past act of cruelty, by the overwhelming losses she had endured, or by the slow suffocation of my years of neglect. Whatever the reason, there was an unseen wall of separation between us. It was like we were a couple that had divorced peacefully years ago and were civilly working out a joint custody of our child.

Abbie had latched on to knowing what day it was as surely as she had latched on to the necklace that she never took off. I had lifted an old phone book from one of the houses I had marked, and she had torn out the page with the fourteen-year calendar on it. For the next week, she spent every spare moment mapping out the days and years, making lists of birthdays and anniversaries that she remembered, making paper calendars on scrap sheets I had brought home. She took particular pleasure in knowing that it was Wednesday or Friday or Monday and insisted that we talk in weeks and months instead of the numbered day system we had become accustomed to. This led to all sorts of choked off sentences at work as I had to learn to shift from home speak to outside speak. I suspect you had the same problem at school. I will never forget how mad she was at me when we finally got to the cabin and realized that I had missed the solstice by eleven days. But at the time, her self-figured calendar was gold.

It was when she was mapping out dates that she came to the realization that your nineteenth birthday was near and that we faced the possibility of losing you forever. I was a bit embarrassed that I hadn't thought of that on my own, but I had been so focused on her that it hadn't crossed my mind. Abbie was as mathematically inclined as any man, and she became consumed with finding the solution to this problem. Our pillow talk was exclusively confined to endless conversations and schemes on how to keep what was left of our broken family together.

It was a painful time for me and one of harsh self-scrutiny. Every word we shared, every time I looked at her, convinced me that I loved her more and more. Every moment together also convicted me that I had never truly loved her at all in the years past. She had spent years loving me unselfishly, receiving no real love in return. All the gifts I had given her, the physical intimacy we had shared were self-serving acts that I had performed to either gain some pleasure for myself or to avoid anger or conflict. Now that I had come to my senses, I wanted more than anything for her to love me the way I loved her. But every second of pain I was experiencing just reminded me all the more of how I had treated her so poorly in the past. It seemed an irony beyond measure that we could love each other, but not at the same time. I spent many days in self-absorbed depression, wasting time that turned out to be precious. Knowing that she had once loved me convinced me that something had been the last straw; something had pushed her away and used up her graces. So I turned back the clock and played the past over in my mind, searching for a past sin to repent of, hoping that in her forgiveness her love could be resurrected.

Remembering the past proved to be harder than I thought it would be. I knew the big things, but the little details of that terrible day and of the months that followed had become lost in the years of slumber. I spent weeks racking my brain, trying to find the key that would unlock the memories I knew were caged inside. It all came back to me at work on one of the first warm days of spring.

After his training, McAllister had convinced himself he was an expert on structural engineering and took to bossing me around on a regular basis. Since the days leading up to Christmas, I hadn't had a day to myself. He would follow me around, waiting until I put a mark for a charge and then telling me to move it over six inches or a foot to be in the perfect spot. Before I woke up, I might have been ready to fight him over it, but now it meant nothing to me. Whatever he asked, I would just do without argument. He soon became weary of my compliance and found excuses to stay in the truck and take care of paperwork.

On that first warm day, the sun had lulled McAllister asleep in the cab of the truck. I took advantage of the situation and walked around inside the house that was to be demolished the next day. Every house had become to me a potential treasure store, sure to have some little item that might bring a smile to Abbie's face. As I stepped into this home, years of suppressed memories jumped out from their grave. The house we had bought when we moved up from Atlanta had been a spec house built from a mail-order set of plans. The house I was walking in that day was either from a modification of our same floor plan or at least from the same architect. The rooms were in the same order, the walls and halls were spaced the same, it just felt like the same house. As I stepped into the living room, a chill came over me and a scene from the day exploded into my mind. Everything that had happened came back to me at once.

You were just nine, Jack, so I don't really know what you remember about that day. Why we never talked about it once we left the city, I don't really know. Abbie and I rarely spoke of it either. It was a day of heaviness, full of regrets and pain. It hurts to even write about it now. I guess it all started at a bit after seven that morning. I was getting ready to leave for work, and Abbie was helping you pack your books for school. The television was on with the local news, just like it was every morning. In the midst of the weather report, the national anchor broke in with a picture of a mushroom cloud over what they were almost positive was Houston. It had hit only minutes before. The anchor was stumbling, in shock, searching for something to say when a similar picture came through again, this time, they said, from a traffic surveillance camera outside of Detroit. Thirty seconds later, the national feed was gone and the local newswoman was left sitting there with her mouth open.

They kept playing the two pictures over and over for about ten more minutes when one of the producers popped in front of the camera and handed the poor lady a piece of paper. It was an e-mail to the station from the local head of homeland security. We were to stay inside, tape off our doors and windows, and wait for help to come. She read the message through about three times before the satellite feed flickered and went to a black screen. I turned around to see Abbie standing behind me, half-dressed, crying and scared to death. You were jumping on your brother's bed and singing something about not having to go to school that day. I walked past Abbie without saying a word and yelled at you and your brother to either sit down and shut up or go upstairs to play so I could hear the TV.

I went back to the television and went through the channels on the satellite about three times and then spent another twenty minutes trying in vain to hook up some old rabbit ears. I left it with the fuzz on the screen and the static sound turned up and gave up, walking back to see what Abbie was doing. She was getting together some wet towels and a roll of duct tape. "I tried to call Mom," she said, "even on the cell phones, but all the lines are dead."

We obeyed the frightened news lady and went around the house sealing off the doors and windows. "It's not going to do any good," I kept saying over and over. "We are not going to get a good enough seal." She chose not to argue with me, and I kept on taping, complaining as I went. We ran out of tape before we got to all the windows, so we shut off one of the boy's bedrooms and closed off the door to the basement, laying a towel at the base of the door. About a half hour later, the power went off.

I suggested we get some water stored up before the waterlines lost all their pressure when the pumps shut down. We filled up all the containers we could find and both bathtubs with water. The water only came out as a trickle the size of my pinkie finger by the time we finished. Abbie sat down on the couch and stared up at the ceiling. She was terrified. I just paced, talking mostly to myself, running through the possibilities of who might have set off the bombs and guessing how many cities were hit. You and Jeremy had picked up on your mother's anxiety and snuggled up against her on the couch, petting her hair and feet and telling her it was going to be all right. I don't know why that bothered me so much, but it did. I avoided you three for the rest of the day, pacing from room to room, staring out the windows and fussing with a battery-operated radio that wouldn't pick up anything.

School had started back a few weeks previous, and it was a very hot day. With no air conditioning and no circulation, it got hotter and hotter in the house as the day went on. Abbie had slipped into a forced peace, probably a motherly instinct to calm you guys down. She spent most of the day reading stories to Jeremy and playing board games with you. Against my wishes, she gave both of you a bath in the cold water of one of the tubs, which you loved. You two boys were excited to sleep in the same bed together but complained incessantly about the heat. As usual, Abbie took care of bedtime. I just didn't have the patience to be much of a father to you two. All of your talking made me nervous and annoyed me. It was easier to just find something else to do when parental duties called. The heat and stress of that day just made it worse. I don't remember speaking more than a word or two at a time to either one of you the entire day.

I was sitting in the dark at the kitchen table when Abbie came back in after laying you two down. She was sweating, just like I was, but had pulled her hair back in a pony tail. She was about four months pregnant and was just starting to show. Her face was beautiful and her figure still looked great, enhanced by her growing belly. Your mother just couldn't help but be pretty; she always was. She had made the best of it that day, without any help from me. She pulled up a chair and forced a worried smile. "What are we going to do?" she asked.

I hung my head. "I guess we just wait," I said. "Homeland wouldn't have made that announcement if they didn't have a contingency plan in place." That was all I said. She tried to talk with me some more, but I didn't have anything else to offer. I answered all her questions with one or two words, never adding anything to the conversation. I don't think she wanted my answers, I think she just wanted to talk. In all the years we had been married, I had never taken the time to be her friend. It was my loss for sure; your mother was, and is, a wonderful person, and I wasted most of our marriage before I figured that out.

I didn't even answer her last question, something about wondering how her sister's family was handling things, and Abbie got up from the table, giving me a peck on the cheek as she walked away. She went back to your bedroom, stopping for a minute to encourage the two of you to go to sleep and stop talking. I could hear her dipping a washcloth in the tub water, presumably to wash off her face. She paused at the edge of the kitchen where I still sat before going off silently to bed.

I left her like that on many nights, using my silence as a means to gain the solitude I wanted. I had spent most of the day mentally listing my projects at work that would be probably be put on hold for weeks or even cancelled while all this got sorted out. I pondered how the crushed economy would affect our workload. I tried to do the math in my head as to how many cities could be destroyed without sending us into a full-scale depression. "We made it through pretty well after 9–11 and after the hurricane flooded out New Orleans," I reasoned to myself. In all these thoughts, the family had barely entered my mind. I didn't even think about my own parents and what they might be going through. Abbie's questions embarrassed me.

I tried to think about what the next day might bring, tried to plan out a path for the family, but I couldn't focus in on anything. Abbie had made all the decisions for so long, I just couldn't bring myself to lead, no matter how much she needed me to. If only I had used that time wisely, I might have changed all of our lives completely. So many things could have been done differently, been done better. I can make the excuse that I didn't know any better, because I didn't, but honestly I didn't really even try. I know now that I was just as asleep then as ever and really didn't care about anyone but myself.

I tiptoed into our bedroom and heard Abbie's slow exhales as she slept, but it was just too hot for me, so I made a place for myself on the kitchen floor. The vinyl was cooler, but I still got up every couple of hours to walk around. Abbie had lit a candle when it first got dark, but the moon was nearly full, and so much light came in through the windows, we really didn't need it. It looked so peaceful outside in the moonlight; I spent the early morning hours just staring out the windows, waiting for the dawn. As the first light warmed up the eastern sky, I slid the towel away from the door at the top of the stairs to the basement, tiptoed down, and slipped out the back door.

Our dog Rusty met me at the door and slid his head under my hand. We hadn't thought about him. "You're doing pretty well, old boy, so maybe a few minutes out in this air won't hurt me either." I took a couple of deep breaths, wondering what radiation would smell like. It seemed like a normal morning to me. I had put on a pair of slippers, and the morning dew was soaking through the cloth sides. It had to have been at least ten or fifteen degrees cooler outside than it was inside. With all the heat and the stress of the day, it drove me insane to be cooped up in the house for so long. It was so good to be outside again. I felt like a body exhumed.

I followed the dog around to the garage. He was obviously hungry, stopping every few steps to push his head against my knee, steering me toward the food bowl. We had gotten him when you were six, to give you a friend to play with when Jeremy got here. At least that was Abbie's reasoning. You barely noticed the dog and wanted to spend all your time fussing over your baby brother. As soon as he could walk, he followed every step you took, trying his best to keep up with you. You were his hero and everything that he wanted to be. Even at three, Jeremy had figured out that you were a better man in the making than his dad. He took some of your attention and even more of Abbie's. I guess it was petty for a grown man to be jealous of his own son, but it wasn't far from the truth. When Abbie found out she was pregnant again, I knew for sure I would be the odd man even further out.

I took my time feeding Rusty, taking an extra minute to fish some pieces of grass from the water bowl. I had found my excuse for being outside and didn't really want to go back in just yet. On a whim, I decided to pull a couple of steaks out of the box freezer in the garage, reasoning to myself that they would be going bad anyway. They were still quite cold but were soft and thawed, perfect for cooking. I stuck my head and shoulders down in the freezer for just a second, drinking in the cold air. As the sun peeked up over the hill, I fired up the gas grill and cooked the two steaks for breakfast. I was enjoying myself so thoroughly, I didn't notice all three of you watching me through the window until the steaks were done.

I didn't have a plate of course, so I killed the grill and wrapped the steaks up in a wad of paper towels from the garage and brought them back in through the basement so I wouldn't break off any of our tape around the doors. Abbie gave me a look and a half when I brought the steaks in and set them on a plate on the kitchen counter. "Come on, honey," I reasoned. "The steaks were shut up in the freezer all day yesterday. They weren't soaking up any more radiation through the freezer walls than we were in here." I assured her two times that they were still cold when I got them out, and she was convinced. We all had steak for breakfast. Even Jeremy had a bite or two to go along with his Pop-tart. The refrigerator had lost the battle with the heat, so we opened up a bottle of warm apple juice. It was an odd breakfast to be sure, but probably the best meal we had together until we made it to the cabin. It was the last time we would be together as a whole family, with number five tucked safely away in Abbie's belly.

After we finished breakfast, I was wiping down the dishes and cups with paper towels. Abbie had found some batteries for your headphones, and you had retreated to your room to try it out. Jeremy was hanging around Abbie's feet, begging for more juice. She reached down for his cup when the knock came at the front door. I walked over to the door and looked out the side glass. Two men in SWAT uniforms and gas masks stood on the front porch. They both were carrying what looked like M-16s. They banged on the door again, this time with some urgency. The hackles rose on the back of my neck. Good guys or bad, I didn't like them coming to my house this way.

"Open the door, Mr. Wilson," they shouted through their masks.

"Hold your horses, I'm breaking the seal," I snapped back. Abbie came up behind me and helped me pull off the duct tape, Jeremy still clinging to her leg. The two men pushed into the house, barely looking around before one of them grabbed Abbie by the arm.

"You have to come with us now," they growled. I brought my forearm up under the man's gloved hand, breaking his grip on Abbie as I stepped between them.

"You can give us a minute to get some things together," I said. I was inches away from him and could see his eyes through his mask.

He yelled in my face, "You don't have a minute," and reached again over my shoulder for her arm with his right hand, yanking at my arm with his left.

It all happened in a few seconds. It was a moment that I have replayed over and over in my mind, wondering what I might have done differently. I ripped my arm free from the grasp of the hooded man and shoved him back against the door frame, trying to get my hands up around his neck. He pushed me clear, spinning me half around, nearly knocking me over. I caught myself from falling and looked up from a crouched position in time to see his partner uppercut swing his rifle at me. I rolled out of the way in time to miss the heavy butt end, and it caught Jeremy full in the face. I turned in time to see his face caved in, the front of his skull crushed. It was the last thing I saw before another swing of the rifle came down on the top of my own head, knocking me out cold.

I came to in the window seat of a bus, sitting next to Abbie. She had a black eye, and I had a headache. From the look on her face, she was in severe shock. I looked back over to the seat behind me. You were sitting next to a young woman who shared the same look on her face as Abbie. You stared out the window and didn't notice me looking at you. The morning sun was on the opposite side of the bus, the right side, so we were going north. I felt at the gash on my head; it wasn't bleeding, but it had been. The hair on that side of my head was matted down and sticky. We were riding on a school bus. It was hot and stuffy inside and the windows and the back safety exit door were taped all around. The bus was about three-fourths full of people—all of them with dull, shocked looks on their faces. No one said a word.

I looked down and noticed straps around my chest, tying me to the seat. A man at the front of the bus in a black uniform saw that I was awake and walked back to our seats, leaning between Abbie and me. He spoke softly and firmly, "Your son is dead. Unfortunate to be sure, but there is nothing that can be done about it. It isn't safe to go back. You have to think about what is best for everyone else."

He stopped and nodded toward another man in black standing near the front of the bus, leaning on his rifle to steady himself. He was one of the men that had come to our door, but not the one that had killed Jeremy. "Mr. Wilson, if you promise to be a good boy, we'll take off these straps and no one else will have to get hurt."

I nodded silently and he loosened the straps, returning to the front of the bus without saying another word. I suppose they thought I might put up a protest, but the blow to my head had knocked the fight out of me. Abbie's pleading and terrified eyes gave me a good excuse to sit still and do nothing. I looked away and stared out the window.

I recognized the road as the bus drove north on the interstate, but I didn't recognize the city where we finally stopped. The driver was wearing a gas mask and handed us wet washcloths to put over our faces as we stepped out of the bus. We were herded by two more men in masks into the lobby of a roadside motel and on into an inner room where another collection of haggard-looking people were also waiting. All the while, you clung to your mother's side as she walked along in a trance. The two men left their gas masks on and gave us a paper with instructions on it and a key card to room 119. The three of us shuffled down the concrete walk with the washcloths over our faces and on into the small stuffy room, one of the men in a mask shutting the door quickly behind us.

The drapes had been taken down and the windows and air unit were covered over with plastic and taped all around with a strange type of tape that I hadn't seen before. There was another roll of it lying on the table and our instructions called for us to seal around the door. The tape didn't seem to stick well, but sealed off tight when I ran my fingers over it. The power was out, and no water came from the tap in the bathroom. Abbie lay down on the bed, and you snuggled up next to her, crying softly in kind of a whimper. The pretty glow of her face from the night before had faded into a blank, sweaty, hazy stare. I started to ask her about how she got the black eye, but thought better of it. I just didn't know what to say.

A stack of water bottles sat in the corner of the room along with about a dozen boxes each of graham crackers and saltines. I read the paper with the rationing instructions out loud to no one in particular and did the math in my head, counting out crackers. They were planning on several weeks it seemed, or "Maybe they were just being cautious," I said out loud. I looked back to see if Abbie would reply. The two of you were sleeping, the painful, wrenched expressions replaced by more peaceful looks.

There were two holes in the wall, each about the size of my hand with a filtered cap over the opening. The distant sound of an engine came from the direction of the office, and a few minutes later air began to blow out of the upper hole. I stepped around the end of the bed, trying not to wake the sleepers, and felt at the air. It wasn't cold, but it was definitely cooler than the steamy air in the room. The lower hole had a light amount of suction. *How did they install an isolated hvac system in two days?* I wondered to myself. I wandered the perimeter of the room, feeling at the tape for the seals. It was spongy and stretchy, but the outer side was slick and looked to be airtight. They had created a little cocoon for us.

The peacefulness of your sleep was broken by a knock at the door. I broke the seal on the door, this time without protest. The tape pulled back more easily than I thought it would, and I opened the door to see a plastic pocket about two feet deep wrapped around the entrance to the room. There was a man in a yellow plastic suit and a hood under his arm. "You're Jack Wilson, right?" he asked in a tone of voice that indicated his question was rhetorical. "We need engineers," he continued, "to help us rebuild the city," and he handed me a suit that looked just like his. "You have to leave now." I had fought enough today and knew the consequences. There was something about being called out as an engineer, as someone needed and important, that made it seem okay.

I pulled the suit over my clothes, stopping to kiss Abbie on the cheek and pat you on the head before putting on the hood. She had sat up in the bed, her arm still around your shoulders. "How long will you be?" she choked out, struggling to keep herself in sense of consciousness.

I looked over my shoulder at the man. He shook his head. "I'm not sure."

"I won't be long," I said to her. "You'll be fine here." Both of those were pure speculation, and she and I both knew it. I pulled on the hood, the man sealed it off to the suit, and we were twins. I turned and tried a smile that the two of you never saw through the hood and headed out the door, feeling the tape reseal as I pulled it tight. Leaving you two behind to an unknown fate, I stepped into the small plastic chamber and out into the world.

The next four weeks were the oddest I had ever experienced. I was ushered into another bus with a group of yellow-hooded men, and we were driven to a warehouse building downtown. The building had already been wrapped in plastic. We passed through another little plastic door stoop and stepped into an enclosed room past the entrance. In that room, we were stripped naked and hosed down one by one in businesslike manner. I was handed a towel and a jump-suit, not unlike the ones we wore for so long in the city. Once inside, our names and faces were matched to a list, and we were sorted into different rooms around the edges of the building. In the main open area of the warehouse, tall pallets of food and building supplies were stacked in neat rows with huge rolls of plastic wrap filling the gaps in between. It was a bizarre scene and hard to absorb.

The room I was herded into was not nearly as well lit as the warehouse, and it took a minute for my eyes to adjust. There was a large folding table in the center of the room with seven men seated around it in fold-ing chairs. I shut the door behind me and took the last seat at the table. Each man introduced himself around the room by last name only. By the looks of the faces around me we were all in our thirties, none younger, none older. I spent every waking hour with these men for the next four weeks, yet I can to this day remem-ber none of their names. Over the next ten years, we would pass each other often on the streets of CR12.

In all that time, never once was a word spoken, a head nodded, or even an eyebrow lifted in recognition. It was as if we belonged to a secret sect that was never to be spoken of.

A short fellow with some leftovers of reddish curly hair was our leader. It quickly became apparent that he had his hands full. Each of us was a structural engineer and thought we were the best in the room. Every idea, argument, and counterpoint was defended vigorously. No suggestion was raised without someone playing the devil's advocate and trying to shoot it down. But in the midst of the arguing our way through each aspect of the design, we really did a great job. All in all, it was the best experience of my engineering career.

We had been given the task of designing the support arms for the plastic canopy that would be draped over the city. We weren't bound by building codes or by plans reviewers. We didn't have to meet OSHA safety standards or stay on a strict budget. We just had to make it work, with no room for error and no time to spare. Sketches and schemes were scribbled on paper and drawn out on laptops. We would slip off to eat or to grab a nap one by one, but the work never stopped. By the end of the first week, we had a working design for the entire city. Two days later material lists were compiled and the details were fine tuned. Over the next three days, simple computer drawings and hand sketches were hammered out even as the construction had already begun. The last two weeks had us out of the little room and onto the street that would become CR12, supervising the work, each of us so deeply in tune with the design that we inspected and corrected as if we were one man, making decisions and recommendations from the single symbiotic collection of our minds.

While we worked on the canopy, other crews were going just as fast on building the apartments, putting together the air and water purification systems, and compiling stockpiles of food. There were four men in charge of meshing all the systems together into a working, breathing, living city. When it all came together, it was a thing of beauty. We had poured every ounce of our training, experience, and energy into this one project, working with more intensity and focus than we had on anything in our lives. We were soldiers, leaving our families behind to give all of our being to a noble purpose and cause.

For me, this enlistment had fed something deeply sinister in my soul. I was separated from all the encumbrances of relationship and responsibility. My engineering decisions could be defended on the basis of science. Each step was sequenced by reason and experience. It was much more comfortable than all the complications of emotions and hurt feelings. I saw some of the other men slipping off during a break, trying their cell phones in vain, pulling out photos from the wallets, burying their heads in their hands and crying, but not me. It is embarrassing now to think how little I missed you and your mother, how little I mourned Jeremy's death. Even in the shadow of the horror that had just proceeded, even in the confines of the radiation suits and the plastic-shrouded buildings, I felt freer than ever. The portion of my soul that had long desired to be in full charge of me had finally won an outright victory. All that was human and of any worth within me was utterly crushed. I had been asleep before; now I was very near to being dead.

At the end of the four weeks, our city of refuge triumphantly completed, the buses were sent to collect our families. I was waiting for you and your mother as you came from the building that would become my workplace, freshly showered and dressed in your jump-suits. I was proudly waiting to show you both what had been built and take you to our new apartment where we would be safe and could start a new life. Abbie fell into my arms, crying, holding on to me tightly. She looked up at me with tears in her eyes, pleading for some sort of comfort and said through choking sobs, "Honey, I lost our baby."

I can remember my reply, but it was as if it came from someone else's mouth. "Just as well, this is no place for a baby." Her arms went limp, and she backed away from me. I looked into her loving, beautiful, gentle eyes full of tears and watched the lights go off inside as surely as if I had reached into her soul and turned off the switch. And, at that moment, I didn't very much care.

I was so deeply entranced by the disturbing glimpse into my father's soul that I had completely lost touch with everything around me. I was slowly absorbing the last sentence read when a short kick to the bottom of my feet brought me back to the real world. "Curfew," the night watchmen said abruptly. "Pick up your paperwork, and get on off to bed." And so I did, folding the papers into their bag and grabbing up my things as I stumbled off in a stupor to Davis's apartment.

CHAPTER 8

"Oh, I remember you like yesterday, yesterday.
And until I'm with you, I'll carry on."

The street was silent and still as I walked under the dim lights and found the door to the apartment building. The watchman had gone on his way and trusted me to find my own. There was a deep, oppressive sense of aloneness that took me back to the early days in that other city. As my father had revisited his own feelings, my own dark, repressed memories of the day had been pulled out into the light. Turning the doorknob on Davis's apartment, I was walking again into our little apartment in CR12, and further back to our time of hell in that tiny motel room. Dad had been there for only a matter of hours, but Mom and I had suffered in that awful room for what seemed like much longer than four weeks.

When Dad had kissed Mom on the cheek, put on his strange suit, and left us in that room, it was as if he left my life forever. He had never been that close with me, but after that day, it was as if I didn't exist to him. Mom was still in some short of shock, and for the rest of the afternoon she just sat on the edge of the bed, staring at the door. It didn't seem right for me to bother her, so I just wandered the room, trying to see out the window, stopping to read the yellow pages in the phone book. When it began to get dark, and I realized that there were no candles, no lights, and no lights from outside, I broke the silence and asked, "Mom, what are we going to do?"

"Sleep," she replied. She pulled back the sheets on one bed for me and on the other for herself, took off her shoes and socks and climbed into the bed, motioning for me to do the same.

The vents were blowing, but it was stuffy and hot in the room, and I didn't stay under the covers for long. It just didn't seem right to complain to her, and even at my age, I was old enough to realize that there was absolutely nothing she could do about the situation. So I just lay there with the images of the day running through my mind. I had seen or heard nothing of the fight at the front door that morning. I was listening to my headphones in my bedroom when Mom slammed the door open with a wild, panicked look on her face. There was a huge bruise on one side of her face with blood running down it. "Honey, we have to go now" was all she said to me. She was looking around my room frantically; I am not sure for what, but she finally grabbed my pillow and yanked it out of its case. I reached down and picked up Jeremy's stuffed rabbit and said, "He will want this."

Mom stifled a whimper and pulled the pillowcase over my head mumbling, "You will need this to breathe outside." She led me out the front door, slowly down the steps, and into a car I didn't know.

We were pulling down our driveway when she took off the pillowcase. The three of us were in the back seat, and there were two men I didn't know in the front. I was in the middle of the back seat. Dad was unconscious and leaning on the window on one side of me, blood running down the side of his face. Mom was on the other side, less blood on her face. I still had Jeremy's bunny in my hand, and I slipped it into the pillowcase, twisting it tight in my hands and holding it against me as I pulled my knees up to my chest. We weren't buckled up, and I felt uncomfortable riding without it but didn't want to say anything. I turned back to Mom. "Where is Jeremy?" I asked.

She paused and looked at me, trying to smile but not able to. Her lip was shaking and tears were in her eyes. "He's not here," she whispered, her voice breaking. "I hope we can come back and get him real soon." She put her arm around me and pulled me tight against her. I remember laying my hand on her large belly and rubbing it. I really liked that, and she never seemed to mind me doing it. I want to think I felt the baby kick, but I can't remember for sure. Everything from that day is still a little mixed up in my mind.

We didn't drive far when we came to the bus that would take us to the city. Dad was still unconscious, and the two men carried him up to his seat. I wanted to sit next to Mom, but I ended up behind her with some lady I didn't know. Nobody said a word on the bus, so I just stared out the window like I always did when I was riding in our minivan. Riding in a car was such a part of life back before that day, but I hadn't ridden in one since. Walking had become so normal and natural that it never seemed slow or difficult to go for miles and miles to get from one place or another. The three of us had walked out of CR12 down the same road that the bus took us into the city on that day. Walking out had been like traveling into a third world, different from both the world before and also from the world within the city.

As I lay in that hot bed in the motel room, trying to go to sleep, I pulled out my brother's bunny from the pillowcase. It smelled like home. I kept it wrapped up in the case for years, just to try and hold on to the smell. Of course, it lost that smell within a few months, but my mind would remember the association and create it for me. That little blue bunny became a symbol to me of a forgotten life and a reminder of my lost family. During our time in the apartment, I would put the bunny in the pillowcase, twist it up tight, and rub on the case every night as I went to sleep. It was something a three-year-old would do, but it worked for me at nine. After a few years, the pillowcase was threadbare. Mom threw it away one day while I was at school and she had the day off. She let me keep the bunny. Maybe it reminded her of Jeremy too.

Leaning against the door inside Davis's apartment, I wondered what she thought of all that, or if she could even remember what she did at that time while she was "sleeping." I resolved to ask her about it when I got back to the cabin. We would have a lot to discuss.

We woke in the motel room to the sunlight the next morning, and Mom had regained her wits. Dad was gone, and it was her job now to keep things together. He had commanded us before he left not to flush the toilet and so we didn't. Mom took a wash cloth and wet it from the tank in the back, and we wiped ourselves down. We split a bottle of water and had a few crackers. She found a pen from the drawer and challenged me to count how many t's there were on pages 65 through 67 of the phone book. Then she began to pace the room, much like Dad, thinking and talking to herself. She rummaged through the water bottles and boxes of crackers twice, counting each cracker and making notes on a pad of paper. By the time I had discovered that there were more t's than there were s's and m's, she sat back down again, looking less rattled, focused of course on me and trying to help me feel more at ease.

She passed the afternoon reading stories to me from the Gideon Bible. I loved to hear her read, and I remember how she would pause and convert the King James English into words and phrases that I could better understand. We spent the evening looking at the channel guide for the television and a menu from a local pizza place, talking about what shows we wished we could watch if the TV worked and what we might order on our pizza if we could have one. There were more crackers and another bottle of water before it got dark and we were off to sleep.

That was every day for the first week. Mom took the little pad of paper they had given us and made a calendar, marking off each day as it passed. By the end of that week, the bathroom already smelled foul, and we kept the door shut all the time with a towel across the crack at the bottom. We only had a roll and a half of toilet paper left. We had been putting our used toilet paper and the cracker packages in a pile behind the trash can in a corner of the bathroom. We stacked the empty water bottles in the bathtub.

By the end of the second week both our sanity and the bathroom situation were getting worse. By then we were used to the smell, but the toilet was full. We moved out the empty bottles to a corner of the room and resorted to using the bathtub for our toilet. Our last roll of paper was gone, and we were using pages from the phone book. The water from the toilet tank was gone, and Mom refused to use the bottled water for washing, so we just sweated and got dirty and smelly and sticky.

With what was left of the phone book, I had been filling in the inside of the *o*'s and drawing pictures in the borders and used up the pen. I was very disappointed and remember throwing a fit, the only time I had done that since we had been cooped up in the room. Mom just let me go, and I ranted and raved for four or five minutes straight before collapsing into the bed in tears. She came over and lay down next to me, hugging me close and crying with me. It was nearly dark, and we just fell asleep that way. I remember that being the fourteenth day, because it was the last day Mom had marked her little calendar with the pen.

I woke in the dimness of the predawn to the groans of Mom from the bathroom. I went to the door and asked her if she was all right. She didn't answer and I tried the knob, but it was locked. I hit the door once with my shoulder to try and force it, but I wasn't strong enough. She called weakly from inside, "Honey, please don't come in now." And so I went back and sat on the bed, unsure of what was happening in the bathroom, but certain that it was something bad. I was troubled for Mom, and the beginnings of manhood within me felt compelled to protect her and help her. I remember distinctly being embarrassed of the fit I had thrown the night before.

Her groans were mixed intermittently with unrestrained wailing. She was obviously in pain. After about an hour, I went back to the door and pecked softly. "Let me get you some water," I said.

"Yes, please," she replied, "and bring me the pillowcase and sheet from my bed." I delivered the items as requested, placing them into her shaking hand protruding from the door.

I heard her grunting and the sound of the sheet ripping. "Let me help you with that, please," I offered, but she didn't reply, only stopping to lock the door again. I went back and sat on the bed again, wondering what would come next.

Her wailing intensified and then began to taper off, finally coming to a stop. About an hour after that, she emerged from the bathroom, barely walking, leaning on the walls, clearly spent of all her energy. "Have you eaten?" she asked. I shook my head no, and she gave me my ration of crackers and water. She sat on the bare mattress of her stripped bed and lay down on her side, obviously still hurting.

Since we left the house, we had both been sleeping and wearing what clothes we had on when we were taken away. Her t-shirt had dried stains on the shoulder from her head wound. Her jeans were dark with blood and water down each leg. There were flecks of paper on the jeans where she had tried to rub out the blood with the pages from the phone book. I was staring at her, and she spoke to me as sternly as she had since we had left. "Jack," she said, "you cannot go into the bathroom, no matter what. Promise me."

"But where will I go?" I asked.

"Promise me," she said. And so I did.

Each time I would need to use the bathroom, she would go in and produce the little trash can that was in there. I would go around the corner of the room and do my business and bring it back to her, and she would empty it in the bathtub, I suppose. I kept my promise and didn't go into the bathroom, but with nothing else to occupy my thoughts, the morbid curiosity was difficult to bear. It was years before I figured out that she had lost the baby that day.

Mom was very weak and didn't eat much and rarely got up from the bed in the first few days following, but by the end of our third week there she was able to get up and move about again. She was obsessive about me not going into the bathroom and went in there herself for long stretches of time, with sounds of the sheet ripping coming from inside. Usually I could tell that she had been crying when she came back out. I loved my mother and was terribly worried for her. In a strange way, my worrying had taken my mind away from fretting over how many more days we were to be there or from thinking about Dad or Jeremy.

On the fourth day of the fourth week, there was a knock on our door. Mom rushed to the door and tried to look out the peephole. She began to pull off the tape when a voice came from outside, "Don't open the door yet, it isn't safe. It won't be long now, just a few more days; hang in there." And then whoever was there was gone.

Mom had quit eating for the two days previous and had only been taking sips of the water. I noticed what she was doing, but I was so hungry and thirsty. I couldn't help from eating my share, though I was ashamed to do it. Our ration of crackers had never been enough to fill us up, and my stomach had shrunk with the daily hunger. The night the man knocked on our door, we had a little cracker and water party. We each ate twice as many crackers as usual and drank two bottles of water each. It felt like a feast. She smiled for the first time since the day in the bathroom and said to me, "Hopefully we will get to see your dad soon."

She was right. They came to us on the last day of the fourth week. We had eaten down to our last package of crackers and had four bottles of water left. When they knocked on the door, they pushed it open, ripping the tape. There was a man in a yellow suit and hood with a suit for both of us in his hands. He dropped our suits in the floor, stared for a minute at Mom's blood-stained pants and then turned away, telling us to suit up and to hurry about it. So we did, finally leaving that room behind, and leaving behind what was left of my dead baby brother or sister. We rode the bus to the city, and I saw the plastic draped buildings of CR12 from the outside for the first and only time until the day I glanced back over my shoulder as we were leaving for good ten years later.

We were led through the doors and plastic wrap with the rest of the motel refugees. Once inside, we were split into a group of boys, a group of girls, and a group of women. There were no adult men with us. I went to a dressing room and was lined up in a row with about ten other boys. We were stripped, handed a bar of soap, and hosed down unceremoniously. It was a bit degrading, but I didn't care. It just felt good to wash off the filth of the last four weeks. I toweled off and put on my blue jumpsuit. I never saw the clothes I was wearing. I was handed three changes of clothes, a pair of shoes, and a small bag. I had laid the pillowcase with the bunny inside against the wall and was able to snatch it up and stuff it into my bag before anyone said anything. We were herded out onto the street where I met Mom, and we were reunited with my dad. It wasn't until they each awoke years later that either my mom or dad would say more than two words at a time to me again. I was like an orphan in my own family—the only one awake while they passed away the years in their subconscious sleep.

The remembrances of those days were broken by the blinking of the computer screen on the wall opposite the door. It had been blinking in the darkness since I came back into Davis's apartment, but I hadn't noticed it until I paused the story playing in my head. I went to the screen and read the message. A box with the word "accept" filled the center of the computer screen. I read the lines above; it was the invitation to the meeting in the City Building about the wrecked truck. Several names and titles were listed, none familiar, of course, except for the name Wigginton, chief assistant to the mayor. That would be the little weasel from the encounter that morning. I accepted the invitation to the meeting with no intentions to go, but with the achieved purpose of stopping the blinking on the computer. There was no option to decline the meeting.

I sat down on the couch and leaned back. It felt good to sit down; it felt good to take my feet out of those crazy shoes. It had been a strange day to be sure, a disappointing day, but a day of purpose. For all the empty faces scanned and all the corners of the city searched, I had gained a strange peace about the situation that I could not understand. I was absolutely sure that I would find Lori tomorrow. I had no reason to believe it and no plan to achieve it. All the facts indicated that she wasn't in this city, but I knew without a doubt that she was. It wasn't intuition, it wasn't a gut feeling, it was just an inner assurance—a feeling within that came from without.

Remembering the time in the motel room drew me back to a childhood lost, a childhood alone. Alone, that is, until I met Lori. So much of our last times together had been soured by my pining over her, but she herded my emotions and hormones between wonderful conversations and we developed a trusting friendship. Sitting in Davis's tiny apartment, I just missed her. I wanted to hold her, to see her, for sure, but really, I just missed her. She understood me in a way that no one else did. I missed being understood.

I hadn't thought about that blue bunny since we left the city. I had kept it in my room for years after we got to the CR12. Even as a teenager, I would rub the ears as I fell asleep each night. After a while, I stopped associating it exclusively with my brother, and it became a reminder of all things lost, a symbol of a world I missed terribly and a contrast to the pale, gray life that had adopted me.

My grandmother, I called her Mamaw, had given blue bunny to Jeremy for his second birthday. It had become his chosen toy, and he never let it out of his sight. Jeremy would carry it around the house by its ear and tuck it under his arm each night when he slept. The words "Jesus Loves Me" were embroidered in blue across its chest. I can remember lying in my bed in the apartment each night, looking at the little pink smile on its face and reading the words out loud, always following it with the question, "Does he really?" and then, "Probably not." That was my bedtime prayer each night. I would rub his ears and go to sleep.

About four or five times Lori had stopped by the apartment for a few minutes after school. We had classes the same length as the work day, and I would get home about the same time as Mom and always about an hour before Dad. Lori had no home to go to except her little room with the other orphans. I can remember always hoping that Mom would set an extra plate for her and invite her to eat with us, but she never did. I don't think she ever said anything to her other than "hi" and "bye." By the time Mom and Dad had woken up, Lori just wouldn't come by anymore, except to wait at the door if we were going somewhere together.

I remembered the first time she came by. We were in either the eighth or ninth grade, I think. She and I were just getting to know each other as friends. No boys were allowed on the floor at her room, but she had told me about it. All of the rooms in her building were just large enough for two beds with a small dresser and a built-in wardrobe. The bathroom was down the hall, and there was a cafeteria on the bottom floor. She had roommates off and on, but by the time she and I were friends, so many of the girls her age were gone that there was plenty enough space for every girl to have her own room. Our apartment was the first one she had seen in the city. As she walked from room to room, she whistled and wowed as if we lived in a palace.

She came to my bedroom door but wouldn't go in at first. When she saw the bunny on the bed, she couldn't help herself. "Where did you get this?" she asked, pulling it close to her chest as she sat on the bed. She sat near the end, knowing I would stay at the door and not crawl around her in the narrow room to sit down next to her. Mom was in the kitchen, but Lori always kept things proper. She smiled and hugged the little bunny, looking for the moment like a little girl at Christmas. It was good to see something that made her so happy, and I said impulsively, "You can have it. You need it more than I do."

"Really?" she said, forgetting her first question for a minute. She looked at the bunny, studying its features. "Are you sure?" she asked, hugging it close to her. There weren't any toys in the city. Holding the bunny had temporarily transformed her into the little girl she used to be. Her smile turned serious again. "Was this yours, you know, before?"

"It was my brother's," I explained and went on to tell her how I had snuck baby bunny into the city in the pillowcase. She had heard the story of Jeremy's death before. I had told her many stories about him, but hadn't brought up the bunny until then. It hurt me at first when Lori would ask questions about before the day, but she would always prod me gently to get me talking. Lori had been an only child and my stories of how Jeremy and I would play together and the little things that brothers do filled an empty place in her soul. Talking about those days filled holes in my own soul, replacing painful memories with peaceful ones. She was a better therapist than she knew.

"I can't take this from you," she said, handing the bunny up to me with tears in her eyes. She could always cry, always share the pain of another without letting it break her down. I think it was how she coped. I remember seeing her talk sometimes under the trees at school with the younger girls, asking them questions, crying with them, hugging them. I would stand to the side where she couldn't see me and just watch her. She loved everyone, but never had any real friends, except for me. She needed that bunny.

"Borrow it for a while," I said. "You'll take good care of it."

And so she smiled sweetly at me and took blue bunny with her as she went back to her building. "Good-bye, Mrs. Wilson," she called as she skipped out the door, waving good-bye to me over her shoulder as she slipped out the door. Mom just looked down at the dinner she was preparing, pretending not to notice her.

Sitting on Davis's couch, I wondered what my mom thought about Lori. She didn't say much about her when Dad and I were preparing to leave. Even after she woke up, Mom kept her contemplative side. She was thinking about things always, but you had to ask if you wanted to draw out those thoughts. I don't think she meant to be rude to Lori in those days before she woke up. She either just couldn't process who she was in her mind, or she couldn't put together the pieces to even be able to communicate. It was a strange thing to live for all those years with my parents, not knowing why they would never speak with me. I had learned more about what was going on inside their brains from reading my dad's papers these last few days than I was ever able to figure out living with them, even during the better days at the cabin.

Remembering Dad's papers, I pulled out the pouch and lay them on the floor in front of me. I also pulled out the pretzels I had wrapped in the napkin that afternoon. I had been carrying the bag from my morning's visit to the store under my armpit all day. These jumpsuits definitely needed bigger pockets. I opened up the bag of goodies and looked inside. A toothbrush, a razor, some shaving cream, and some socks. I pulled off Davis's socks and stood up, wiggling my bare toes. They had suffered in those shoes all day and deserved a break before putting on the new socks.

I held up the shaving cream and razor and considered trying to shave again. My first shave had been at fourteen. I didn't really need one but thought it would make me more grown up. I remember standing at the bathroom door watching my dad shave and asking him to teach me how. He just looked at my chin with a blank look as he toweled off his face and replied, "You're too young to shave; you're just a boy." Dad went by me, zipping up his jumpsuit without looking back as he walked straight out the door to work. He was right, but I picked up his razor anyway. I wasted about a fourth of his can of shaving cream, cut myself in about ten places, and got yelled at that night when he got back home. I shaved quietly and quickly from then on, using soap and my own razor, and continued to cut myself mercilessly. From the day we left the city until Dad and I had embarked on our journey, I had proudly sported a beard. I rubbed my chin and felt the roughness that had drawn the attention of Wiggington that morning. I needed a shave, but it could wait.

The new toothbrush I had bought that morning was too much to resist. Using toothpaste was maybe the only thing I actually missed from the city when we had gone to the cabin. Mr. Harkey had taught us how to make a sort of paste from some roots, but it wasn't the same clean feeling as toothpaste and a toothbrush. I used some of Davis's paste and brushed my teeth for about five minutes, cleaning off the nasty aftertaste from the bad beer. I wished I had eaten one of the pretzels before brushing, but I set them on the countertop for later. I had a long night of reading in front of me and would be glad I had something to eat. Dad had written a lot. There were still more pages to go than had been read. I sat back down on the couch and found the place where the watchman had interrupted me in the park.

Jack, I put down my pen for a while and went back and reread the last few pages. It hurts even now, all these years later, on the back side of the darkness, to remember what a nasty, depraved man I was. I would like to say that I can't identify with the thoughtlessness and coldness that defined me in those days, but they are still all too close. It is a fight to me, it seems, to even be a human. The animalistic selfishness and cruelty within is always near at hand. Never fool yourself into believing that you aren't capable of all the same sins I have committed, or even worse. You have to struggle and fight each and every day to not let yourself falter. Son, never lose hold of who you are and whose you are. You will always belong to your mother and me; you will always be my son, even if you are a murderer, even if you are a liar, even if you are cruel and full of hate. And you will always belong to God, whether you think you do or not. You can run all around this world and never escape those two facts.

In the days following my recollection in the living room of that house, I certainly didn't feel like I belonged to God. I was crushed by the weight of my regrets, buried at the bottom of a deep pit, staring upwards at a hopeless climb. Each night as I closed my eyes I heard the screams for help and saw the smashed faces of little Jeremy and the baby I never knew. Jackson's crushed body and pleading face had returned again to my dreams. I blamed myself for all of their deaths.

Every time I saw you, it reminded me of all the years I had lost and of the terrible dad I was. It was the first time I had really even paid attention to you since you were a baby. It was as if you had transformed from a toddler to a grown man, and I had missed everything in between. Being a father was the most important job I would ever have to do, and I had let it pass through my hands like sand through a sieve. Your childhood was past, your personality set, and I had no part in the man you had become. Every good trait in you had come from somewhere other than me. Every weakness I recognized I blamed on my lack of fathering. I wanted desperately to start again with you, but I didn't know where to begin.

Seeing Abbie each day was even worse. She had continued to blossom as she woke from her sleep. Her smiles and positive attitude just made my own depression seem all the worse. She was a kind, wonderful person; I was selfish and cruel. She was beautiful; I was hideous. I longed to escape from the pit I was in, I wanted so much to hold on to her and love her and be the husband I never was, but it seemed impossible. I had done too much to be forgiven. I had broken her heart too many times for her to trust it to me again.

More than anything, I wanted to go backward and fix my many mistakes. I wanted to erase the years wasted pouring my heart and soul into a job that didn't exist anymore and into projects that had been reduced to rubble. I wanted another chance at that day, to be the leader of our family, to stand up and protect the lives of our two youngest children. I wanted an opportunity to act decisively and take us from the house before the men had come and it was too late. Now that I finally cared, all the things I cared about were either gone or out of my reach. I was like Casey at bat after the third strike flew past, standing at the plate, holding onto my bat, watching the stands empty of fans, and wishing with all my might for another swing that would never come.

Just as Jackson's death had abruptly ended my years of slumber, the recollection of those terrible days and of all my failures had plunged me into a different type of darkness. The lack of awareness that defined most of my life was a painless, narcotic-induced, dreamless sleep that silently consumed years without feeling or perception of the time that passed. The depression of those few weeks was in its own way much worse. I can look back upon that time and flit around the edges of it, painting the corners of how things were, but it just isn't something that is properly put into words. Thinking now of the self-hatred and inward consumption I was feeling at the time is embarrassing to me. I know better now than to slip that far into myself, but at the time, it was very real. When you see a shadow in the room at night, you can believe with all your heart in monsters until the light comes on again.

I don't really remember when or why the lights came back on and the darkness faded. Abbie helped a lot. She had taken an interest in cooking and tried a new recipe every other day. There weren't many ingredients to work with, so she sent me out each day with a list of seasonings to bring home if I happened to see them, always with an admonition to be careful and not risk anything on her account. Anything I brought home, spice or trinket, was met with as much appreciation as there had been indifference before. I don't know if she saw my depression and was trying to help me out of it or if she was just reveling in her newfound awareness of the world around her, but it helped me greatly to be needed. If I couldn't do anything else right, at least I could bring home a little bit of paprika or a sealed-up jar of pickles.

Abbie helped, but I don't think that was what shook me out of my funk. I think I needed to get that low to finally stop taking myself so seriously. Strange as it seems, and as dangerous as those wasted weeks of precious time were, I wouldn't go back and undo them. I had been so self-consumed for so many years, I needed to know that, deep down inside, I was pretty lousy and the world would seem much brighter to me if I would pay less attention to myself. For all my life, I had been in charge of my life and no one else. I worked my way through college, I built up my career, I earned a living for my family, and I helped to build that city. I needed that time of darkness to open my eyes and realize that everything I thought I had accomplished had come to nothing. All of my life's efforts were dust. I was rolling in that dust, unable even to pick myself up off the ground, left with nothing to do but call for help. And at the bottom of the pit, at the end of my rope, just like the prodigal's father, God was waiting for me saying, "Now, John, are you ready to really live?"

I didn't hear a voice out loud, of course, but it was just as real to me. I had seen the mountains and the stars and touched my baby's cheek and felt the happy little warm feelings of being blessed, but this was something new. It was a hand reaching down to help me stand; it was a call to arms; it was a reason to hope; it was a mission instead of an obligation. Even as I write this, I don't fully know what that mission is, but it feels good to be a part of it, to know that my efforts are for something that will last, a project with an expected life of forever instead of fifty years. And what beat it all was that I knew that God knew me for who I really was. He knew how selfish and cruel I was. He knew how cowardly and weak I was. He knew I would probably run when the battle got tough. He knew all that, but he picked me up anyway. And at that, I stopped crying and started laughing—not every day, but most days.

And so, when all those wasted, useful days were past, I was left with you and with Abbie and with not a whole lot of days left to figure out what to do with my family. Lori was gone, and you had descended into your own sort of darkness. Abbie and I pondered and schemed on how to leave the city and came up again and again with nothing. When the days were done and everyone was asleep, I found myself staring at the ceiling, thinking again of the life I had lost, seeing Jeremy's face and hearing his laughing and crying in the darkness, but crying myself with a smile on my face. I just missed him and missed the life that had been in my grasp that I never had the sense to hold onto. Those types of nights have never gone away. I carried them with me to the cabin and suspect I will have them forever until I finally go on to a place without tears.

One morning during our time in the apartment, after one of those nights of crying myself to sleep, I woke a few minutes before Abbie. It was a quiet and poignant moment. The morning sun filtering through the plastic over the window cast a soft, gray light over her beautiful face. I lay there silently, thinking of all the pain I had caused her. She opened her eyes and saw me looking at her in a way I suppose she had never seen before, even in our early days of courtship. "What is it?" she asked.

"I'm sorry," I replied without even thinking if it would be best to broach the subject with her. "I am so sorry for everything I've done to you. I miss our Jeremy; I miss our baby; I miss you."

She looked back at me and didn't say anything but leaned forward and kissed me on the cheek tenderly, sliding from beneath the sheets and slipping on her bathrobe before I could reach for her. She stopped at the door and whispered softly without turning to face me, "All that was a long time ago. We can't undo what happened." She turned back toward me and smiled. "Go wake up Jack. Let's get some breakfast. I made a bread pudding last night, and I want us to try it out."

So that was as close to forgiveness as I got for a while, but it was still pretty good. Where things went next I will never really understand. I had no clue how to love your mother. I guess I had to keep messing things up to learn anything. If you don't get anything else out of reading all this, please don't make the same mistakes I have made. If I haven't been able to teach you much else as your father, maybe I can teach you that.

CHAPTER 9

"My wife was at the door ... My heart beat once
or twice, and life flooded my veins.
Everything had changed ...
What was once routine was now the perfect joy."

I set down the papers and stood from the couch, stretching and thinking. Dad's story seemed to be a sort of confessional, leading me from one failure to another. He was sharing more about himself than I had heard before, more than I really wanted to know. No matter how rebellious, every son wants to look up to his father, wants to believe the best in him, wants him for a hero. It was really rather disturbing to hear one failure and weakness after another from someone who I loved so much, especially in light of seeing him die just two days ago. I knew some of the story, but not most of it, and of course I had no clue as to what had been going on inside my dad's head through all that. The man he described was a stranger to me, but I knew that it was all true. It was too much to deal with at once.

I paced the tiny apartment from room to room in the foggy oblivion of my thoughts. I found myself back in Davis's bedroom, absently lying on the bed, staring into the dark reflection of the window when the memory came rushing back of Davis' body lying facedown in the bed of his grave as I covered it up with dirt. I had adopted his home for my own and was entirely too comfortable lying on the bed of a man I had murdered just two days previous. It was disturbing how quickly I had adapted to the new environment, how natural being back in the city already felt. Not speaking to anyone, not having some other soul to connect to was already taking its toll. Being so engrossed into my dad's papers only made it worse. It was easy to see how someone could unplug from reality and fall asleep in these conditions.

I jumped up from the bed, wanting to change the subject in the conversation going on in my mind, and decided to go ahead and shave. I stepped into the bathroom and plugged the sink, waiting for the water to get hot first. The newer razor was much better. The whiskers pulled and hurt, but I didn't cut myself more than just a few normal nicks. I let the water out of the sink and rinsed off my face, looking around for a towel. I had used the last towel with my shower, so I stepped to one side and closed the door to look behind it. Up to that point, I had no reason to close the door and hadn't noticed the small window in the bathroom. It was a tiny window, not even two feet wide, just enough to let some light in if the door was shut.

There wasn't a towel behind the door and I was just about to open the door back up and check in the kitchen when some clear tape in the corner of the window caught my eye. The corner of the glass had broken out and been patched up with the tape. I wouldn't have thought much of that, but the humidity of the bathroom had peeled up the corner of the tape just enough that there was an open gap about the size of the end of a pencil.

I looked harder at the window, forgetting about the water dripping from my face. It was a standard window with a single latch in the middle. This window was made to be opened. There was no screen and no storm window behind the panes to seal off the gap in the tape. The next thing behind the window was the plastic of the canopy rippling loosely in the light evening breeze. I pushed open the gap in the tape, pulling it back some, and pushed my index finger out the window, barely touching the plastic canopy as it swayed back and forth. No alarms sounded. No flashing lights came on. I hurried back into the kitchen and found a table knife. I pulled the tape off of the hole, which was several inches wide and poked the dull knife through the gap, jabbing at the thick plastic. I poked my fingers back through the hole. The air outside the window was a little cooler than the air inside the apartment.

I set the table knife on the window sill and went back to the kitchen again, digging through drawers until I found a sharper knife and a pair of scissors. The latch on the window opened easily, but the window wouldn't budge when I tried to lift it. I was convinced now that the system wasn't rigged to detect changes in air pressure, but I didn't want to risk the sound of breaking glass. It looked like the window frame had been painted. I took turns with the knives and the pointed end of the scissors and dug around the edges of the window frame, chiseling out the layers of paint. A rough couple of wiggles and a hard jerk lifted the little window open, letting in a rush of colder air. I wanted to think it smelled fresh, but it was still the dry, stale air of the city. The cold had added a bit of spice to its smell and gave me a false sense of hope.

I reached out through the window and grabbed a handful of plastic. It was slick, but not slimy, and surprisingly clean considering how long it had been hanging there. I pulled on it, gently at first, and then harder to see if I could feel any give or stretch in the plastic or in whatever was holding it up. It was loose and free moving from side to side but barely moved downward from my tugging. I smoothed and folded a handful of the plastic canopy and took up the scissors to cut it. The blade was on the plastic when I thought better of it. "What will this accomplish for now?" I said out loud. It would be good to know if I could cut the plastic without being detected, but if it was on some other type of sensor, I would be throwing away any chance of seeing Lori again and all of this, including my father's death, would be for nothing. I set the scissors back down on the sill and closed the little window.

It was a terribly exciting moment, but it seemed quite useless at the time. Still thinking, but now about different things, I wandered back to the kitchen and ate the last pretzel. Whole new options were on the table for our escape. *There won't be an "our,"* I thought as I slumped back down on the couch, *if I don't find Lori.* I picked up Dad's papers again and read the next paragraph where I had left off without taking in a single word, thoroughly distracted. I read the same paragraph over and then the next and the next and was soon lost again in his story.

Your mother's forgiveness and gentle kiss should have nurtured kindness and tender feelings from me, but as usual, I went exactly the opposite from the direction I should have. I realize now that I had never really loved her, or anyone for that matter, up to that time in my life. When she and I were first married, if I wanted to be with her, I would just compliment her on the way she looked or on the supper she had cooked that night. I might rub on her shoulder for a few seconds or give her a kiss on the cheek. All of that was just leading up to where I wanted things to go that evening after the kids were in bed. I was gone so often with work or late getting home or back on the computer after dinner checking e-mails, that she was willing enough to take the attention, even though I am pretty sure she knew my true intentions. It wasn't that I didn't care for her, it was just that all the affection I gave her was only given to gain what I wanted for myself.

In the days after I achieved my goal, I was satisfied enough and would slip back into my world of self and work, paying little attention to her at all for several days until my urges would come back. Looking back on it, it seems so petty and childish; it had to have hurt her feelings. I am saying all this to remind you to always check your motives. Our hearts are wicked and selfish to the core, and we will never get better and be set free from ourselves until we start being honest about whom and what we really are.

So in those days and weeks after her forgiveness, I had it in my mind that our relationship was somewhat restored. I wanted nothing more than to take the next step, but I had no idea how to make that happen except to fall back on the old tricks and enticements I had used before. I was so thoroughly asleep for all those years after we came to the city that I honestly had very little desire to be with Abbie or with anyone for that matter. I know that is probably hard for a young man of your age to understand, but it was true. When I awoke from my sleep, that part of me woke up too. The fire kindled slowly at first, but it built steadily, especially as Abbie's personality began to come alive.

At first, I was flirting with her, like a teenager might. I would compliment her and tell her how pretty she was. She would catch me looking at her too long. The apartment was so cramped that it was easy to find excuses to bump into her and get in her way so that we would be close, even if only for a few seconds. I think she liked that, or at least she didn't push me away at first. I had flirted with her in much the same way when we were dating, and it was like we started that over again.

But sharing the same bed with Abbie became a torture to me. I was obsessed with seeing her, with touching her, with holding her, and it began to consume me. It took hours for me to fall asleep at night. I would lie awake in the bed, hoping and wishing that she would roll over and reach for me and using all my effort to keep myself from reaching for her. I would listen to her breathing in her sleep, wondering if she were dreaming, hoping she might awake and forget where she was and when it was. I would act like I was asleep and let my foot or elbow drift onto her side of the bed, hoping I could brush up against her leg or the side of her breast. She never said a word about it, but she began to take a fold of the sheet and tuck it under herself before she went to sleep, making a wall between us that could resist my crude gropings.

I would always wake first and just lie there, watching her sleep in the morning light, silently excited to see a glimpse of her shoulder or thigh poking from under the sheets. The look of love she saw that morning of my apology had turned into leering, I am afraid, and the purer and truer love that was growing within me was souring and turning into something else—and she knew it.

For all the years in CR12 that we had been in our state of dull existence, we had changed clothes in front of each other without a thought. We were, after all, married, and had seen each other thousands of times. We would change into our jumpsuits each morning, stripping to our underwear or even to the skin, only a few feet from each other, neither of us even wanting to touch or embrace or even look at the other. Apparently my lingering stares had become so obvious that Abbie refused to change in front of me anymore. She would wait in the bed until I changed and left and then get up and shut the door behind me. A few times I went into the bathroom while she was showering, using the excuse that I needed to brush my teeth or shave. She began to lock the door each time she went in.

After the Christmas morning, I began to tune in on finding some clothes for Abbie. We spent most days in our jumpsuits, putting them on in the morning when we got up and taking them off in the evening when we went to bed. We just didn't have anything else to wear. I found several pairs of shorts and t-shirts and more comfortable clothes for her to wear around the apartment, and she loved it, taking each gift with a smile. One day I found a silk nightgown, with thin shoulder straps, low cut and only just covering down to the thigh. It was a mint green color and would have fit her perfectly, and she would have looked beautiful in it. I was smiling as I gave it to her, but she didn't smile back. She wadded it up with a scowl and tucked it away when I wasn't looking. I couldn't find the nightgown anywhere in the apartment (I looked pretty hard, too), and she didn't speak to me for the rest of the day.

It wasn't that I wanted to push her away; it was almost as if I couldn't help myself. I knew that I was annoying her, and I knew that it was hurting our relationship and damaging what good had been built, but I wanted to be with her so much. I really did love her, and this time I loved her for the right reasons. I just didn't know how to show that love in a healthy way.

After two weeks, I couldn't handle the intensity of the feelings. I at least could read the situation enough to know that I needed to back off. I started staying up later, letting Abbie go to bed first, and then just sleeping on the couch. A few times she woke me up in the morning and would look at me with a puzzled look, but she never asked me why I didn't come to bed. We both knew why. I knew in my mind that she just wasn't ready to be with me, but in my heart, the rejection hurt badly.

It was in the midst of this inner turmoil that a young lady named Leslie Fox came into the picture. She was a new inspector, just out of school, and was being rotated with different teams as part of her training. I was accustomed to the procedure and had directed new trainees for many years before I was demoted. When she came into the group, all of our inspector teams were in pairs, so she became a third for a five-day set at a time with each team until a spot came open. There were rumors that the head of our department was tapped for a position at City Hall. Everyone in the department except me, it seemed, was positioning themselves to take over as head. When the shift came, Leslie would move into the empty spot.

I had trained practically the entire department, so having her along with us was nothing new. She was, however, the first woman inspector I had worked with. It was rather cramped being three wide in the little truck, and she insisted on sitting in the middle since she was, she reminded us each time she climbed into the cab, much smaller than either of us. She talked incessantly about nothing, asking easy questions about what we were doing that day and constantly telling us how much she appreciated working with two men that were so smart. She was a very attractive young lady, a little ditzy, but very pretty in the face. I would be lying if I said I didn't enjoy the compliments, but she was so much younger than me, practically your age, that I just didn't see her as someone I should be interested in. McAllister was only a few years older than her, and he gorged himself on her compliments, swelling up more and more each day that she was with us.

Once his initial training period was over, McAllister and I were scheduled with different fifth days off, so that our team could work continuously with no downtime. The day after my day off was always tough, because I had to go back and catch up the work he hadn't done and fill out all his paperwork. His day off was always a joy, and I looked forward to it each time it came around. By myself, I could search the houses freely for Abbie's treasures and, if demolition crews weren't around, take off my hood and enjoy the real air. The fourth day of Leslie's set with our team was McAllister's day off. I woke up that day with dread at having to put up with her tagging along behind me like a puppy, asking a thousand questions.

I should have been tipped off to how things would go that day when she walked up behind me just as I got to the locker room door. I was always early to work, getting there fifteen or twenty minutes before McAllister, mostly just to get everything in order with the tools and directions to the work site since he wouldn't be helping with either. The locker room was empty as we walked in together, and she smiled and said, "Looking forward to learning some more from you today, chief."

Her locker was on the next aisle from mine, but she walked back toward me as she was changing from her gray jumpsuit into the light blue outdoor suit, using the excuse of asking me questions about where we were going and what we would be doing that day. We were all used to changing in front of each other, but the few women that shared the locker room always kept their distance, and no one ever spoke—that was an unwritten rule. Before that morning, I had never seen Leslie in anything but the bulky outdoor suit. Standing in front of me in just her underwear, I couldn't help but notice her striking figure. The gray jumpsuits were not flattering, but the one-piece underwear hugged her body tightly, covering everything, but showing off every curve and revealing every unseen feature. She smiled as she noticed me staring.

As usual, she talked nonstop in the truck the entire trip to the jobsite, filling between her questions about the work that day with compliments about how smart I was and how thankful she was for me teaching her so much. She guessed my age at ten years younger than I was. Two or three times she speculated that I was sure to be assigned to the head of the department, after all, she said, "I knew more about inspections than everyone in the department put together."

By the end of the day, she had my attention. I know I shouldn't have fallen into such simple traps, but I did. I talked more with her on the way home, falling into an idle and aimless exchange. As we got back to the city, she reached over and squeezed my arm with her gloved hand. Her eyes caught mine as she said, "Thanks, John, for a good day. You taught me a lot today, but I would love it if you would come to my apartment some evening so you could teach me more. I never do anything in the evenings and have so much to learn about this job." Her squeeze loosened and she rubbed her hand lightly up and down my arm as she spoke. "I am in the same building as you, on the floor above, in apartment number 21. Please come up if you have the time." And that was that. The invitation was set.

The next day was the last day of Leslie's rotation with our team and was my day off. I hadn't slept much the night before, tossing and turning on the couch. Abbie was working and you were at school. Needless to say, I was thoroughly distracted. I tried to nap and to catch up on paperwork but couldn't focus on either.

I knew Leslie was too young for me and I shouldn't be interested in her. Her personality was actually irritating to me, but I couldn't help but be attracted to her physically. Even through high school and college I had never been propositioned like that. Abbie had been a lady; I had courted her, slowly working toward our engagement. In all the years in the city and in my engineering career before, I had almost exclusively worked with men. The only other woman I ever spent more than a few minutes a day with was one of the CAD technicians at my first job in Atlanta, and she was old, ugly, and mean.

That night over dinner, I tried to focus in on Abbie and put Leslie out of my head. Abbie was just as pretty as her and ten times as smart. I loved Abbie; I liked being with her; she was my wife; she was everything I was living for. After dinner she and I spent an hour going over a plan she had worked up that day for us leaving the city. In the end, I shot it down. She hadn't considered a few things, and I knew it wouldn't work. I must have been too harsh and hurt her feelings, because she was dressed and ready for bed by eight. It wasn't even dark out yet. I went to the bedroom to try and apologize and found the door locked. As usual during that time, you were already shut up in your room, working on homework or sulking over Lori being gone. I went back to the couch and laid down to try and sleep, but I couldn't. I had napped a few hours that afternoon and just wasn't tired.

After lying on the couch for a half hour, I couldn't take it anymore. Except for the sound of the refrigerator, the apartment was completely silent. I went back to the bedroom door and listened. Abbie wasn't making a sound. She was already asleep. I grabbed my badge and my shoes and slipped silently out the door, locking it quietly behind me. A few steps later I found myself on the floor above staring at the number 21 on Leslie's apartment door. I stood for a moment with my knuckles a few inches from the door, trying to decide whether or not to knock. I could hear Leslie walking around inside, humming quietly to herself.

The lines and curves of her body, so close to me the previous morning, were burning in my mind. I spent a few minutes outside her door imagining myself going inside and being with her. I knew without a doubt that she wanted me to come inside; all I had to do was open the door and take what she was freely giving. If she had heard me outside the door and opened it at that moment, I don't know where I would be now. Thankfully, she did not. After a few minutes, my mind cleared, and I lowered my hand from knocking. I turned away from her door and walked down the hall, nearly running by the time I got to the stairs.

I would like to say I made a morally superior decision and that I walked away because it was the right thing to do. A closer truth is that I was just flat-out afraid. Afraid of what I was about to do and afraid of losing Abbie forever. I knew I couldn't trust myself to stay in the apartment building, so I just kept walking down all the stairs and out the main doors onto the street. The farther I got away from apartment 21, the safer I felt. I kept walking all the way to the end of the city and found myself at the door of the entertainment building.

I wasn't much of a drinker, and even if I had been, I wouldn't have wanted the beer they were serving. I decided to go inside anyway in the hopes that a few drinks might take the edge off my feelings enough to go back to my own couch and sleep off my temptation. Not good reasoning, but I wasn't making good decisions that evening. Turning right and getting on the elevator instead of going into the bar was an even worse decision.

I stepped out of the elevator onto the second floor into the hall of what had once been a very nice hotel. Dimly lit lights lined the richly papered walls with dark wood paneling on the bottom. The carpet was lush and soft underfoot with a beautiful red and black oriental print runner centered in the aisle. Each room in the hall had a small sign and a badge scanner next to the door. I walked along the hall looking at each closed door. Most of the rooms were marked "in use" or "reserved," but one of them was marked "available." I wasn't really sure why, but I scanned in my badge, and the door released and opened just a crack.

I pushed it open and stepped into a nicely furnished hotel room, certain to have been ranked as four stars in its day. A voice came from the bathroom, "Take a seat, honey. I'll be ready for you in just a minute." I was sure then where I was and kept standing near the door, not replying, undecided what I should do next.

In just a few minutes, but what seemed to me to be an eternity, a lady came out from the bathroom. She was wearing a thin bathrobe that hung loosely over pink silk that left little to the imagination. The nightgown was very similar to the one I had given Abbie, only pink instead of green. She was about my age, prettier than most women, helped by her makeup and neatly fixed hair that fell past her shoulders, a luxury that no other women in the city enjoyed. Her forced smile helped to hide the weariness in her face. Her eyes were dull and lifeless, and I could tell immediately that there was nothing inside. She was asleep, to be sure.

I stood there looking at her, wondering how I had come to this place, thinking to myself without saying a word. She let me stand there silent for a minute and then said, "You paid for your time here; you might as well enjoy yourself."

I paused for another moment, looking at her. She was a very attractive woman, and part of me wanted to stay for a while. *Abbie would never know,* I reasoned. Just the thought of Abbie extinguished the desire I had for this woman. I dropped my eyes to the ground and asked the only question that came into my head, "Don't you have a husband?"

In a flash, her eyes came to life, glaring first with anger and then melting into pain. She sat down on the edge of the bed and wrapped the thin bathrobe tightly around herself, putting her face in her hands. "My husband is dead now for ten years," she whispered. "If he were here, I wouldn't be doing this." Her quiet sobs covered the noise of me slipping out the door and shutting it quietly behind me as I headed back to the elevator.

As I stepped back into the lobby, I looked back toward the bar where I would have been much better off going in the first place and decided against it. I had been in enough trouble for one night. The lonely couch seemed pretty good to me at that moment.

Walking up the hill, I determined to tell Abbie the whole thing the next day and come clean with her. I rationalized myself into a sense of pride. After all, I had conquered the temptations of the evening and remained true to my wife. But the victory was thin and unsatisfying—I knew Abbie would not see it that way. I knew also that the short meeting in the room would show up on our expense sheet. I would have some explaining to do anyway when she found it. I looked at the clock on the street as I neared the apartment. It was barely past nine, I hadn't been gone long at all. I quietly unlocked our apartment door and tried to slip in without making much noise. When I turned around, I was more than surprised to see Abbie sitting at our kitchen table, wrapped tightly in the fuzzy bathrobe I had brought home to her the week before, with a very perturbed look on her face.

I stood there, waiting for a "Where you been?" or "What have you been doing?" but none came. She just looked at me expectantly. I didn't know what to do but start at the beginning, telling her the whole story about the past few days with Leslie and the poor decisions of that evening. I spelled it out much as I just did to you, Jack, trying to be as honest as possible, not leaving out anything. When I finished, she sat there glaring at me silently with a look somewhere between hurt and anger. "Abbie," I pleaded, "you can't be angry about this. I didn't do anything against you. I never touched either one of them. I didn't cheat on you. I came back home."

She stood up from her chair and turned her back to me, taking the two steps into the kitchen she had available to her. When she turned back around, I could see a tear running down each cheek as she said, "John, you cheated on me when you got up from that couch and laid your hand on the door. Everything after that just makes it worse. Sit down and listen to me. I have my own story to tell you." So I did. She gathered herself and began, pacing back and forth as she spoke.

"John, you told me about the man you met, Wiley Fisher, and how he said that people are awake and asleep. I would agree with that and I am very grateful that you worked so hard to help wake me out of the state I was in. But I would add that everyone doesn't sleep in the same way. For all the years that I was asleep, I was still feeling and thinking inside. I knew what was going on around me; I could see the hurt that Jack was going through; I watched and saw how you ignored the both of us; I could see the blank faces scattered all around me on the street and at work. I knew those things inside of me, but I couldn't get anything to come out. I wanted to speak, I wanted to cry, sometimes I wanted to scream, but nothing could escape. It was as if I was trapped inside myself with no way to break loose. The tears I cried when you gave me that locket were a key that opened the door to the prison I had been trapped inside for so long.

"When I walked up to you on my first day in the city, I wanted so badly for you to reach out and hold me. I needed that more than anything at that moment and you just turned away. That hurt me more than you can understand. I missed my children, I missed my parents, I was cramping and in pain from losing our baby. I wanted a shoulder to cry on, I needed someone to share my pain with and there just wasn't anyone. I felt so alone.

"I guess I got used to you not being around. After we were married and you started to work, we drifted further and further apart. I remember you going back to work a day earlier than you had to after Jeremy was born. I remember you coming home late for work and saying you were too tired to go to Jack's school program. I remember you forgetting my birthday and then how miserably you tried to make up for it. But most of all, I remember how you would look over my shoulder while I was talking with you, obviously thinking about some project at work instead of listening to what I was saying. Something inside me hoped that everything that happened when we were taken to the city might bring you back to me. It wouldn't have brought back everything that was lost, but at least we could have gone through it together.

"I am sure you don't remember everything that happened in the first days that we came to the city. I was still bleeding from the miscarriage and had to wait two days before I was allocated any sanitary napkins. On the second day we were here, they cut my hair shorter than it had ever been. These jumpsuits they gave us are the same as they would be for a man. On the third day we were here, I was assigned to my job in an office full of men. In short, I felt like I wasn't a woman anymore. You didn't help. You never looked at me, you barely spoke to me, and you never ever touched me. At least before we came to the city, you would want something from me every once in a while. As far as you were concerned, we might as well have been two men sharing an apartment with a nine-year-old boy.

"And seeing Jack every day just made things worse. I could see how much he was hurting. I wanted to be a good mother to him, I wanted to hug him and comfort him, but I just couldn't. Every time I saw him, I thought of Jeremy and of our baby, and it just opened up the pain of the memories and the things that were lost. It was easier to just stay away and keep Jack and you at an arm's length. It was easier to disengage than it was to hurt all the time.

"All this was part of who I was when Jeff Tribbett was assigned to be the head of the accounting and records department. I had been working in that department for about a year when he came. He was about my age, I guess, and not particularly handsome, but there was something different about him. He was what you would call a riser, I suppose, and he stood out from all the other men I was in contact with, including you. In fact, he reminded me of you when we first met in college. He was assertive, smart, and decisive. He stopped to talk to each person in every cubicle, asking them how they were doing, offering to answer any questions they might have.

"When he stopped to talk to me each day, he called me Abbie instead of Ms. Wilson. It was the first time I had heard my first name spoken out loud in over a year. He insisted that I call him Jeff. I was good at my job, and he always took a minute to compliment me and point out how accurate and neat my bookkeeping was. He would be standing and I would be sitting when he would stop and speak with me, and he would always pat me a couple of times on the shoulder while he was talking. It wasn't much, and I felt silly for feeling that way, but just that small bit of touch was electrifying. I was definitely attracted to him and wanted to talk more, but I never did anything but answer with one or two words, trying my best to muster out a smile."

I shifted in my seat and looked at her nervously. I didn't want to hear what I knew was coming next.

"After about a month of the same routine, he stopped before going to the next cubicle and complimented me on how pretty my smile was. Before we came to the city, you had always told me my smile was pretty, even when you barely noticed anything else, and his compliment was more than welcome. It was nice to feel pretty again, to feel like a woman again, even for just a few minutes a day. I always tried to smile my best when he came by each day, even though I could never bring myself to say anything more than a few words when we spoke.

"One day, just after lunch, I was in a back room alone, digging for a record. The file room was well removed from the rest of the office, and no one ever went back there, so I was surprised when Jeff walked into the room. 'Hi there, Abbie with the pretty smile. What brings you back here?' he asked with his normal upbeat confidence.

"I stood up from the cabinet I was kneeling in front of and turned to face him. I could feel my cheeks burning as a warm feeling came over me and hoped he wouldn't notice. 'Just looking for a file,' I replied and smiled back at him.

"'Me too,' he replied, pointing to a file cabinet behind me. His eyes were locked into mine as he squeezed past me. I could have moved over more than I did but stayed close on purpose, letting him brush against me as he passed.

"He must have seen in my eyes how much I enjoyed him being that close to me. As he was about to pass by me, he stopped and put his hand on my waist. I let him pull me against him, and he kissed me on the lips. I tried to kiss him back, but I just didn't have it in me. His embrace loosened, and he backed away. He didn't say a word, but his thoughts were shouting out loud and clear from the expression on his face. He looked at me as if he had just kissed a corpse. Any attraction he had for me melted away in an instant. He quickly grabbed his file and nearly ran from the room. Jeff barely spoke to me again after that, often skipping my cubicle, until he was promoted to another department about a year later.

"To be honest with you, John, that hurt me almost as much as you had. More than anything, I just wanted Jeff to want me. If he had closed the door in that file room and pulled me into a corner, I wouldn't have fought him off. If he had invited me to come to his apartment, I think I probably would have gone. If he had offered to have you transferred away and asked me and Jack to move in with him, I would have considered it. He made me realize that I just didn't love you at all anymore and made me question if I ever really had.

"I tell you all this not to hurt you or to give you an excuse for what you did or almost did tonight, I tell you this to try and explain how mixed up things are inside me right now. I made a promise to be your wife in front of God and my family. I had every intention of keeping that promise forever, but when push came to shove, I was ready to throw it away." She paused for a minute and I thought she might cry, but she only steeled her resolve and stood a little straighter.

"John, I loved you the best I could for all those years without you ever loving me back. In truth, I don't know if that is even love at all. I don't know what love is anymore.

"You and I are like little babies right now. We have only been awake for such a short time, and neither one of us is anything like the same sort of person we were before all this happened. I am still committed to being your wife. I will do my best to forgive you for what you have done, and I ask to you try and forgive me for what I have done. I just need some time to get my head on straight and so do you.

"I see how much you want to be with me. I see how you look at me now, I know the little things you are doing to try and get me to be closer to you. I know you have needs, so do I for goodness sake. The bottom line is this: I refuse to just have sex with you. We did that for years before we ever came to this city. I don't want to do that anymore. Until I love you and you love me and we can truly make love together as God intended for a man and wife, you will not touch me or kiss me or even look at me like you want to, much less anything else. Until that time, I would ask you to control yourself and act like a man instead of like a teenager pumped up with hormones. I promise you that if you can be patient with me, it will be worth your while. If you need to sleep on the couch to control yourself, I understand."

With that she stopped pacing and sat in the chair across the table, finally letting a smile break through the seriousness on her face. It had been an effort for her to get all that out, and she looked relieved that it was over. "Are we okay, dear?" she asked me earnestly.

I was overwhelmed with all that she said and all that had happened that night. I wanted to scream or break down and cry, but mostly I was just relieved. It was good to have everything laid out on the table. I looked back at her and waited just long enough to hold the moment. "Jeff was right," I said. "You do have a pretty smile."

That was enough for her. She stuck out her tongue at me as she stood up from the chair and headed off to bed. I went back over to the couch and slept better than I had in a long time. I felt like a real man for the first time in years. In a sense, I had been released from all the insecurities and feelings of inadequacy that had consumed me for so long. Don't get me wrong, I stole a glance at Abbie whenever I could. Your mother is a beautiful woman. Sometimes she would catch me staring at her, but then she would just smile and wag her finger at me like she was saying, "No, no," and tap her wrist like it was a watch. Things were clear between us. She was still my wife, I just needed to wait.

It was just a few days later that the plan that ultimately gained our escape from the city came to me. I had made a career out of solving problems and was definitely gifted in that way. I think I just needed to really give my full attention to it in the same way that I had poured myself into waking up Abbie. In the end, it was simple; I finally looked at your face and saw you as more than the little nine-year-old boy that you were when you came into the city. When I saw the man that you are, it all came clear.

The day after that ill-fated evening, I was back in the truck with McAllister. Leslie had rotated on to another group. "Hey, Wilson," he boasted, "guess where I was last night." He didn't wait for my reply but went on. "I guess your day off was all Leslie needed to see me for who I am. She says I am sure to be named head of the department. She and I discussed things a little more in detail at her apartment last night, if you know what I mean."

I laughed and smiled, not at his conquest of well-trodden lands, but rather at relief for not having knocked on her door the night before. What strange confusion that would have thrown into the mix! It was just a few weeks later that another riser in the department, even younger than McAllister, was named chief.

Leslie was thankfully assigned to another team and was seen in common company with the new department head, leading to many disparaging comments from McAllister.

I have often thought of the strange fate of the two ladies I came into contact with that week. Perhaps it is better to describe them as one woman and one lady, or two women and neither a lady, who is to say for sure. I think Leslie was really a riser in her own way, just like McAllister but with different methods. She must have found out somewhere along the way that she could get what she wanted if she used the only thing she thought she had to give. The other lady of that evening, so to speak, I pity in a much different way. I have often wondered if my thoughtless and hastily spoken question about her dead husband only served to bring her to a temporary stirring from her slumber or if the pain and tears of the moment woke her completely to find herself in a hell, of sorts, here on earth. Once again, never underestimate the collateral damage you leave behind when you treat those around you with only your own selfish desires guiding your decisions and actions.

In all that happened on those days, even with all the pain I caused, I don't think I would change a thing. It was exactly what Abbie and I needed to get us through those times. It is beyond my understanding how God can take even my sins and failings and form and mold them to fit his own perfect plan. Through the whole episode with Leslie, I never even considered to back away from things for a minute and ask for God's help. He helped me anyway and worked it out better than I deserved, much better than I could have done on my own. I do wish I could have gotten through all that mess without all the regrets; maybe that would have happened if I had stopped and prayed before I got off the couch that night. Jack, I sure do wish you would go to God with your problems instead of plowing through them on your own.

I don't mean to preach at you; that isn't what this is all about. You know I love you, and you surely know better than ever after reading all of this that your old man is anything but perfect. We are all working out our own journeys, and I just want to help you avoid some of the same pitfalls that I have fallen into. I know that as you read this you are in the midst of intense decisions and conflicted feelings that you have never experienced before. I just wish I could be inside the city to help you with it. Since I can't be there, you should try going to the one that can help you a lot more than I can.

I do want you to know that Abbie was certainly true to her word. It was six months to the day after we reached the cabin and well over ten years since she and I had been together. It was the middle of winter by then and was a cold night. I was sleeping on the couch as always in front of the fireplace. By this time, you had already made a place for yourself just down the valley from us, and Abbie and I were living alone again. You and I had spent the day working together outside, and my muscles ached as I finally relaxed on the couch, wrapping up in a blanket as I fell asleep.

Abbie came into the living room a little past midnight and woke me gently, letting her fingers trail through the edge of my hair. "John," she whispered in my ear, "I'm ready." Her words woke me instantly from my sleep, and I opened my eyes to see her kneeling in front of me on the rug in between the couch and the fireplace. She was wearing a bathrobe that we had found on our hike from the city to the cabin, and she loosened the tie in front of it and let it slip off from her shoulders. The firelight was dim, but I could clearly see that she was wearing the mint green silk nightgown I had given to her back in the city. It complimented her eyes and slid around her body even better than I hoped when I found it.

I smiled and sat up from the couch. "But how did you?" I began. She put her finger over my lips and took my hand, leading me back to the bed she had left, still warm in the spot she had been. No dream could have been that sweet.

Let me just say that she was definitely worth the wait. It was the first time we had truly made love together. We had never touched and caressed and held each other this way before, meeting the needs of the other without needing to worry about meeting our own. In the weeks and months that followed, we explored and discovered each other, finding great joy in learning how to bring pleasure and contentment to the other. What was unexpected, at least for me, was recognizing how she and I had been growing closer in spirit and soul long before we joined together in body. That bond continued to flourish even more as we became closer to what God intended a husband and wife to be.

Jack, it is a hard thing to put in words. Maybe I have already said more than I should. Don't tell your mom I have been talking about her this way. I just want you to be able to enjoy your wife one day as I do my Abbie. It was and is a true and wondrous joy to be the husband of my wife. What is most exciting is that I feel like I am just getting started. As you read this, you can be assured that I am eagerly waiting for you and Lori to meet me outside the city so I can get back to the cabin and pick up where Abbie and I left off.

The stinging thought that my dad and mom would never see each other again tore me from my reading, and I laid the papers aside and looked up at the ceiling. If I had only been content to stay at the cabin, Dad would still be alive. How much more pain and loss would Mom have to suffer? As I read of the love of my parents, I couldn't help but hope that Lori and I would have the opportunity to love each other in the same way. How can you measure the value of one life against another? Wonderful and painful hopes and regrets swirled around in my head. I have no idea what time it was when this strange mix lulled me to sleep.

CHAPTER 10

"In this life, you're the flower and the thorn.
You're everything that's fair."

The most gut-wrenching day of my life began with being ripped out of my sleep by a blood-curdling scream from the apartment across the hall. I had been in the midst of a peaceful dream. Dad and I were chopping firewood on a wintry day in front of his cabin when Mom and Lori called from the front porch for us to come in and wash up for dinner. The shrill voice of the scream brought me back to a strange world I didn't want to be a part of and to a sad realization that my dream could never be reality. Dad was dead and buried, and Lori might as well be for all the chance I had of finding her. I tried to force myself to think more positively as I jammed on my shoes and grabbed the badge from the counter, having enough sense to quickly lock the door behind me as I rushed to the apartment of the scream.

Considering the situation I was in, I probably should have thought twice of answering a total stranger's call for help, but to be honest, I never even considered doing anything other than what I did. The scream that woke me was incoherent, but the second time she screamed clearly, "Someone help me! He's dying!" I shoved open the door, almost knocking her over in the process. From the look of her hair and the lines on her face, she had also just been sleeping. Her eyes were wide open now as she pointed to a man leaning against the kitchen wall, grasping at his throat, gagging silently, turning a deep shade of purple. He was obviously choking.

Some public service announcement that was played between the cartoons from my early youth must have kicked in, because I quickly moved over behind him and performed the Heimlich maneuver. An indistinguishable wad of something doughy popped out of his mouth onto the floor. He bent over, his head between his knees, gasping for air. It must have been a late-night snack that went horribly wrong.

I turned toward the woman, his wife, I supposed. She had fallen to her knees with her face toward the floor and was sobbing heavily, whispering, "Thank you, thank you," over and over again. By this time, the man had regained the oxygen in his brain, and he stood up straight and said, "I'm going back to bed." The woman continued crying, now lying on the floor, saying nothing more and not even looking at me, so I backed up from the bizarre scene and walked out into the hall, closing the door behind me.

It was such a shocking way to wake up, I just couldn't go back to sleep. Curiously, no one else was in the hall, despite the huge ruckus that had been raised. I decided to walk outside and try to get my head screwed on straight. Slivers of the gray morning light were beginning to puncture the darkness that covered the canopy like a heavy blanket. I wandered up and down the street in front of the apartments, looking back at the building I had just left. I could count the windows in the dim streetlights and found the apartment where the man was choking. Its lights were on, but every other window on this side of the building was dark. No one had even gotten out of bed to see what she was yelling about. *Maybe I should have just let him choke to death so he could be put out of his misery,* I wondered silently. Feelings of guilt washed over me at the thought. His misery would be much worse where he might have gone.

Judging from the streaks of daylight over the canopy above, it would be less than an hour before the city would begin to stir. I decided to just wait down on the street and take one more stab at picking out Lori from the crowd. Maybe she was an early riser that got out before everyone else. It seemed odd that it was my last day in the city. The next morning, according to our plan, I would get into Davis's new assigned truck and drive until the gas tank ran empty. Desperation wrestled with a thin hope that was forced at best.

The light was on at the little convenience store. Another cup of coffee would be the thing to get things started. I might as well spend all of Davis's money; neither of us would need it after today. I stepped inside the store and scanned up and down the aisles, looking for something rare and expensive. Maybe a pack of peanut butter crackers or a moon pie. I was surprised when I heard the deep, Southern drawl of the man working the counter. "You're in here a bit early this morning, Mr. Davis. Getting ready for your date tonight?"

I jumped a bit hearing the name of my victim, wondering how the clerk knew it. I had been in his sight for only a half second when I walked in, turning immediately away from the counter. *Maybe they have scanners that picked up the badge when I walked in,* I wondered. That was a scary thought. I could hear the sound of his shoes on the floor. He was walking toward me. He obviously knew who Davis was. I tried my best to be casual and turned around to face him, looking for an avenue to make a quick exit if needed.

He saw my face just as I read the name on his badge, "W. Fisher." "Little John Wilson," he whispered just as I said, "Wiley Fisher," under my breath. He was as startled as I was, but he caught his composure first, laying his big hand on my shoulder and guiding me to walk down the aisle. "Can I help you find something, sir?" he said casually in a normal voice just before whispering "cameras" in a low voice.

I struggled to think of something. "Do you have socks?" I mustered. It was a stupid question. I had just bought a pair the day before. If anyone was paying attention, which was unlikely, they would have known I knew better.

Wiley played it cool and flipped me a pair in my size. "How about a cup of coffee with your socks?" He grinned. I could see him staring at the numbers on Davis's badge as he scanned it across the machine to pay for the items. "I get off early shift this morning at eleven," he said. "You're off all day today, aren't you, Davis?" I looked back at him and nodded, trying not to act very interested. His eyes caught mine in a glance that was short but firm and somehow I understood his motives completely. Another early riser passed me as I walked out of the door. I could hear Wiley greeting him in the same casual way. I felt sure the rest of the day would be as bizarre as that early morning, and it gave me a strange sense of hope.

I sipped the coffee slowly and leaned against a tree, looking for another vantage point for the parade that was about to begin. I found my spot on the side of the street, this time more toward the school. From there I could see everyone as they exited the apartment buildings, both those going toward the school and those headed down the hill toward the rest of the city. As the commuters filed past, I saw many faces from the past two days: several men from the bar, the secretary at the school, my nemesis from the mayor's office, and even the lady that worked the desk outside the locker room that I had slipped past on that first morning in CR18.

I watched the little girl that walked barefoot in the grass in the park being escorted by her mother toward the school. They stopped halfway and exchanged hugs before her mom turned back down the hill to her work. Both of them were clearly awake, sticking out like a sore thumb in the crowds. I slipped into the throng as she walked past and picked casually between the walkers until I came up beside her. "Don't look up at me," I said in a voice that I was afraid she wouldn't hear.

"Why are you talking to me?" she whispered back.

"I am looking for a lady named Lori Applegate," I replied softly.

She paused from walking for just an instant but caught herself before she caused a pile up in the traffic. "I don't know anyone by that name," she said and then paused. "But there is a little boy with the last name Applegate in my daughter's second grade class. Gotta go," she whispered as she turned toward a nondescript brick building and reached for the door. I could barely hear her say to herself as she stepped inside, "I wish someone were looking for me." I almost followed her into the building but thought better of it. I had put her in enough risk already by just talking to her.

I followed the crowds to the end of the road and headed back up toward the apartment again, my feet howling in protest all the way. No one looked up at me as I walked up the hill, thinking to myself. My heart had leaped when she mentioned the little boy, but I knew that he was much too old to be Lori's son. That was a relief in a way. I had always feared that she would find someone else and be married. The foolish thought that he might be her stepson lasted only for a second before I realized that no child that age could belong to her and still have her last name. Still, just hearing her name acknowledged, just saying it out loud to another person, added fuel to the fire of hope that was kindled that morning by seeing Wiley.

The streets were nearly empty as I passed the convenience store again on my way back to the apartment. The strange run-in with Wiley was a shock to be sure. What was he doing in CR18? It was too much to be a coincidence. I could barely wait until eleven. His eyes had told me he would come to Davis's apartment. I hoped I was reading them right. It would be a huge relief to talk with someone other than the one-sided recollections of my father. Based on my dad's brief description of him, if anyone knew if Lori was in the city, it would be Wiley.

The computer was flashing with another reminder of my meeting at the city building the next day. I hit "accept" again and looked over at the clock. It was only eight thirty. I had a long time to wait, too long with everything I had to think about already this morning. I slipped off Davis's shoes and sat back down on the couch. I still had some reading to do.

I looked again at the stack of papers, finding my place just past the middle. I wasn't going to finish this before it was time to leave the city, much less before I found Lori, if I did find Lori. "Too much sleeping when there are important things to do," my dad would have said. Despite my rude awakening that morning, I felt surprisingly fresh, better than I had since I had arrived, and my mind felt sharp. Something told me I would need it. I hoped it wasn't just the coffee kicking in. I picked up the papers, starting back into Dad's story.

Jack, I suspect that as you have been reading all this, you have wondered why I even wrote it down. Sometimes I wonder myself. Things can be hard to explain in talking sometimes, and I have a hard time getting my thoughts in order while I am listening to someone else. Writing things down helps me to make sure I am saying everything I mean to. Even with that, as I finish writing to you, I am not at all sure that I have accomplished what I set out to do. I wanted to tell you our story so that maybe you would understand a bit more what it really means to love someone. I can certainly tell that you have a strong intention to love Lori and that you care a great deal for her. What I hope is that someday you can love her as I have just begun to love Abbie.

You cannot possibly love Lori yet. I don't say that to put you down. You are a long way ahead of where I was at your age and you have a heart for people that I have never had. This is a hard thing to explain. Love is a very difficult thing to put into words and an even harder thing to actually do. If I were a poet, maybe I could choose a phrase that would make it come alive, but I am not. I tried writing a poem to your mom once. When she got done reading it, she smiled and patted me on my shoulder. No, I am not a poet or a painter or even much of a writer. I am an engineer. When I want to describe something, I try to make a sketch to show it from three different angles, put labels all over it, and then write some notes to describe it more. This is not working well. If I am confusing myself, I must be confusing you.

Let me put it to you this way. For years and years I saw the stars just as anyone would, only occasionally stealing a fleeting glance through the streetlights, rarely giving them a second thought. When we came to the cabin, it was the first time that I had really stopped and studied the stars, and I was taken away by their beauty. When I look up at them on a clear night before the moon has risen, it is like I can see a glimpse of the soul of God. He is the artist and the sky is his canvas. If I look at the stars every night for a month straight, I am no less amazed. It just isn't something you can get tired of.

Love is a little bit like that. For years and years I saw Abbie as a beautiful woman. I might have looked at someone else and thought the same thing. But when we suffered through things together, when we found a way to get out of the city with you, when we worked so hard to get things up and running at the cabin, it just bonded us together. I saw the good and the not-so-good in her, but I began to see the real her and not just a fake screen with a smile on it that she put up in front of me. Now I still think she is beautiful on the outside, but when I saw the real her, maybe a glimpse of her true soul, it was even more beautiful and I loved her. Like the stars at night, I never grow tired of seeing that glimpse.

Of course, those feelings aren't for every day. Most days having a relationship with anyone, whether you love them or not, is just a lot of work. What is wonderful about a marriage is that nothing else that we can experience on this earth is better at revealing to you how selfish you truly are. It hurts to see the truth about ourselves, but being honest about my own selfishness is the only way I can ever get free of it. The short times we stop thinking of ourselves are the only times we can truly be free, and truly be happy. One part of love is when you can want some other person to have joy, to be at peace, to have comfort and pleasure and fulfillment, more than you want those things for yourself.

That seems easier than it really is. Even when we think we are being selfless in how we are dealing with someone else, those inner motives will come out in the choices we make. Often an act of kindness is only done to feed our own pride, or to assuage our own guilt or, worst of all, to fertilize some sort of sick self-martyrdom, which is really just another twisted form of pride. You can only love someone in a selfless way by accident, unintentionally, without meaning to. You won't even know that you have done it until later, and then the pride can try to work in there again.

So the moments of true love are fleeting and hard to hold onto. Love is a strange thing, rarely seen on this earth, never really done right except by God. The best we can do is to approach it from the side and sneak in for a quick taste. But when we get close to it and can be on the edges of truly loving someone and being loved back, there is nothing sweeter or more satisfying that can ever be experienced in this life.

You might think that the evening I just described to you when Abbie came to me in the cabin would have been the consummation and pinnacle of our marriage, but that would be wrong. As a man, and I think you know what I mean, I loved her more in the weeks leading up to that day than I did that night. I had begun to stop obsessing about making love to Abbie, not because I wasn't attracted to her, but because I just loved her in so many other ways. Maybe she sensed the gradual change in my attitudes and that was what allowed her to let down her walls and open her heart to me. At any rate, I never really thought about what I was feeling until much later, it just happened that way.

When you find Lori, and I am confident that you will very soon, first stop and examine your own heart. Try to make decisions and actions and to speak words that are in her best interest, not just in your own, and not just what might seem to make her happy at that particular moment. And when you want to run away from her, run toward her instead. One thing that I did learn from all this is that you don't really love someone if you don't love them when they aren't loving you back.

So that's it, Jack. I have written a lot more than I intended to. You now know a lot more about me, mostly bad things. I certainly want you to think well of me, but it is always better to know the truth. The very worst things I have ever done, the things I have imagined and been too scared to do, you still don't know. Those same sorts of things are in your mind too, I suspect. I hope that all this has been of some help to you, and I haven't wasted too much of the short time you had inside the city. Most of the time, we think things are in a huge hurry. They really aren't. God works things to happen just when they should and just when we need them, which is usually much later than we would like.

I hope that you and I will see each other again in a very short period of time, but I fear that will not be the case. This is a dangerous thing you and I are doing; most things worth doing are. I think that is still hard for your mother to understand. The pages following are for her to have in case I don't make it back with you. Please don't read them, just deliver them to her. I am confident that you and Lori will make it back safely, and I don't want your mother to read what I have written to her if I am coming back. If I had left it for her, she surely would have read it while we were gone, and it would have just made her worry more.

So, my son, Godspeed. I didn't say good luck because luck is for suckers. In my heart I know that God has planned out this entire adventure in a way only he can do, full of surprises and with a meaning much deeper and far reaching than you and I ever intended when we set out. You are a man now, not a boy at all, and I am so very proud of my son. My strongest desire as I set down my pen is that you will fight this fight before you in the way that God intended and with the strength that only he can give you.

So that was it. Dad had ended the last sentence in the center of the page. I turned the page and read the first sentence: "My dearest Abbie, I am so sorry for the pain that you are feeling as you read this, but I look forward with great anticipation to the day that you will join me once again." I closed the papers and folded them shut. Dad had asked me not to read the rest, and I wouldn't. That was between the two of them. I could close my eyes and see my mother's face before me, stained with tears as I walked up to the cabin alone. I dreaded that look on her face and have never to this day lost the feelings of guilt for taking her husband away from her.

The papers in my hand had been a part of my father. They oozed of his personality, deliberate and ordered, but full of love and compassion and honesty. While I was reading, it was if he were still partially alive and talking to me, giving me advice as he told his story in much the same way he had sprinkled our long hike to the city with stories and nuggets of wisdom. Now that his story was over, his candle was snuffed. He was completely and truly dead to me forever. I wanted to keep reading more, to hear his voice in my head, just to keep him alive for a few more minutes. I opened the papers back up but let my eyes blur instead of reading. I folded the papers and put them back into the plastic bag Dad had put them in before giving them to me. I wanted to cry and to fold up like a child, but it wasn't the right time yet. There was work yet to be done.

I found Davis's little duffle bag in the corner and put Dad's notes inside. It was a little bag, much too small to work for the plan that Dad and I had originally laid out. When he and Mom and I had left CR12, we had used a full-size tool bag, complete with a spare shovel and axe inside. Mom had squeezed inside the bag next to the tools. Dad had walked on one side and I walked on the other, he and I each holding a handle. Mom was light enough for the two of us to carry easily, but it was a bit difficult to balance as we walked. A policeman had actually stopped us on the street and asked us what was in the bag. Dad had been cool as could be and just said, "tools," shaking the bag to make the shovel and axe clank against each other. That was enough to satisfy the policeman and no one said anything else to us, but Mom had reminded Dad more than once how much that little shake hurt.

After Dad's night of temptation (which I had known nothing about at the time), he finally stopped and noticed how much I had grown. For the two days following, he went on and on about how much I looked like his partner McAllister. I guess that was when the plan clicked for him. He brought the bag of tools home the next day, supposedly so he could sharpen them. We practiced carrying Mom inside and just like that the plan was set. That night, the three of us mugged and tied up McAllister in his apartment, stealing his badge and jumpsuit for me to wear as we left the next day. Dad was kind enough to leave a time-delayed e-message on the computer for his supervisor, telling him where they could find McAllister. We walked out of the city, loaded Mom into the back of the truck, drove right out of town and just kept going past the job site scheduled for that day, driving until we ran out of gas. It was surely uncomfortable for Mom in that bag, but she was so excited to breathe real air and look at the sky that she didn't complain a bit when we got out and started walking.

Dad had driven in a direction completely opposite the direction of the cabin with the intent of throwing off anyone who might come looking for us. We picked our way around the searched and demolished perimeter of CR12, sleeping during the day in borrowed houses with each of us taking turns at watch. We walked together on the highways mostly at night.

When we finally made it to my grandfather's cabin, we were pleasantly surprised to find the small community of people already living around it. We had carried the tool bag along with us, filling it with supplies we knew would be hard to find at the cabin. We gladly shared our things with our neighbors, coming out far ahead in the bargain with the help they gave us in that first year.

Looking at Davis's small bag, I knew that I had messed up. This bag was only big enough to carry a small child. Even with the full-size bag, I was probably kidding myself to think that I could have carried Lori by myself. I just shook my head. Nothing had gone according to plan so far, so why should this be any different?

I rummaged through Davis's bag to see what was inside. There was an extra suit of underwear (that would have been useful), a clipboard with some working notes on it, a couple of small screwdrivers, and a chisel. Attached on the front of the clipboard was a smaller handwritten note, kind of a to-do list, but with only two items on it. The first item said, "Get some groceries." That explained the empty kitchen. The second note said, "Date, day 72, 18:00." I looked at the day listed at the corner of the computer screen. Day 72 was today, and the time was tonight since they used military time. I looked at the standard issue calendar with the days listed in rows of five each, set to match the modified work "week" they had created. Day 72 was circled in red, as was a single day in every other row up to that point in that year. His "date" of interest was once every ten days.

I was just pondering to myself why Davis would say "date, day" in his note like that when a knock came at the door. I glanced at the clock, 11:12 it said, this was sure to be Wiley. The morning had passed away without me realizing it. I gathered myself and went to the door, opening it to his smiling face. I surely didn't expect for Wiley to have someone with him. He shook my hand when I opened the door, "You must be John, Jr.," he said.

"Call me Jack," I replied. "You must be the famous Mr. Wiley Fisher."

He stepped quickly inside the apartment and shut the door behind him, holding a small boy by the hand. He patted him on the head and said, "Now go play," handing him a half-dozen unsharpened, yellow, number two pencils from his pocket. The little boy obediently took the pencils and sat in a corner of the kitchen, quietly making shapes and wiggling the pencils in the air as if they were people having a conversation with him and with each other. Wiley and I both stood still, watching him for just a minute before I asked, "Is this your grandson?"

He sat down on the couch as I pulled a chair from the kitchen table. He looked at me and grinned, "How old do you think I am, Jack?" I smiled but didn't answer; it was hard to tell. He answered his own question before I had a chance. "Too old to have a baby boy, I suppose. This is my son, Lucas, and he has just turned two years old last week." At the sound of his name, the boy turned toward his father and smiled. Wiley continued, "I have been praying for someone to come for about six months now, so you are here a bit sooner than I thought you would be."

His words puzzled me for sure, and about ten different questions bounced around in my head. I picked one of them. "I'm sorry, but I didn't come here to see you. I had no idea you would be here. My dad and I had planned on coming here for another reason and you had nothing to do with our plan. How did you get here anyway?"

"You look just like your father, and you talk like him too," he replied. "Of course you didn't plan on seeing me here. It isn't your plan. Not mine either, for that matter." He paused and looked at his son, now back to playing quietly in the corner. "Let me tell you a little story, Jack, and I think that it will answer some of your questions.

"I am guessing that somewhere along the line that John, I mean your father, told you something about how he and I met, or you wouldn't have recognized my name. I went in for my little meeting just after your father, and it didn't go so well for me. They had been onto me for a while, and this was the last straw. I figured they would just snuff me out like they did most older folks or anyone who caused them any trouble. I am not really sure why they didn't; I guess God had something else in mind. Right at the end of the meeting, I was led to small dark room down the hall where I spent the night. Early the next morning, they tied my hands behind my back, put a hood over my head, and led me off to a truck. I didn't hear anyone as I was being led along, but I've always wondered if anyone was watching an old black man being led around the City Building with a hood on his head. Doesn't matter if anyone saw, I suppose, I'll never be back to that place. Anyways, I rode in the back of that truck for the better part of the day, and they didn't let me look around until they let me out here. I figured out later from talking to folks that I was in this CR18 somewhere in South Georgia, but at the time I as well could have been on the dark side of the moon. I did notice that things here are just almost exactly like they were back in CR12. You noticed that too?" I nodded but didn't speak.

Here he paused for a moment, "Could you trouble yourself to get me a glass of water?" I got up and filled a glass, wondering to myself if Lori had been put through the same ordeal and what reason they might have had for moving her. Wiley took a few sips and continued, "Thank you, Jack; you're a good fellow. Anyways, I hadn't been here for just a few weeks when I started back into seeing awake people. I just couldn't help myself from talking to them. Working at the store just makes things all the much better for seeing folks. I reckon I've seen about every person in this city. We started meeting together, but a lot more in secret than we did in CR12 and in a lot smaller groups, no more than six or eight at a time. So far we've appointed about a half dozen group leaders and things are going well. I don't think they are on to us much yet."

He stopped for another drink, but I didn't try to break in with questions. Goodness knows I had a bundle, but he was still in the middle of his story. He gulped twice, paused for a second, and went on. "I guess things moved awfully fast, but I met Lucas's mother the first day I was here. She came into the store, and I could see from a mile away that she was awake. Her eyes just shone; she is a real beauty for an old gal. She and I got married, or at least as married as they let you get in these crazy places, after only a few months. She is a few years younger than me, but she is still too old to be having babies, or so we thought. God likes surprising people a lot; it's just one of his ways."

I couldn't help but break in, "Mr. Fisher, um, Wiley, what does this have to do with me? You said you were waiting for me."

He smiled and looked right through me with his eyes. I almost looked behind me to see what he was looking at. "Jack, I'm getting there. You not going to let an old man finish his story? You got somewhere to be?"

Well, I surely didn't, so I leaned back in my chair and waved my hands for him to continue. He looked over at Lucas again. "You notice what a good little fellow he is? You hear him crying or whining or complaining about anything? Have you been around little boys enough to notice something's different about him?" I looked over at the boy; he hadn't made a sound since they came into the room. Wiley put his hand behind his back and snapped his fingers loudly. Lucas looked at him right away. "There's nothing the matter with his hearing," he said, "and he's plenty smart; he just won't talk. In fact, he won't make any sound at all. It could be lots of things causing it, and so far the ladies at daycare haven't said anything about it, but he is getting old enough for it to be noticed. You and I both know that the folks in charge of this place won't let anyone with any sort of defect go along. He'll be singled out soon for sure."

At that point he stood up and put his hand on my shoulder, looking me right in the eyes, but this time with a softness I hadn't seen from him. "Jack," he said, "if he stays here any longer, they'll kill him. My wife and I have been praying for God to provide some sort of help for six months now. And here you are. I saw the name on the scanner when you walked into the store, and I see the name on your badge right here. You must have done something with Mr. Davis. I don't know how you got in, but I figure you must have gotten out of CR12 somehow and that you are probably planning on getting back out of here too. Am I right so far?"

"Yes, you are," I croaked. "I am leaving the city tomorrow morning first thing." I was beginning to see where this was going. I knew the answer I had to give to his next question before he asked it, but I didn't like it. I didn't come here to do this; this was not the plan. I looked over to where Lucas was playing, right next to the open bag I had just been looking at. I sized him up; he would certainly fit inside. I thought of my father's comparisons of luck and providence. Yes, I knew the answer to his question, so I didn't give him a chance to ask it. I swallowed a dry gulp of air and spoke, "I'll take him with me in the morning. I'll be leaving at six, so have him here before then. Don't ask me how we'll be leaving or where we will be going; it's safer for all of us if you don't know."

Tears welled up in Wiley's eyes, and he turned away from me to wipe them. "You don't know," he said, "what this means to me, what it means to his mother." He gathered himself. "He goes to sleep at twenty-one hundred, I'll bring him over just before then tonight." He paused again, looking me in the eye. "Jack," he said, "raise him up right. Teach him about God as best as you can. Tell him every day that his momma and daddy love him. I can see in your eyes that you have a good heart. You wouldn't be doing this if you didn't. I trust you completely. Let your father help you; he's a good man."

I looked to the ground at his words. "Dad is dead," I whispered. "Davis killed him, and I killed Davis."

Wiley reached out and lifted up my chin. "Don't kick yourself, son," he said. "Desperate times require desperate measures. You did what you had to do, and your dad is a grown man. He didn't come here because you forced him. Now, I'll leave you be. You came here for a reason other than the one I am giving you, and I'll let you get back to it with what time you have left before we come back tonight."

He reached over and scooped up his son and the pencils, making a small grunt noise as he lifted him in his arms. "Getting too old for picking up," he said with another grin as he turned for the door. I came to my senses and the flurry of questions rushed again through my head.

"Wait," I said. "When you were first talking, you said you have seen about everyone in this city. I came here looking for a lady about my age name Lori Applegate. She and I were close friends back at CR12, and I've come here to look for her."

He turned back toward me with a puzzled but compassionate look, searching his mind for names and faces. "I can't say for sure, Jack, but I seem to remember a pretty young girl about your age named Applegate that came into the store a few times early on, maybe about a year after I came here. That name is different enough anyway, but I seem to remember that she had long hair, which is real odd, you know. I didn't attach her face to anyone I saw back in CR12, but you know with the hair, it's hard to say, it could have been her. I could see that she was awake and tried to talk with her and even invited her to our meetings. She would always hang her head and turn me down. Since those first few months, I haven't seen her one time." He stopped and looked at me, his face softening as he saw the pain in my own. "I hope you find her. I should let you get back to looking." He turned back toward the door.

"Wait," I said again. Even more questions were bouncing around my head. The question that came out of my mouth surprised me. "Davis has got an appointment down at the City Building tomorrow for something that I did after I killed him. I don't want to go, I am planning on being gone before then. But something tells me I should go. If I do go, they are sure to know who I am, and they will kill me. I can't go to that meeting, can I? I mean, especially not now, with your son involved in all this."

Wiley stared to the side against the wall, his gaze steeling as he thought. "Jack," he said, "you and your dad didn't pick out Davis—God did. He wanted you to become Davis for his own purposes. It doesn't have to make any sense to us. When you took on his badge and uniform, you became Davis. That appointment is yours now to keep or to break. I won't tell you what to do about that; you'll have to work it out on your own. We live at apartment building five, room two twenty-eight if you need to change your plans. Just bring Lucas back over there if that's what you feel like you need to do, and me and the wife and everybody we can round up on short notice will be praying for you."

Before I could stop him with another question, he had turned and was gone. I had a thousand more questions for him, but I let him get away. I stood there with my mouth open for what seemed like an hour, boiling inside with frustration and confusion, when my legs went weak. I had been standing in front of the chair and now I dropped to the ground and lay down with my face on the floor. "God," I prayed, "what in the world are you doing?" I clenched both my hands into fists and pounded once on the floor. "I don't know what your whole crazy plan is here, but I didn't sign up for any of this. I don't even know this man. Dad only talked with him for ten minutes. How am I supposed to look after a two-year-old who can't even talk?" I unclenched my fists and just lay flat on the floor, letting myself get quiet as the anger subsided. "I suppose you are too big to argue with and you have a better look at things than I do. You've brought me this far, let's just finish this thing up. I sure haven't been getting anywhere without you." And with that I stood up and took a deep breath.

That was the first real honest prayer I suppose I had ever prayed. Not the last to be sure. I felt a little silly laying there on the floor talking out loud with no one in the room, but I couldn't deny feeling a strange sense of peace all the same. I grabbed Davis's badge, jammed my aching feet back into his shoes, and headed out the door with a bit too much spring in my step. I only had a few hours left in the city, but I figured I might as well pick up the cards I had been dealt and see how they played.

I spent the afternoon walking up and down the streets one last time. I went back through the school again and even walked into a few of the factories to look around. I went down to the City Building and found the room where the dreaded review would be held, stopping along the way to explore all the levels of the building, looking into offices and work rooms. I got a lot of odd looks from people, but no one said anything to me. I had a peaceful sort of boldness that I hadn't enjoyed the past two days, but it neither caused me any trouble nor gave up any hints to Lori's location.

I took my last chance at the evening rush hour, but gave up early when the crowd started thinning and went back up to the room about half past five. As I walked in, I saw the computer screen blinking again, reminding me once more about the meeting the next day with the weasel and his gang. "These reminders must be set for every couple of hours," I thought. I hit "accept" again, not really sure if I would be there or not. After I hit the button, a different type of screen came up. This one was a self-reminder, kind of like an alarm clock. Davis must have set it for himself. This one had both "accept" and "reject" boxes under the words, "Date, Entertainment Building, Room 205, 18:00." This time I paused, using the arrow to light up the accept box but not hitting enter just yet. Wiley had said that I had become Davis for a purpose. Maybe taking on his life would somehow lead me to Lori. I accepted the "date" just as I realized I only had a few minutes and a long walk to get there. I went to the bathroom and splashed some water on my face, looking myself over to make sure things were more or less in place before hurrying out the door and down the street to a meeting that I never expected.

CHAPTER 11

"Let your love be strong, and I don't care what goes down."

I would like to say that I saw it coming, but I really didn't. As I walked down the hill one more time, my thoughts were consumed with thoughts of little Lucas. I imagined putting him in the bag, loading him into the seat next to me on the truck, and driving right out of the city. I considered driving in the wrong direction, but thought better of it. I had so far to go that I wouldn't be tipping off my final destination at all by the direction I took. I thought of the long journey ahead and decided that the five or six days of walking I would save by driving would be well worth the risk of being followed.

The review meeting scheduled for the next afternoon also was on my mind. One minute I felt a strange sense of duty to attend, and the next minute I was sure I shouldn't go. If I went to the meeting, I was surely dooming the future safety of Lucas. If I didn't go, I might be passing up a chance to find Lori. I was swaying back and forth between my two choices as I walked along. In a moment of clarity, I decided to give it over to God. *This is too big for me,* I thought as I pushed the button on the elevator. *I will leave it up to you. Your problem, not mine.* And that was that. Part of me was relieved, and the other part felt that I was just using the little prayer as an excuse to dodge the issue. It's strange what you think to be a problem before the real problems arrive.

When I stepped out of the elevator into the hall of the second floor of the entertainment building, the reality of the situation smacked me in the face. The scene before me was almost exactly the same as the hall my dad had described at the entertainment building back in CR12. Even the rug in the center of the floor had the same colors he had described. Wiley must have been onto something when he said that the two cities were the same. I walked down the hall, much more slowly now, and found myself in front of room 205.

I was beginning to realize how foolish it was to have followed through on the appointment. Whatever "date" Davis had planned, the person on the other side of this door would know that I wasn't him. I looked down at the scanner to the side of the doorknob. It read "reserved." I pulled out my badge and paused. I could pretend that I wasn't Davis and that I had just come to the wrong room, but the scanner wouldn't lie. If this woman on the other side of the door wanted to make something out of this, this one move could end the entire journey. *You chose Davis for a reason,* I thought to myself and swiped my badge under the reader. The scanner beeped softly and read "Reserved, 2 hrs" as the door clicked and opened just a crack. I paused again, drew a breath, and pushed the door open just enough to walk into the room, shutting it quietly behind me.

It was a beautiful room that must have once been used by a hotel, small but immaculately furnished. A tall dresser stood in the corner with an antique lamp on top and a square lace doily turned diagonally so that the corner hung just over the edge. The two end tables on either side of the bed and the little desk near the door had the same turned doily and matched the rich dark brown walnut of the dresser. The large king bed had a richly carved headboard and four corner posts that almost reached the ceiling. Two high-backed chairs filled the only empty spaces in the room, with ivory satin upholstery trimmed with gold patterns that matched the heavy drapes on either side of the window. Only the thick plastic that could be seen through the window panes betrayed the fact that I was still within the wretched confines of the city.

I sat in the seat nearest the door, ready to make a run for it if I needed to, still unsure of where this was leading. The light of the bathroom in the rear of the room painted a swath of light on the dimly lit carpet in front of me. The high-pitched whining sound of a hairdryer was reduced from high to low, and a voice called out over the top of the sound. "Mitchell, you're early," she said. "Give me just a few minutes." The hairdryer went back to high, and I could hear it waving it back and forth as she dried her hair. I hadn't heard that sound since I was a young boy, when Mom would fix her hair at our old house. No one had a hairdryer in the city, and we had no electricity at the cabin.

Mitchell, I thought. *That must be what the* M *stood for.* The realization that this was no random date came over me. This woman knew exactly who Davis was and would know immediately that I wasn't him. I looked to the door and considered leaving before she came out.

The hairdryer switched back to low, and she called out again, "Did you work hard today? Can I get you some water?" I didn't know what to say and mumbled a "yes" right before she switched off her hairdryer. I knew she didn't hear me and started to say it again when I heard the sound of the tap water filling a glass in the sink. "Here you go," she said just before she walked into the room. With no sound to mask that last sentence, I recognized the voice as Lori's just before she stepped out into the room.

It is certainly true that your mind can think many thoughts in a terrifically short period of time, but it would be hard to describe the rush of feelings as "thoughts" in that split second between the time I recognized her voice and saw her face. All the blood in my body rushed to my head, and I think I might have fainted if I hadn't been sitting down. I had realized the moment I stepped from the elevator that I was going to a meeting with a prostitute but never dreamed it would be Lori. It made perfect sense, of course. I had scoured every inch of the city, and this was all that was left. When she had met with the city officials that day back in CR12, they hadn't seen the good marks on her school records or recognized her intelligence, they only saw a pretty face and bright eyes. Without thinking twice of it, those men had sentenced her to a prison they would never be able to comprehend. Their only act of mercy was to allow her to be in a place where no one knew her name.

She saw me as she walked into the room and gasped out, "Jack," as she dropped the glass to the floor, putting her hand to her mouth. I instinctively leaned forward in the chair and watched the glass as it fell. It hit the carpet at an angle and splashed water against the wall without breaking. I brought my eyes back up to her face but knew I had lingered too long as I raised my head. She was wearing a tiny negligee that just barely covered her at all. In all the time back at CR12, I had never seen her wearing anything other than the standard issue jumpsuits. For two long years I had wanted nothing more than to see her again, but this was a shocking way to be reintroduced.

When I finally looked again at her face, I saw that she was gripped with a look of horror. She was wearing makeup, which she had never needed, and her mascara was streaked with the tears that were already streaming down her cheeks. She was choking off sobs and grunted as she pulled at the sheets on the bed. I stood from the chair when I realized what she was doing. "Let me help you," I said quietly, and reached to loosen the sheet and bedspread from the end of the bed. She pulled it quickly around herself and sat down on the edge of the bed, shaking all over, sobbing uncontrollably now, and staring at me with her big eyes full of tears.

I wanted to console her and sat on the end of the bed. She shuddered as I drew near her, so I slipped back slowly to sit in the chair. I opened my mouth to talk but really didn't know where to start, so I just sat there looking at her, letting her collect herself and trying to pull myself together at the same time. It is hard to explain how I felt right at that moment. I was looking at a shadow of the person I once knew. She looked much the same as when I saw her last and was certainly as beautiful as ever, but she was not the same, and understandably so. I believe she was still awake, and the light still shone faintly in her eyes, but it had faded from its former brightness. When we were at CR12, she had always had a joy within her that just seemed to flow out to everyone she met. Sitting there wrapped up in the bedcovers, that joy was gone, replaced by a deep sadness that resonated in her sobs.

Suddenly she lifted her head and looked to a small clock on the nightstand next to her. She turned to me with a fearful panic that broke through the tears. "Jack, I don't know if you are real or a dream, but right now you have to go. Mitchell will be here any minute, and you will be found out. They get very upset with me if I don't keep my reservations."

I sat still in the chair without moving, and she looked at me with a puzzled look, waiting for me to explain. I leaned forward in the chair, trying to decide where to start. "Davis is dead," I said. "I killed him three days ago and kind of took over his identity." I held up his badge so she could see the picture. Her eyes fell to the floor and the look of fear on her face was replaced by sadness. Her response surprised me. I have to admit that I wanted her to be grateful to me that he was dead. "Did you care for him?" I asked.

"No!" she said strongly, with an anger I had never heard from her. "No," she said again, less strongly this time with her eyes still toward the floor. "I don't guess I care for anyone anymore, Jack." She reigned in her emotions and tried to regain her composure as she spoke in a flat voice. "Mitchell loved his wife very much. He talked about her a lot. She died about three years ago." I thought back to the picture taped up in Davis's locker; that must have been his wife. She continued, "He was at least not cruel to me. Most of the men are so ... " Her voice trailed off at the end, and she looked back down to the floor, not wanting to make eye contact with me, choking off tears again. "Why did you kill him?" she asked, almost in a whisper.

"We didn't want to," I replied. "Dad and I came here to find you, to take you back with us. We jumped Davis in a home he was marking for demo and tried to grab him. He pulled a gun on my dad and killed him. I just reacted and hit him in the head with a shovel." She looked at me in surprise when I said it. "We never meant for anyone to die," I said quickly. "We were just going to tie him up."

"Came here? You came here?" she said with a puzzled look on her face that stopped the tears for a moment. "What do you mean? How did you and your dad get transferred to the same place? Is your mom here too? Mitchell killed your father?"

"Let me back up a little," I explained. "It wasn't long after they took you away that the three of us escaped from CR12. We left the city and ran away to my grandparents' cabin in the mountains. We found a whole group of people up there living nearby. It's not an easy life, but it's a whole lot better than here. I came to get you out of here and take you back with me." I paused and took a breath. "Lori, you have always meant the world to me. You are the only true friend I have. I've thought about you every waking moment since they took you away. Before we left CR12, Mom found your transfer record and figured out that they sent you here. After a year, I couldn't stand it anymore. I had to come here and try to find you. I wanted you to come back with me. I have been all over this city looking for you for these past three days." I stopped and looked down. "I never dreamed this is where I would find you."

Her face darkened at those words. "I guess you didn't expect that this is what would have come of me?" she said bitterly. "Well, maybe you should just go back home. Maybe I don't want to go anywhere with you."

This was not what I had expected. In all the years I had known her, I had rarely seen her get upset and had never seen her angry, never seen her be anything other than gentle and kind. I knew she didn't mean what she said, but it hurt to hear it all the same. I should have thought before I spoke, but I didn't. "If I had known this is where they would put you," I said in a cold and serious voice, "I would have come sooner. It wasn't easy getting here." It was the wrong thing to say and the wrong way to say it, and I knew it as soon as it came from my mouth.

"Easy," she said through clenched teeth as the tears welled up in her eyes again. "Do you think it's been easy for me? Do you think I have enjoyed what I've been doing? Do you think I was happy when I found out the wonderful career that was selected for me? Do you think it's easy walking down the street and seeing the leering looks of all the hateful men in this city that have come through that door?" She reached up with one hand and pulled the pins that held her hair up on top of her head. It fell around her shoulders as she shook it loose. I had never seen Lori with long hair and felt myself staring at her. "Do you think I look pretty in long hair?" she continued. "Did you know there are only five women in this city who have long hair? Do you think it is easy to see the looks on women's faces when they see my hair? They act like I chose this. I didn't choose to be here. They act like I am a prostitute. I am not a prostitute. These men pay the city, they don't pay me. What little money I have is worthless because I can never buy my way out of this prison cell. I hardly ever leave this room because I am so ashamed to be seen on the street. I sit in here day after day and listen for the sound of that scanner and stare at the door and hope it won't open. I am just as much of a slave as everyone else in this city. Even more so. They stole my life. They killed me."

The light of the fire that had risen in her eyes as she spoke faded to darkness as the words of the last sentence came from her mouth. She stared forward at the wall with a blank and empty look and looked for the moment to have the same sleeping face as everyone else in the city. It was a horrifying thing to watch, and my heart locked in fear within my chest for the few moments before she spoke again. As she sat there silently, her hands were up at her shoulders, kneading the wad of bedcovers she was holding against herself. When she opened her mouth, the words came out with no emotion or feeling, almost in a whisper. "You were always different, Jack—not like all the other men. I saw how you looked at me when I walked into the room. I saw how you looked at me when I dropped my hair. What do you see when you look at me?" She raised her eyes and looked around the room before fixing her gaze on me as she asked the question, "Is this what I've become?"

I forced myself to look down at the floor and was ashamed because I knew in my heart that part of me was guilty of what she had described. I had barely enough time to process and understand what was going on around me, much less to assign to her person the horrifying role she had been cast into. She was truly my best friend in the world, and I had always felt that I connected with her soul on a deep and true level. I had always hoped that she felt the same way toward me. At the same time, I was forced to admit that part of me had always only been looking at her pretty face. Part of me had only cared for her because of what I hoped to receive in return. That part could not be allowed to win the day. I started to speak, but I stopped to gather myself, and I looked her straight in the eyes before answering. "I am not like the other men," I said deliberately. "I came here because I miss you, because I care about you, because I love you."

Her eyes were locked into mine as I spoke, but her face was distant, and she was not really looking at me as she stared. I don't think she even heard what I said as she continued on with the same series of thoughts she had left. "Why shouldn't you see me that way?" she said in a subdued and shaking voice, almost to herself. "Everyone else does." The tears slowly slid down the side of her face, and her bare shoulders quivered as she spoke. "I did love you once. It seems like forever ago. Back in school, there were lots of other boys who were interested in me, but I didn't even want to talk with them. I was waiting for the day that we would get married." She paused to breathe deeply and looked toward the corner of the room. "When they first brought me to this place, I tried to save my heart for you. It was all I had left to give you. I fought as best I could and tried to hold on to the person I used to be. But it was too much, Jack, too much. I don't even know what love is anymore. There is nothing left of me to save for you."

"Please, Lori," I pleaded, "I've come so far to see you. I've missed you so much. Can you please stop talking this way?"

She was sobbing again, and I sat in the chair silently, neither of us looking at the other. I put my head in my hands and struggled to regain my composure. To think that we had come so far and my dad had paid for this moment with his very life, and this was what it was coming to? Things were coming undone. I scanned around the room, not ready to look at her again just yet. A speck of light blue under the corner of the dresser caught my eye. I recognized the color and got up from my chair without thinking. It was the blue bunny I had given her years ago, covered with dust, but still the same. Her face softened a little as she saw me hold it up. "How did you get this here?" I asked as I handed it to her.

She reached a hand from beneath the covers and took the bunny from me. A tiny hint of the sweet smile I remembered teased the corners of her mouth as she looked absently toward the dresser. "I had packed a bag," she said. "They said I should. I forgot to take it with me on the day we walked down to the city building. When I found out I was leaving, I begged them to send someone to go and get the bag from my room until they gave in. All that was in it was the bunny and a note that you had written to me when we were sixteen. They let me keep the bunny but took the note." I noticed that she had slipped her other hand from beneath the cover and was rubbing the ears of the bunny like Jeremy used to—like I used to.

I sat back down in the chair, determined to regain some sort of productive conversation. "How did it end up under the dresser?" I asked.

The smile faded from her face at the question, and her voice got softer as she continued, "When I first got here, I would hide the bunny somewhere in the room with only the ears poking out. Somewhere I could just barely see it and the men wouldn't notice it. When a man was here, I would look at the bunny and try to pretend I was somewhere else." She paused and looked at me, talking clearly now. "I used to dream that you would come back to save me. But you never came, so I finally gave up the dream and threw the bunny in the corner." She looked back down at the bunny. "I am glad you found this, and I am glad you came, Jack, but you can't save me anymore. You're too late."

She stopped talking, and we looked at each other in silence for several minutes. Any hint of a smile was long gone. Thinking back on the moment, I know I should have said something, maybe tried to comfort her, but I couldn't find the words. Lori closed her eyes for a moment and opened them as she continued. "Jack," she said, "most of the girls down here are half crazy or have just checked out from reality, and I don't think I'm far behind them. They operated on me about a year ago, I guess to keep me from getting pregnant. My body just isn't right anymore. A woman knows about herself, you know. I don't feel like I'm the same person I used to be. You see how I'm acting. I don't want to be like this. They gave me pills to take, they made me feel even crazier, and now I just flush them. And there are other things too. Things I could never tell you. Things you don't want to know."

She sat there, thinking to herself for a long while before a look of resolve came onto her face. She stood up from the bed with the sheet wrapped around her and tugged it from under the bedspread, tying it around her chest so it hung around her like a dress. She straightened her back and gathered herself with as much dignity as she could muster and spoke. "I am not the little girl you used to know. The person you came looking for is dead. I know you went through a lot of trouble to get here, but I can't go anywhere with you. It would really be best if you would just leave now and go back home."

"Lori, wait," I said, standing to meet her. "You aren't thinking straight. Let's talk about this. I didn't come all this way to leave you here."

She grabbed me firmly by the elbow and guided me toward the door. I took a step and dug in my heels. "I am terribly sorry about your father," she said. "I suppose you made a tragic mistake in coming here. You really need to leave now." Her voice was serious but unsteady, and she pulled harder at my arm.

I resisted her tugging and turned to face her, shaking loose my arm. She shifted to one side, and I slid along with her, standing to the side of the chair in front of the door. "Please," I pleaded, "can we talk some more about this?" With a move she had probably used more than once, she reached around me with one hand to open the door and shoved me into the hall with the other, shutting the door back quickly while snapping the lock. "Lori, please," I pleaded through the door.

"I have a button," she said in a shaky but deliberate voice. "If I push that button, men will come through that door at the end of the hall, they will find out who you are and what you've done, and you will die. I am counting to twenty, and I expect to hear the bell on the elevator. Now please leave." She started counting up from one in a loud voice, and I rushed to the elevator to push the down button. It was only a few steps, and I ran back to the door. She had counted to six.

I looked down at the scanner next to the door and ran my badge under it. "Lori," I said as I typed on the keypad, "listen to me. Building five, room three eighteen. Building five, room three eighteen." The screen on the scanner read, "Hours reserved?" and I punched the up button as quickly as I could. It stopped at twenty-four hours. The doors opened on the elevator. Lori had made it to seventeen and was counting more quickly. "Building five, room three eighteen," I said one more time through the door and ran for the elevator. I heard a buzzer sound behind me. The doors at the end of the hall opened, and two men ran out with crowbars just as the elevator doors closed in front of me.

It was still daylight when I hit the street and the brightness surprised me. I walked as quickly as I could up the hill, not wanting to look back. There was no crowd of people to hide in this time. I broke into a half-run, hoping not to draw attention to myself. I made it to to the familiar park and slipped behind a bush, crouching to the ground. The two men came up the hill about five minutes later. They looped up by the store and headed past me back down the hill, nudging each other and laughing. I sat there as they went by, ashamed at myself for running away. I buried my face in my hands and rubbed up and down on my forehead, sitting there for a while but not really thinking anything, not sure what to think after what had just happened.

My stupor was broken by the sound of a little girl laughing. It was the same girl and her mother, walking barefoot in the grass. "Why, God?" I said in a whisper. "Why do things have to happen the way that they do? Why do you let people hurt so bad?" I sat in the shadows and watched the little girl. She was so happy, holding her mother's hand. What would her future hold in this wicked place?

I stood quietly from behind the bush and slipped out the end of the park and into the little store without being seen. Wiley wasn't on duty. I had hoped he would be there. I looked at the clock next to the counter. *I'll be seeing him soon enough,* I thought to myself. I didn't know if I could stand any more of his words of wisdom but wanted more than anyone to talk to him about what had just happened.

I found the item I was looking for and paid for it. Davis's account had just enough money left over after I bought the twenty-four hours with Lori. I walked back to the park and tapped the young mother gently on the shoulder. She was startled until she saw my face. "It's you," she said quietly.

I handed her the little jar of peanut butter and said, "For your daughter," as I smiled down at the little girl. "You know," I added as I turned away, "you can breathe the air outside this place, and the grass is pretty much growing out of control."

I didn't look back to see her reaction and went back up to Davis's apartment. I didn't know where else to go or what else to do. I sat on the couch and tried to collect myself. "What now?" I said out loud. I tried to think but couldn't. My brain was toast. I sat on the couch and stared up at the ceiling.

I was jolted from my trance by a knock at the door. *Lori,* I thought, and my heart leapt until I looked over at the clock. "19:59" it read. Wiley was a minute early. I was surprised again when I opened the door and saw a very short lady who looked to be in her mid-fifties holding little Lucas's hand. Her left hand was free, and she held it out to me, squeezing my hand warmly.

"Mrs. Fisher," she said as she looked me in the eyes. "You must be Jack. I insisted on coming and seeing the man who would save my son." She walked past me and into the apartment.

I stood to the side and watched as she found some clean sheets and carefully made the bed in the bedroom, tucking him in gently. She whispered softly in his ear and ran her fingers across his hair as she spoke. I knew the moment was private, and I shouldn't have been watching, but I couldn't pull away. My eyes filled with tears, and I thought of my own mom waiting back at the cabin as I heard her singing softly to him. I don't remember how long it took, but she stayed with him for a while, singing and rocking the little boy gently until he fell asleep in her arms. She looked for the door that wasn't there as she tiptoed from the room.

"He's a good boy, Jack; he really is," she whispered as she came back into the room. "Take this," she said as she handed me a small bag. "There are diapers inside and a few changes of clothes and some food. Wiley tells me you will have all of that you need once you clear the city, but I wanted you to have it just in case." I had never changed a diaper before, and the thought of having to take care of such a young child brought a new kind of fear into my heart. She must have seen it because she patted my arm and smiled reassuringly. "It's not as hard as you might think, son. Just do what you know to be right, and the Good Lord will take care of the rest." She wiped her eyes on her sleeve and gave me a hug. "Thank you," she whispered in my ear. "This means more than you know." And with that she was gone.

I realized that I hadn't said a word the whole time she was there. I looked in at little Lucas sleeping peacefully and thought that she was probably used to that sort of conversation. There were a million things I wished I could have asked her. I wanted very much to go and talk to Wiley about what had happened with Lori that evening. I looked at the clock. It was already past 21:00; walking the street, even to the next apartment building, would be very risky. It wasn't just about me and Lori anymore.

I paced the little living room nervously and as quietly as I could, not wanting to wake the child. I hadn't made but a few laps when the computer screen began flashing again with the appointment reminder. I went to hit the button, but this time it was different. The message read that the review meeting was postponed indefinitely due to scheduling conflicts with Mr. Wigginton. That little encounter in the park had effectively taken that meeting off the table. *Nothing to keep me here now; no reason to go to that meeting anyway,* I thought to myself as I cleared the screen for the last time.

I started my pacing again but stopped, looking at Lucas as I passed by and thinking of how I had left Lori back at her room. I thought of my dad's words, "When you think you should run away, run toward instead." He hadn't been talking about this sort of situation at all. Lori was awake, she was an adult, she had made her decision, and she knew what she was doing. I couldn't force her to come with me. I had told her where to find me. It was her choice now. *Maybe she really doesn't want to come with me,* I reasoned to myself.

I thought of the conversation, argument really, that we had back at her room. It had all gone so fast. Dad had months to work on Mom, but I had only had a few minutes with Lori. Everything I said, everything I had done, had been wrong. I thought back over the last several months. In all the planning on how to get into the city, I had never really thought about what I would say when I found her.

I kept pacing and let my thoughts escape my control. I thought of how she looked as she first walked out into the room. I thought of holding her in my arms and pulling her close to me and then imagined the whole city of men lined up out the door of the room, each waiting their turn with her. The thought disgusted me, and I was ashamed of myself for thinking it. I tried to imagine the hurt and shame she had endured, a pain I knew I would never really understand. I thought of peaceful nights I had enjoyed in a warm bed at the cabin while she had suffered through each night here. I tried to imagine her ever being able to hold me and love me like I had always dreamed and hoped she would and realized that it would probably never be possible. I thought of the children I had hoped we would share and realized that dream would never be a reality either. Everything I had hoped for, the very direction of my life, had been shattered in that fifteen-minute conversation. I am ashamed to admit that part of me wanted to just take Lucas and go back home to the cabin without her. The other part of me couldn't imagine ever living another day if I left her here at this place.

I sat back down on the couch and rubbed my forehead again with my hands. *This is how people go bald,* I thought to myself. I sat on the couch forever, batting thoughts back and forth, fretting and rubbing my head, before I finally stopped. "God," I prayed, bowing my head, "what do I do?" I waited for an answer, listening carefully, but heard no voice. I know now that God usually answers prayers in other ways.

As I lifted my head, my eyes were drawn to the yellow papers peeking from the bag. I thought of all that my dad had been trying to teach me about what love really means. I remembered his words: "You don't really love someone if you don't love them when they aren't loving you back." I knew that he was right, but I also knew that it was going to be very hard. What had taken Dad months with Mom would probably take years with Lori. There was a good chance that we would never be able to share the love that he described, the love that I had hoped for. I could work my entire life and never break through the darkness that had clouded over her soul. What was most likely to happen was that I would have my hopes shattered and my heart broken again and again. It was a mountain that seemed much too high to climb.

"But," I said out loud, "this is the path that has been chosen for me; this is the reason I am here. I was made to love her. If I only love her for what I hope to get in return, then it isn't really love. If I use up all of my life and all of my heart to reawaken the joy in her soul for just one minute, it will be a life well spent." Hearing the words spoken out loud sounded foolish, but I knew it was true. *I'm going back to her room,* I thought, *because there is no other place for me to go.* I stood from the couch and straightened my back, resolving that I would bring her home with me, whether she wanted to come or not.

I looked in at Lucas sleeping again. *Even if he wakes up,* I thought, *he won't hurt himself and he can't cry out.* Just to be sure, I flipped the kitchen table on its side as quietly as I could and blocked off the bedroom door. I looked again at the clock; hours had passed in my pacing, and it was already after midnight. *If I get caught,* I thought, *Lucas might never be found.* His parents didn't expect to ever see him again. I hesitated, but only for a moment. *If I get caught,* I decided, *I will just tell them where he is and who his parents are and say that I stole him.* It seemed like a good enough plan, and I grabbed up the badge and locked the door before I could change my mind again, stepping out into the darkened hall.

The hall seemed darker than usual, and it was hard to see. I made my way to the door at the top of the stairs and stopped. What would I say when I got there? Would they even let me back into the building at this hour? Would the two guys still be looking out for me? I was afraid. There was a lot to lose. Wiley and his wife were depending on me. Mom had already lost so much, and she would have no one left if I died too. She would never get to read the papers Dad had written to her. I knew that everything I was thinking was just an excuse. It was my fear of facing her again, my fear of being rejected that was holding me back. "I will try to love her," I whispered to myself in the dark, "even if she can't love me back."

I stepped into the stairwell and realized why the hall had seemed darker than usual. Someone had turned off the light that was usually on at the bottom floor landing. The stairwell was pitch black, even darker than the hall. I grabbed onto the handrail to get my bearings and started down. At the first turn, I felt something different in the air around my body. I didn't hear anything, didn't see anything in the dark, and nothing touched me. Somehow I felt like someone or something was there. I froze and turned around, determined not to be afraid, listening for anything but hearing only my heart beating in my throat.

"Jack?" a small voice said weakly from the corner, "Please be you."

I bent toward the voice and grabbed the person by the shoulders, trying to see their face in the darkness. I knew when I touched her that it was Lori. "Yes," I said, "it's me."

"I changed my mind," she whispered. "I want to go with you. I found the building, but I couldn't remember the room number. I was going to wait here for you until morning." She reached out to find me in the dark and put both hands on my cheeks. "Jack," she said, "you came looking for me. I'm glad you came looking for me."

"How could I ever leave you here?" I said. "I told you that I love you." I grabbed both of her hands and pulled her to her feet. "Now come on; let's go." She put her hand on my shoulder, and I led her up the dark stairs and hall back to the apartment.

When we got into the light of the kitchen, I could see that she had put on a gray jumpsuit. She had washed the makeup from her face and cut her hair as short as I had ever seen it. She looked more beautiful now than she did in the hotel room. She looked like she did before. "You look great," I whispered, "just like the Lori I've always known." I was smiling when I said it and looked at her eyes, hoping for some sort of response. There was still only sadness.

"Jack," she said, dropping her eyes to the ground as she spoke, "I am not the person you used to know. What you did, coming all this way." She paused, tears filling the corners of her eyes. "You're a good guy, Jack. You deserve better than me. My life is wasted now. I've got too many issues." She paused again and almost smiled, but didn't. "I guess you figured that out tonight. I'm sorry for how I acted back at the room. I pushed you away because I wanted you to just go back home and have a normal life. Well, as normal of a life as anyone can have these days. I should've just let you go, Jack. I shouldn't even be here. I just couldn't bear the thought of staying in that room another night." She looked back at me, her eyes glassy with tears but serious and pleading as she spoke. "If you came here to rescue who I used to be, then you got a bad deal. You are under no obligation to take me with you. I'll just go back to the room, and you can go home to your family. I'll understand if that's what you want to do."

She had spoken the last sentence in a normal voice, and I put my finger on my lips and led her to where she could look in on Lucas sleeping. She had a confused look on her face as we stepped backward quietly away from the door. "We don't have to figure all this out tonight," I whispered. I looked at her and smiled. "I definitely want you to come. I want it more than anything in the world. We can talk more about serious things later. Trust me; you'll need your sleep for tomorrow morning. Come and rest."

I laid a pillow on the end of the couch and motioned for her to lie down. She sat down and looked toward the door. "Do you think they will come looking for us?" she said with a worried look on her face.

"If they do, they'll have to come through me," I said as I grabbed the other pillow from the couch and sat in the floor with my back to the door. We sat quietly in our respective seats just looking at each other for a few minutes. I watched her shoulders slowly relax and her breathing become more regular.

Finally, she turned sideways and curled into a ball, laying her head on the pillow. She pulled the blue bunny from her jumpsuit and began to rub its ears. "Jack," she whispered, "tell me about where we are going. I want to know what it's like."

And so I did, whispering in a low voice and telling her whatever came to my mind, remembering details of the cabin and the people that lived around us, listing off the dinners Mom had cooked, trying to remind her how the air smelt in the springtime and how it felt to wade in a stream. I talked and talked about chopping wood and shucking corn and stopping to look at the stars at night. My throat was getting raspy from all the whispering. She shuddered twice and then relaxed. I heard her slow breathing when I stopped to swallow and knew she was asleep.

I sat in that same spot in the floor and stayed awake for what was left of the night. I should have gotten some rest, but I couldn't slow down my brain. I was planning out our escape, running through the details in my mind over and over again. In the midst of the worrying and planning, a strange sense of peace was coming over me. It was good to be near her; it was good to watch her sleep, to look at her face. Only in her sleep could she let go of the burdens she was carrying. She almost looked like herself again—almost, but not quite.

I thought back to the embrace we had shared on the steps of the city building back at CR12. If only I could have taken her away before that day and saved her from all she had been through these last two years. In a way, Lori was right about one thing: the innocent young woman I held in my arms on those steps was gone for good. When we said good-bye that day, we said it forever. But then I wasn't the same person she used to know either. I'd changed more than she knew.

So it was like we were starting over again. Neither of us could claim a clean slate, but at least we had a new day that could be better than the day before. I thought with a smile of how far the two of us had come and how much further we still had to go. The next day would be a day to remember, that was for sure.

CHAPTER 12

"I want out of this machine. It doesn't feel like freedom ...
I want to live and die for bigger things.
I'm tired of fighting for just me."

I wasn't really sleeping, just drifting a bit, but it jerked me out of the fog I was in when I felt my chin bouncing off my chest. I could feel the soreness in my back as I leaned forward off the door. I looked between the rungs of the chair in the kitchen to read the numbers on the clock over the stove: 04:13. Time to get going. I pushed myself up from the floor as quietly as I could, watching Lori closely as she slept to make sure I wasn't disturbing her. This day was by far the most dangerous she and I would face, but just having her back with me again erased any fear I should have felt. As I watched her sleeping, I wondered to myself if her dreams were sweet or full of darkness.

I was able to slide away the table that was blocking the door to the bedroom without waking either Lori or Lucas and quickly found the sheets folded neatly in the corner where Mrs. Fisher had left them when she changed out the bed the night before. That moment already seemed like ages ago. Looking out the window, I estimated that I would need about twenty to thirty feet of rope to get Lori to the ground. I grabbed up the fitted sheet also.

I stepped into the bathroom and found the scissors on the window sill where I had left them. I opened the window as wide as it would go and peered down to the ground below, convincing myself that thirty feet would work fine. I took the sheets and scissors back to the living room and sat down to my work, cutting strips in the sheets about four inches wide, concentrating to try and keep them all the same size. When I had cut up both sheets, I tied the strips end to end, measuring out three lengths of thirty feet by assuming the spread of my arms to be six feet. I tied one end of the three lengths together and began to try unsuccessfully to weave them into a braid. I huffed in frustration at myself, too loudly, and looked up at Lori to see if I woke her. She was looking back at me with no sign of sleep in her eyes. She must have been watching me work for a while.

"What are you trying to make?" she asked, propping herself up on one elbow.

"A rope," I replied, "at least, it is supposed to be a rope."

She sat up from the couch and took the strips of sheet from me, quickly unraveling what little I had done. "My dad taught me to braid ropes for our horses when I was a girl. Just hold this and keep some tension in it when I get started," she said, handing me back the knotted end. She rolled the three strands into three balls and began to weave them around each other, her face gripped in concentration. In just a few minutes, she was done. With a look of satisfaction, she whispered under her breath, "Dad would be proud."

I stood on the chair and lifted the new rope as high as I could, letting it hang to one side of me. Hold onto the rope," I said. She was thin as a rail, but of course I couldn't pick up her full weight in that position. All the same, the strips of sheet didn't tear at all and the knots didn't pull loose. I needed a better test. I wrapped it around two legs of the couch and sat on the floor. With my feet pressed against the front of the couch, I pulled as hard as I could on the rope while pushing with my legs. It was hard to tell how much tension I was putting on the rope, but it surely seemed like more than what she weighed. I tested the rope along its length, trying out each knot. I wasn't sure if it would be strong enough, but when I looked at the clock again it read 5:12. This would have to do.

I hadn't noticed, but Lucas was awake and had slipped over to the corner of the room, watching my strange experiment. His eyes lit up when I handed the rope to him, but he immediately stuck it in his mouth and started gnawing on it. *Not what Mrs. Fisher would want him to be doing*, I thought to myself as I emptied the few contents from Davis's bag.

He was so contented with his chewing that he didn't object when I picked him up and laid him inside the bag. I saw the fear in his eyes as I took the rope from him and zipped it up. If he could have, he surely would have cried out. I needed to know what he would do, so I went ahead and picked up the bag with him in it and walked around the room. He began thrashing his arms and legs. "Stop it, Jack, you're freaking him out," Lori pleaded.

I set down the bag and unzipped it enough for him to pull out his head and shoulders. Lori immediately bent over him and began to hug him and whisper in his ear, stroking his hair gently with her hands. I looked at the clock again; we needed to leave in fifteen minutes. "Lori," I said, "I think I have a way to get us out of here, but I am going to need you to trust me." I proceeded to describe my plan to her in quick steps, giving her the basic overview.

She continued to hold and pet Lucas while she drank in every word. When I finished, the blank stare from the night before had come over her face. "I can't do this," she said. "You should just take Lucas and go without me."

I looked over my shoulder to the bedroom window. It was still dark, but the first hints of light would be breaking through soon. I could hear the sound of showers coming on and people moving around in the apartments around us. We needed to leave now to beat the crowds. I stepped in front of Lori and squatted down to the level where she was sitting so I could look straight into her eyes. "Lori," I said, "I am not going anywhere without you. This will work, I promise." I stopped and looked down at Lucas hanging half out of the bag and laying across her lap. "Do this for Lucas. I need you to help me with him. I can't do it without you."

She looked down at the little boy in her lap and shook the empty stare from her face. I could see the resolve building within her. She reached over and took the blue bunny from the couch and put in his arms. "Help me tie him," she said, gathering the leftover strips of sheet. "It's the only way." She gently turned him onto his side and tucked him into the fetal position, leaving the bunny in his arms. We wrapped three or four strips around his arms, tying them loosely, but in a way that he couldn't wiggle much. I tucked Dad's papers to one side of him and wrapped up what food I could grab in the leftover strips of sheet, stuffing the wads on each side of him, careful to keep things away from his face so he could breathe. His eyes were gripped in fear and tears rolled down his cheeks, but Lori kissed him on the forehead and whispered quietly to him as she slowly zipped the bag up, leaving the last inch of the zipper open. "Be gentle with him," she implored before grabbing the rope and hurrying toward the bathroom.

I looped the braided sheet around her waist and tied a knot in it as best as I could. "Hold on to the knot with one hand and to the rope up higher with the other," I suggested, not really knowing what was best myself but trying to sound confident. "Try to use your feet to kind of walk on the wall, but watch out for the windows. There will be two other bathrooms right below us, and people are already getting up." She nodded, trying to look confident, but I could see the fear in her eyes. She climbed up to sit on the window sill. "Wait," I said, grabbing the knife that I laid aside to the sink, "you'll need this if the plastic is attached at the bottom."

She took it from me and started to put in her pocket before changing her mind and stabbing it between the braids in the rope a few feet above her top hand. "Please don't drop me, Jack," she whispered before swinging her legs around and crawling out of the window.

I braced myself against the wall and let her down as slowly as I could, surprised at how hard it was to hold on to the rope. In just a few seconds the rope went slack, and I knew she had made it safely to the ground. She tugged twice on the rope, and I pulled it up quickly, hoping no one in the floors below had noticed it dangling. I stuck my head out the window and saw her standing below in the gap between the wall and plastic, holding the knife against the canopy. I wanted more than anything to yell out to her but was forced to watch in silence. She pushed the knife through the plastic and cut a slit about four feet long before silently disappearing into the darkness. It was an act of unbelievable bravery on her part, and I wanted to cheer and clap, but there was no time. I shut the window as quietly as I could, whispered one last word of encouragement to Lucas through the bag, and hurried out the apartment door for the last time.

The streets were empty when I stepped onto the pavement. I was still ahead of the morning rush. I resisted the temptation to stick my head into the convenience store to see if Wiley was there and just walked as quickly as I could toward the bottom end of the city. Lucas wiggled a little as I walked along, but no one was out on the street to see it. They probably wouldn't have noticed even if it was the middle of rush hour. I cringed at the sight of the entertainment building, but immediately put away the events of the previous night as I opened the door leading to the locker room.

By now Lucas was still. *I hope he's asleep or at least settled down a little,* I thought to myself, worried that he might have gone into shock or passed out from lack of air. Despite my fears, I was thankful that he wasn't wiggling as I stood with my back to the woman in the green uniform in the office next to the computer. *Why is she here already?* I wondered to myself, hoping that she hadn't come in early to catch Davis before he went out. I was a lot more nervous than I had hoped to be, but I was able to scan my badge and get the day's assignment. *Good,* I thought as I read the screen in front of me. *He's got a new truck, and he's scheduled for another solo. Maybe things will work out for a change.*

I clocked in and logged off the screen, picking up the bag again and walking away from the green lady into the empty locker room. I remembered Davis's locker number and walked over to it, trying hard to act nonchalant even though no one was watching. A clean, blue uniform hung inside the locker with the picture of Davis and his wife still taped to one side. The thought of him with Lori mixed with the image of his body lying in a pool of blood next to my father. I turned away from his picture and shut the door to the locker, hoping that his face would one day fade from my memory.

I dressed efficiently into the light blue inspector's uniform, going over each step and snap in my mind as Dad and I had rehearsed them. Davis's boots fit much better than his shoes. It was good riddance to leave them behind. I remembered to flip on the little exhaust fan this time when I was done sealing off the hood. I picked up the bag with Lucas inside and walked through the air locked doors of CR18 into the real world. I had only been inside for three days, but it felt like a lifetime. So much had changed in only a few days. *Truck seventeen,* I reminded myself as I walked through the parking lot. The crunching of the gravel under my boots sounded hollow and distant through my hood. Lucas wiggled in the bag. He was getting his first breaths of real air.

I found the truck and slipped into the cab, setting the bag on the seat beside me and unzipping a few extra inches before shutting the door. The key was in the ignition and I turned it to the "on" position, pausing as the air pumps whooshed out the good air and pumped in the stale. I considered taking off my hood, but thought I might wait until I passed the guard post at the gate. The sinking realization that I didn't know how to drive came over me as I turned over the ignition and started up the engine.

I rifled through the files of information in my mind, looking for the instructions Dad had given me on driving before we left. I closed my eyes and remembered sitting in the cab of the old pickup truck in the field next to the cabin. As I opened my eyes again, I saw familiar markings on the dashboard. I found the lever on the side of the steering wheel and pulled it roughly so that the light switched from *P* to *R*. The truck lurched backward faster than I thought it would, and I fished around the floorboards with my boots, finally finding the brake pedal. I shoved it to the floor, jerking the truck to a stop in a shower of gravel. So much for a quiet exit.

I held my foot on the brake this time before shifting the lever back to *D,* easing off slightly as the truck crept forward in a crawl. Steering was easy at this speed, and I rolled past the guard house as smoothly as I could, too slow, I knew, but trying not to draw any more attention than I already had. The paved road leading away from the city was intersected by the perimeter road much too close to the guard house for my comfort. I had to turn and tried to do so nonchalantly, but I saw a set of eyes watching me in the window as I drove past the guard house back onto the gravel road that went—I hoped—all around the perimeter of the city.

I was breathing heavily already, and my visor fogged up in spite of the fan. I unsealed the hood and pulled it from my head, trying to keep my eyes on the road as I accelerated as much as I dared. The perimeter road was elevated and narrow, much too narrow for someone who didn't know how to drive. There was a shallow ditch on the side near the city and a much deeper ditch on the other side bordered by high weeds and overgrown bushes. I was struggling to keep the truck in the center of the road and backed off the gas a little—wrecking would stop us before we even got started. I had never seen the outside of the city from this direction, and it was hard to get my bearings. The dawn was just beginning to break, and I could barely see the outline of the buildings through the thick plastic. The road suddenly bore to the left, swinging out wide around a protruding wall that let me know I had made it to the apartments. I eased onto the brake as best as I could and slowed to a crawl, counting buildings and windows and looking for Lori.

I quickly found building number five and rolled to a stop in front of the slit Lori had made in the plastic. I shifted into P, letting off the brake slowly until I was sure the truck wouldn't take off without me. I saw a break in the weeds and looked down to see Lori sitting at the foot of the slope, staring straight up. I slid about halfway down into the ditch and offered my hand to her. "What were you doing?" I asked as we climbed back up to the road and got into the truck.

"I hadn't seen the sky since I was a girl. I had forgotten it was so high," she said. She unzipped Lucas and untied him, pulling him into her arms before shutting the passenger door. I remembered to step on the brake before putting the gear into drive, and we took off back around the perimeter road. Lori looked back over her shoulder, and I stole a glance at the mirror. We could both see the dust rising back near the guard house. "What's that?" she asked.

"They're after us already," I said as I pushed on the gas, driving faster than I was comfortable going on the winding gravel road. "Watch them for me," I said. She didn't answer right away, and I glanced toward her. She was hugging Lucas against her and had braced her feet against the dash. Her eyes were wide with fear as she pointed ahead. We had looped around to the other side of the city and were barreling down the hill on a long straightaway toward the paved road that would lead to our freedom. A large yellow dump truck was being moved into place to block the road just before it widened out to pavement. I looked back up at the mirror; there were three trucks right behind us. It had seemed like such a good plan the night before.

"Hold on," I yelled as we approached the dump truck at full speed. Lori had closed her eyes and gritted her teeth. I thought just for a second that we probably should have buckled our seatbelts. Just before we would have hit the dump truck, I yanked the steering wheel to the right where the ditch seemed shallower. We swerved off the road and bottomed out hard. Even with all her bracing, Lori's head hit the roof of the cab. I was holding onto the steering wheel, but we slammed against each other at the impact. I struggled to get my feet back around the pedals as the truck bounced through the ditch onto the gravel road coming from the other side. I thought I had the brake, but hit the gas instead. The truck's wheels dug into the gravel and found enough grip to shoot us out onto the pavement. We whipped behind the dump truck, and I grabbed both hands on the wheel just in time to avoid going off the other side of the road. I checked the rearview mirror and could barely see the first truck that had been following us dipping slowly down into the ditch. We were clear, for the time being, and with a bit of a head start.

I looked over at Lori. She was rubbing her head and breathing hard. She looked at me like I was insane. "I told you to hold on." I grinned and looked back at the road ahead of me. I knew I wanted to go north and east, and the rising sun was to our right. *Good for us,* I thought. *Somebody's on our side today.* We were on a main road and heading in the right direction. Lucas was unhurt but would have been crying if he could. Lori just stared straight ahead, clearly afraid, still bracing herself with her one free hand, turning to look over her shoulder at the three trucks lining up on the road behind us. I was afraid, yes, but exhilarated also with the rush of adrenaline at having cheated death.

The plastic dome of the city was still in the rearview mirror when the speed limiter kicked on and fixed the truck's speed at forty-five miles per hour. I pressed hard on the gas, but it was locked into place. Dad had included the limiter in a list of a hundred other things, but I had forgotten about it. I checked the rearview mirror, looking longer at it than I should have and nearly weaving off the road. I finally convinced myself that the trucks behind us were not gaining. I just hoped their forty-five was the same as ours.

The ring of destroyed buildings around the city roughly formed a radius of about forty miles. Dad had told me that each morning the trucks were filled with just enough gas to get to the job site and come back to the city that evening. By that figuring, we should have been able to drive eighty miles before running out of gas, while the trucks chasing us would only want to go half that far. They might send out another truck after us, but we could surely be hidden somewhere before they caught up to us. I checked the odometer and looked at the clock on the dash. This just might work.

We had found the interstate highway going north and rode steadily on at our limited speed for a half hour, not saying much to each other, constantly checking the progress of our pursuers. The straight road and steady speed made driving a lot easier for me and riding a lot easier for my passengers. Lori rocked Lucas gently in her lap, occasionally whispering something reassuring in his ear. The fear on their faces had faded somewhat, and I caught both of them staring out the windows at the sky above and the mesh of trees and bushes lining the roads. I had forgotten how long it had been since Lori had seen the real world. Her last glimpses were likely from a bus window on the way to CR12 as a newly orphaned little girl.

My confidence had been rising steadily as the miles piled up, but my fears took back over when Lori broke the silence. "What is that?" she asked, twisting herself around to get a better look out the back window. I looked in the mirror and then over my shoulder and saw an orange van gaining quickly on the three trucks.

I remembered more warnings from Dad. "It's the recovery crew," I explained. "They send it out after anyone who is lost—or who has escaped." They obviously did not have a speed limiter and would be overtaking us any minute, but I didn't say that out loud. "We are going to have to go to plan B," I said as I skidded off onto the exit ramp without touching the brakes.

The van was now in front of the other three trucks. It was turning onto the top of the ramp as we hung a sharp right at the bottom. "Their speed won't help them much in here," I said as we turned down a side street. I was trying to act confident, but I don't think Lori believed the act any more than I did.

"What do we do when they catch us?" she asked as she pulled Lucas close to her. We were sliding all over the road, and she was trying to brace herself again. The van had closed the gap completely and was just a few feet off our back bumper.

"Hold on," I said through clenched teeth and swerved onto a side road at the last instant. The truck skidded and crow hopped but didn't flip, and I mashed the gas again once all four tires were back on the road. The van had missed the turn, and I saw them backing up in the rearview mirror. I was still working on Plan B in my head but went ahead and took the first side road we came to. From the rows of driveways leading to demolished heaps of former houses, I could tell we were in some sort of subdivision. I took the third driveway we came to and skidded to a stop behind a row of trees. I could just see the orange van driving slowly past the road we had taken.

"We've lost them for a minute," I said, rolling the truck slowly up the driveway, trying to size up the area around us. I looked over at Lori. "When we find a place to stop, we are going to have to hit the ground running. I'll carry Lucas, and you use the bag to help you get through any briars, okay?" Her eyes were saying no, but she nodded in agreement. I drove the truck past the rubble of the house and into the bushes as far as I could before the wheels started spinning in the weeds and mud. We were able to kick open Lori's door, and we plowed together through the undergrowth for only a few feet before coming out into open space beneath some trees.

There was another road ahead of us with more bushes between, and I turned around to shield Lucas and forced my way through the bushes with my back, Lori following close behind. I looked to the right and left as we crossed the road and saw no one. I could hear the sound of the truck engines driving up and down the roads in the subdivision as we ran down the driveway on the opposite side of the road. I found a gap in the growth at the back of their yard and pushed through it into a long space with no roads or houses.

This was the end of the subdivision. We were in a huge stand of tall pine trees with only a scattering of undergrowth around us. It was easy to run through, but afforded nowhere to hide if someone else joined us beneath the canopy. We were still heading north, by my reckoning, and I could see a long fence to our left and up a hill, probably an old barrier for the interstate right-of-way. I came to an open patch where I didn't need to weave between the trees, and I shifted Lucas to one side and glanced over my shoulder. Lori was bent over and waving one arm at me, about twenty yards behind us.

I hadn't thought of the fact that she would be terribly out of shape. When I got to her she had her head between her knees, gasping for air. "Stand up," I said. "You can't breathe that way." She stood up with a pained and pleading look on her face, still searching for oxygen. "We'll slow down," I conceded, "but we have to keep moving." I knew from my dad that the rescue crew was more like a hit squad; they were on orders to shoot all three of us at sight. I didn't think it would help to tell Lori.

She found her wind after a few minutes, and we jogged slowly. The end of the trees was ahead of us, and I looked one more time behind. We had probably covered about a mile since leaving the truck and had seen no one yet. I could hear the sound of loud speakers far behind us. "If we can get just a little farther, I think we'll get away," I said, trying to encourage Lori. She was gripping her side, obviously in pain, as she struggled along.

There was a thick layer of bushes in front of us, and I traded Lucas for the bag, using it to try and push back the briars. She led him by the hand, and we broke through into the bright sun-light onto a shoulderless two-lane road, nearly running into a light blue truck parked in front of us.

A man in a matching blue suit stood in the bed of the truck and pointed his gun in my face. His words came muffled out through his hood. "How is it you can breathe the air out here?"

I was shocked enough to see him there, and his question surprised me all the more. His tone of voice was neither superior nor aggressive. He asked the question as if he really wanted an answer. It wasn't the sort of thing someone would ask if they were about to shoot you. I decided to take a chance. "There's nothing wrong with the air," I said, trying to smile as I spoke.

"Look at how we are huffing and puffing from all the running. You can breathe it too. Take off your hood if you want to."

I could see his black eyes studying me through the visor, trying to gauge if I was to be trusted. He reached for the seals around his hood with one hand, still holding the gun near my face with the other. I considered for an instant trying to grab the gun away from him but thought better of it as he slowly pulled the hood from his head. He stared into my eyes and drew a deep breath and then another as a smile bent up the corners of his mouth. He was a young man, not much older than Lori or me, with a dark clump of hair messed into a wad by his hood.

I stuck out my hand to him with a smile. "Jack Wilson," I said. "Welcome to the real world."

He shoved his gun back into his pocket and shook my hand. "George Rivera," he answered. "I always thought they were lying." He paused and looked back up the road listening for something. "Where you running to?" he asked.

"Away from here," Lori answered. "Come with us." It wasn't what I wanted her to say, but it wasn't a bad idea. If they found him talking to us without his hood, he would be killed along with the three of us.

"I can't," he said as he looked down at Lucas standing next to Lori. "I can't leave my wife behind. She is all I have left." I smiled and thought of how Lori and I might have found a way together if she had stayed in CR12. George stepped down from the truck and looked me in the eye. "Jack," he said, "wherever you're going to, come back for me and my wife."

I could hear the sound of a truck coming up the road. "I'll try," I said, reaching for Lori's arm and nodding at her to pick up Lucas. We started to move toward the bushes on the other side of the road, but George reached out and grabbed me firmly by the arm.

He looked me in the eye, but it wasn't a look of a threat, or even of fear, but the look of one man to another man when he means serious business. "Don't say you'll try," he said. "Promise me you will."

I looked him back in the eye. This time it was my turn to gauge his character. "I promise to come back for you, George," I said. "I don't know when, but I will—I promise you." He released his grip on my arm, and we disappeared into the bushes just as another light blue truck skidded to a stop behind the first. George was left standing in the middle of the road with his hood in his hand and his head uncovered. We crouched in the bushes and watched, hoping we hadn't been spotted and terrified at the scene that played before us.

The second man stood from his truck, pulled out his gun and pointed it at George. "Rivera," he said gruffly, "I always had my doubts about you. Tell me where they are before I kill you." He touched a button on the side of his belt and talked into his hood as he walked forward. "They are in the northwest quadrant. Send up reinforcements." George just stood there silently, not moving to put his hood back on, not looking from side to side for an escape, not showing an ounce of fear as the man walked toward him with the gun, placing the barrel on his forehead.

I saw him slip his finger over the trigger and could see the muscles in his face tighten as he prepared to fire. Lori whispered in my ear. "Jack," she said, "we can't let him die!"

I had decided what to do before she spoke. I set down Lucas next to her and was out of the bushes before she finished her sentence. "Hey!" I yelled. "You looking for me?"

The man stepped back and lowered his gun as he turned toward me. I didn't realize that Lori had stood up in the bushes behind me. The man looked over my shoulder at her standing there. He paused for a minute and then laughed. "You?" he sneered. "Who let you out of your little cage? I was planning on coming to see you again soon."

I glanced back to see Lori cringing at the words as she sank back deeper into the bushes. As he was speaking, I circled slowly down the road to draw his fire away from her. The man followed me, pointing his gun towards my head as he walked. I had one thought—to break his neck before he shot me enough times to put me down. I walked toward him, watching his finger on the trigger. I could see the muscles in his hand tighten and the same tension in his face, and I ducked and bolted toward him just as he fired the gun.

I heard the sound of the retort and then another closely following and felt one bullet rip through my left shoulder, spinning me half around and nearly knocking me off my feet. I put my hand to the ground to catch myself and dove forward into his midsection, tackling him to the ground. I rolled over and got to my knees, pinning his body to the ground with my right hand on his throat when I noticed the hole on the side of his hood. His arms hung limp by his side. I pulled off his hood and saw a bloody mess on one side of his head. His eyes stared up at me blankly. I turned and looked in the direction of the second gunshot and saw George facing us with his arm still raised and the gun pointed forward. "Is he dead?" he asked as he lowered the gun and walked toward me.

"I'm pretty sure he is," I said, pushing to get up off my left arm and sitting back down as I realized how much my shoulder hurt. George reached out his hand and helped me up. I squeezed his hand as we stood. "You saved my life," I said as Lori ran up to us with Lucas in her arms. "You saved all of our lives."

"Maybe I was just saving my own," George said, but added with a grin, "Now you owe me. You have to keep that promise." He paused for a minute and looked down the road. "You guys had better get going; more of them will be coming soon." He reached over and picked up his hood and handed me his gun. "Take this," he said. "It will be like you shot him. There is some rope in the cab of the truck, tie me up." He stopped and thought and smiled as he spoke, "Even better, take the truck. That'll give you a good head start."

Lori had already grabbed the rope from the truck, and we looked at each other with wonder as she handed it to me. I handed it back to her and took the gun from George. "You tie better knots than I do. Make it look real." I pulled at his badge on his uniform as he was sealing off his hood and quickly read his apartment number out loud three times, trying to burn the numbers in my mind.

As Lori tied his hands behind his back, I looked at him through the visor. It was a look that I hadn't shared since my dad decided to go with me to look for Lori all those months ago. It was a look of two men that understood each other. "You guys had better get going," he said with a smile. "Remember your promise."

"You're awake," I said to him as I helped him sit down. "Go to the little store early in the morning, and keep your eyes open—and watch your back."

"Jack," he said as I started to walk away, "That was the first time I ever fired a gun. No way I'm hitting him with one shot like that. You must be the luckiest man on the earth."

Lori and Lucas were already in the truck, and she was waving for me to hurry from the back window of the cab. I looked down at George. " Luck is for suckers."

I ran and jumped in the truck, and we sped off, leaving George sitting tied up in the middle of the road. "God is good," I said, almost to myself.

"Sometimes, I guess," Lori replied quietly.

We stuck to the back roads for the next hour, always trying to stay near the interstate and always working more or less to the north, not seeing anyone the whole time we drove. We were clearly outside the perimeter of demolished buildings when we ran out of gas. We pushed the truck down a little hill into some bushes on the side of the road, hiding it better than I hoped. I considered taking some time to try our luck at a few gas tanks, but decided against it. The clothes and food they had left behind when they rounded up the people, but the gas they collected to the last drop. Lori was exhausted, and it was tempting to stop and rest, but I knew we needed to cover some more ground before nightfall. We stayed within sight of the interstate to keep our bearings, walking on side roads until well past sunset, still seeing no one.

The moon had risen, and it was already getting cold when I saw a single set of headlights coming up the interstate from the south. "Sit down and be still," I said. "That is their last runner." We watched silently as the truck passed in front of us on the road and sped out of sight to the north. I measured the time in my head as best as I could until we saw the truck coming back the other way. I guessed that it had only gone a few miles before turning around. My heart rose as the truck passed over the last hill to our south, and I realized that we were finally free.

That night was much like most of the others for the next two months as the miles between us and home steadily dwindled. We would find a house near the road and break in through a window. There was usually some sort of canned food to be found and many nights we even found a house with a fireplace. Never did we see another soul, and never did we see a dead body or even any signs of a struggle in any of the houses we came to. Eventually we replaced our clothes and shoes with more comfortable and warm versions of the proper size. After only a week we had found a little red wagon, perfect for pulling Lucas along on our long walks each day.

The bullet had passed through my shoulder without damaging anything severely and healed quickly, but since that day, it has always been a little sore. Lori quickly got stronger, and I could tell that she and Lucas were enjoying the fresh air and the sights around them. It was a whole new world for them. Most nights were spent with me stoking the fire and rummaging up some food while she prepared a place near the fire for each of us to sleep. Lori collected several books along the way and always ended each evening by reading Lucas a story. She was kind to me, and we talked some about the cabin and a little bit of the old days at CR12, but there was a distance between us that I couldn't completely understand. One time I did try to ask her about her time at CR18 and one other time about her family before the day, but she made it plain she didn't want to discuss either. I respected her space and left her to her own thoughts, focusing instead on finding the way home.

We did find our way home—finally coming to the bridge at the river and up and around the old, winding back roads to the cabin. It was a cold, gray day, near to the start of winter, and we could see the smoke rising from the chimneys of the scattered houses of the settlement between the leafless branches of the trees. I could see my breath in front of me as I huffed to pull Lucas in the wagon up the last few hills. As we turned the corner to start up the driveway, I could see my mother stand up from her chair with one hand on the top of her head and the other hand over her mouth. The driveway to the cabin was long, and her chair was about halfway up the drive where she could be in sight of the cabin and still see up the road just a little. She had made herself a little shelter around and over her chair out of scrap lumber and an old blue tarp to keep out the wind and rain as she sat.

She was shaking just a bit, and I could see in her face that she was fighting off tears as the three of us walked up the driveway to meet her. "My Jack," she choked out with a smile, hugging me close as I came to her. "Your father?" she whispered in my ear as she released the hug.

I felt my own tears rolling down my cheeks as I spoke, not knowing what to say. "I was there with him. I tried; there was nothing I could do. It was quick. He didn't suffer." I paused and reached into my pocket, drawing out her half of the papers. "He wanted me to give you this."

She took the papers from my hand and looked down at them for several seconds, spreading the pages just long enough to recognize his handwriting before slipping them into the pocket in her jacket. She wiped a tear from her cheek with her sleeve and straightened her back, smiling with a quiet and confident peace that I had never seen in her before. "Jack," she said, "as you know, the Lord takes away." She paused and nodded toward Lori standing silently just behind my shoulder. "But he also gives."

She nodded down toward Lucas sitting in the wagon and smiled as she said, "And he also gives."

She looked back toward Lori and placed both her hands on Lori's shoulders as she spoke to her. "You must be Lori. Jack has told me so much about you. It will be so nice to have another woman around here. It has been just me with these men for so long." She stooped over and took Lucas's face into her hands. "And who are you, little fellow?" she asked.

Lori answered for him, "Lucas Fisher. He can't speak yet."

Mom smiled at Lori and looked back to Lucas. "Well, Lucas, I am so glad you are here. We are going to have lots of fun with each other." She stood and turned halfway toward the cabin and motioned with her arm. "Come," she said, "I've been expecting you. Dinner is on the table and ready. I've got a pot of beans and ham on the fire, and the cornbread will be done in just a few minutes. I'll set out a few more plates." She was already turned up the hill and walking toward the cabin as she finished the last sentence. She left us all little choice but to follow.

And so we did. It was the best meal I had enjoyed in months, and the best Lori had tasted in years, which she explained to my mother over and over again. We spent the night in front of the fire introducing Lori and Lucas and Mom to each other, talking carelessly until late in the evening about things that didn't matter, things that weren't so heavy on our minds. Mom settled Lori and Lucas in front of the fire, and I went upstairs and crawled under a pile of quilts on my old bed in the loft. I was exhausted and should have fallen right to sleep, but I couldn't.

It was surely past midnight when I heard Mom's quiet footsteps on the stairs. The moon had risen in the window behind me and cast a silvery glow on her face as she sat in the floor next to the bed. She had been crying. "Jack," she said, "you awake?"

She couldn't see my face, but I nodded. She must have sensed my movements, so she went on, "I just finished the first two pages of what your father wrote to me. It was just too dark to read his tiny little handwriting." She wiped a tear from her cheek and continued, "Don't you blame yourself about him dying. He knew what he was doing, and so did I. We both had a good idea he wouldn't be coming home to me. But I'll be going home to him one day, maybe sooner than I think. And until then, I will keep on loving him, just like always. I loved him when he didn't love me, and he loved me when I didn't love him. Now I will have to keep on loving him until I see him again in heaven."

She stood back up and patted me on my forehead. "Go on to sleep now," she said. "I've got a list of chores for you to get started on in the morning that you wouldn't believe. You've got to start by finding me a good Christmas tree." She stopped at the top of the stairs and looked back at me, now hidden in the shadows. "Those two precious souls downstairs wouldn't have had a chance if you and John hadn't gone back for them. It was worth the risk and worth the loss. I didn't think so when you left, but I sure do now."

"I know," I whispered, but I don't think she heard me as she walked back down the stairs. I did fall asleep that night but didn't sleep well. There was too much to think about.

We woke the next morning to a few inches of snow, the first of the year. It was melted by noon, but it was enough to thrill Lucas and nearly enough to make Lori smile. Mom wasn't lying about that list of chores, and she seemed to have a new list for me each day. By the time spring rolled around, I had cut and stacked enough firewood to last all the way through the next year into the following winter and had dug out and planted our little garden plot, expanding it by a few more rows in the process. After that first night home, I moved back into my little cabin at the foot of the hill, surrendering the loft to Lori. Lori needed her own space, and there just wasn't enough room for all of us. She had adapted quickly to the simple life we had taken on, proving herself to be a great help with chores, both inside and outside the cabin.

She and I spent a lot of time working together and much of the old friendship from our days back at CR12 began to be revived, filling the gap that each of us had for the other. We truly enjoyed each other's company and would talk freely with each other while we worked, but only about the happenings of the day. She would pull me away from my list of chores every so often for a foraging trip. We would travel to the abandoned houses within a half day's walk and pilfer through their things, not for food or supplies, most of those had been long picked over, but for clothes and books for Lucas.

It was on one of those trips that she looked over at me and asked, "So, when are you going back to find George and his wife?"

"I'm not sure," I answered, and I wasn't. It was a thought that I had been trying to push away ever since we returned. His supervisors knew what he had seen, and George was surely a marked man. Any step out of line would serve as an excuse to put him away. My promise to him echoed in my ears. I had no desire to leave, but I couldn't escape that promise. Many cold nights were spent pacing the tight floor of my little cabin, stopping to stare at and stoke the fire, conversing with myself and arguing with God.

To say that I was praying, at least praying as I had been taught as a child, would not be completely true. It really was an argument—an argument with someone that I couldn't see, with someone that rarely talked back, with someone that I really didn't know at all. You would have thought that I felt silly standing there yelling at thin air, but I never did. One thing I had learned from my trip to the city was that God was real without a doubt and that for whatever reason, he had swept me up into some big plan that only made sense to him. It was a plan that I hadn't signed up for, but I knew that there was no escape clause, no option for going absent without leave.

If the cold wasn't unbearable and the night sky was clear, the argument would spill outside. I would stand at the foot of the hill and look up at Lori's candle burning in the loft window of the cabin and then turn my eyes to the sky. Underneath the endless canopy of stars, like my own father and so many others before us, I understood that my rank in the universe was well defined and undeniable. There was no use in arguing. He was a force that couldn't be resisted. Like it or not, my life was not my own. My own plans for my life were much smaller than those devised by the maker of the stars. I gave in and agreed to go back to the city long before I had the courage to actually leave.

Even though she never asked it again, the question Lori asked me on our little day trip stuck with me. In that one question, Lori had made it clear that she expected me to keep my promise and that she didn't intend to come with me. The thought of leaving her terrified me, and more than that, it hurt me that she would be so willing to let me be apart from her, something I didn't want to do at all.

Loving Lori without her loving me back had proved to be harder than I expected. She and I had begun to rebuild our friendship, that was true, but her heart was still distant and cold. I found a very nice sweater that I knew she would like on the way home and hid it from her as a Christmas gift. She accepted it only with quiet thanks and never wore it. The early spring daffodils that I picked for her were dutifully put into a vase and set on the table. She talked of how pretty they were, but it obviously meant little to her that they had come from me. The compliments I showered on her were usually only answered with a nod. She never smiled and rarely seemed happy, except when she was with Lucas.

He had become the primary focus of her life. She read to him constantly, pointing at words and letters as she made sounds. They developed a few simple hand gestures to communicate with each other, and Mom and I had even picked them up. Lori was working on learning sign language from a book she had found and planned on teaching it to Lucas when he was older. She tried fruitlessly to help him speak but was at least able to teach him to make some clicking noises with his tongue and something like a little whistle. He was so excited to be able to produce sounds. The once silent little child was now a constant noisemaker, warning everyone of his presence as he drew near.

I remember well the first really warm day of spring; it was the last week in April. Lori had taken Lucas down to the stream at the foot of the hill to draw a bucket of water, and they ended up in a splash fight. I had just brought up another load of wood to the cabin, and I tiptoed as quietly as I could between the trees to sit on the side of the hill where I could see them without being noticed. The water was still frigid, of course, and Lucas would have squealed if he could have. Instead he clicked and whistled with all of his might, running toward Lori instead of away from her and clinging onto her legs.

She smiled and laughed for the first time since I had found her months before back in the city. Her face just shone—she was incredibly beautiful. It was so good to see her happy that

I clapped and laughed without knowing what I was doing. She looked up the hill toward the sound. When she saw it was me, she stopped laughing and waved. Her smile faded and the same serious look of sadness that she had carried with her all these days fell back over her face. She splashed Lucas one more time as she filled up the bucket, and they walked back up the hill together.

Mom had seen me from the cabin and silently came to sit next to me, nearly startling me as she sat down. "She really is a wonderful young lady," she said quietly to me. "Beautiful inside and out. I can see why you love her so much."

"When she sees me," I said, "it just reminds her of where she came from. I do love her. More than I ever thought I could. But I don't see how she will ever be able to love me back. There's just too much pain for her to deal with."

Mom stared out over the foothills in front of us. A valley cradled our little stream as it flowed between the steep slopes. The treetops were green and blooming dogwoods dotted the hillsides. "All the good stuff is hard," she said, almost to herself. "It's how God teaches us about ourselves. We just won't get it if it doesn't hurt." She paused and looked over at me. "It's funny, you know. All those years John was married to his work, I prayed and prayed for him to come around and be the husband and father I knew he could be. What I didn't know was that the little bit of faith I had was only about an inch deep. It wasn't until after your father and I woke up that we really got into the good stuff, the real stuff. Before we were taken to the city, going to church and being a Christian never seemed real. It was the right thing to do, but it didn't mean anything to me. It wasn't until things got turned upside down that I understood that God was the only thing in our lives that really was real."

She paused for a second before continuing. "Your dad, he knew he was going to die before he ever left with you for the city. It was in the papers he wrote to me. When you left, I was afraid that something would happen of course, but he knew without a doubt he would die."

I looked over at her. "Why did he go then?" I asked. "He didn't have to go. I couldn't make him go."

"What he wrote to me," she said, "was that he thought that if you stayed here and never went and looked for Lori, you would have fallen further asleep here at the cabin than he and I ever were before."

"How can that be?" I asked.

"Your dad understood things pretty well," she continued. "It wasn't the city or the busy life that we lived before that put us to sleep. It was living our lives without any meaning or purpose, living as if there wasn't a God and as if he didn't have a say over our lives. When you don't have a reason for getting up each morning—you aren't really living. And when that happens for a long time, you just get bored until you fall to sleep. The city was designed to put people to sleep, but your father knew that it could happen anywhere to anyone. He couldn't bear the thought of losing you. He was right to go."

She looked over at me, staring right into my eyes. "I don't know if he had a chance to tell you before he left, but your dad thought the world of you. He thought you would really be some-thing special and I do too. I think your trip down there was about a whole lot more than you and Lori and Lucas and John. What exactly that something is, we won't know for a while, but I have a feeling it's something big."

We sat there quietly for a few more minutes without speak-ing. Lori and Lucas had come up the hill and they opened the door and went into the cabin behind us. Mom went on. "Lori told me about your promise. She said you would be leaving soon, that you were just trying to get up your nerve. I guess she knows you better than you might think."

She stood and brushed off her jeans. "If going back down there is what God intends for you to be doing, then you should go on and get to it. I'm done arguing with God about my men. Delaying the trip won't help anything and will probably make things worse. We have more than enough firewood, and Lori and I won't have any trouble with the garden. I can see old Mr. Harkey's house from here, and he still has enough shells for his shotgun to scare off any bears if we start screaming."

She bent over and kissed me on the forehead. "You're a man now, son," she said as she turned. "But please be careful and come home soon." She walked to the cabin, leaving me to ponder my thoughts as I looked out over the beauty of the scene before me.

I packed for the long journey in secret over the next few nights, gathering the few things I knew I wouldn't find along the way. The arguing and pacing that had filled my evenings was over. In finally surrendering myself to leave, I had gained a peace with God and with myself.

In the flickering light of my lamp, sleep calls me relentlessly, and I end this story with a comma instead of a period, pausing due to the necessities of travel, bowing to the demands of life rather than the flow of the story. Who knows by what hand the future chapters will be written? I will leave in just a few hours, striking out before dawn, afraid I will lose my nerve if I try to stop for good-byes. I will slip silently into the cabin, being careful not to wake the three dreamers inside, and set this stack of papers on the kitchen table. Atop the stack is a single page, front and back, with the following words written on it:

Please take this as an "I'll be home soon" instead of a "good-bye." My home is wherever my family is, and you are my family. I leave this story to greet you this morning and to let you know that I have finally left. I hope you enjoy reading it as much as I have enjoyed writing it. It has been a joy to put this to paper over the last several months, resting my hands from the axe handle and resting my mind from the endless worries I foolishly let creep in. There is much more I could have written, but that is always so with every story. It was good to remember Dad, good to remember what we went through to get to this place, good to include his travels alongside mine. They are really very much the same story, and neither story makes any sense without the other.

You two ladies know me better than I know myself. You are much safer in God's hands than you are in mine. And that is where I leave you for what I hope is a very uneventful and much less dangerous trip. I have a better plan this time, so I don't think things will get as mixed up as they did last time. I suspect you are laughing as you read that sentence.

To Mom, I leave you with Lori and thank you for bringing her into our family. I wonder often if the precious child that you lost in that hellish motel room might have been a daughter. Over these last several months, you have loved Lori selflessly and patiently as if she were the daughter you never had, like only a mother can. Just as you have loved me all these years.

To Lori, I leave you with a promise. I will always love you as best as I know how, no matter what you feel toward me, no matter how discouraged I get, no matter if you ever love me back. I know you need time; I understand that much better now. Please take this short time apart from me to try and let go of your past. I know it is hard, but the person you think you see in the mirror isn't the real you. The real you, the person God made you to be, and the life you were intended to live, are so much more than what they tried to force you to be. When Lucas sees you, he sees the real you. When I see you, I see the real you. I see the kindest, most loving, purest-hearted person I have ever met. I wish that you could find the joy in living that you have given me as I have enjoyed the beauty of your smile and the beauty of your heart. You are my best and dearest friend on this earth and my one and only true love and it hurts so much to leave you again, even for a short while. You know better than anyone why I have to go back. Real promises, promises that mean something, must be kept. My promise to you is that I will fight with every ounce of my being to return to you and that I will never stop loving you. You and I are just getting started.

"Do this because we live in an important time. It is now time for you to wake up from your sleep, because our salvation is nearer now than when we first believed. The night is almost finished and the day is almost here."

Romans 13:11–12a, NCV

Made in the USA
San Bernardino, CA
13 February 2018